Unknown Territory

Alistair is one of the most rampant, inventive and enduring lovers that has ever walked this earth. Take off the Savile Row suit (personally, I can't wait), the shirt, the tie, the embossed underpants, the Austin Reed socks – and there is the biggest and the liveliest cock you ever saw in your life. Always active, always ready for you, it can go on all night if needed, never repeating itself, always thinking of something different – a new position, a new rhythm, a new movement. Inside that cool, perfect exterior is the wildest and most athletic lover it has ever been my most intense pleasure to meet. I am a lucky girl.

Unknown Territory
Annie O'Neill

BLACK LACE

Black Lace books contain sexual fantasies.
In real life, always practise safe sex.

First published in 2003 by
Black Lace
Thames Wharf Studios
Rainville Road
London W6 9HA

Typeset by SetSystems Ltd, Saffron Walden, Essex
Design by Smith & Gilmour, London
Printed and bound by Mackays of Chatham PLC

ISBN 0 352 33794 X

1

I've woken up horny again. That means I must have been dreaming about *him*.

So what do I do? I get up, throw on a bathrobe, get into the car and drive to his office. It only takes twenty minutes at this time of the morning, and I get to park right outside.

A sleepy security guard barely gives me a second glance. I press the lift button and, as I wait, I stroke myself gently to keep the momentum going. The lift is slow, so by the fifth floor I'm more than ready for him as I step out and down the long, long corridor towards the great oak door at the end. I fling it open without stopping to knock.

Six pairs of eyes swivel in my direction. Six pairs of eyes set atop six identical grey suits.

He is at the head of the table. His suit is light grey, underneath it a pale yellow shirt and grey tie with dark grey motif. Tasteful, understated, neutral, so typical of him.

Confident that I have the full attention of the room I slip my thumb into the belt of my robe, give it a little tug; the robe falls to the ground and there I am, naked.

Two pairs of eyes focus on my breasts. Others are looking further down. One pair of eyes is fixed on the floor.

But he is looking me straight in the eye.

As I walk towards him he gets slowly to his feet. He is calm, watchful, thoughtful. He's thinking: can she possibly be about to do what I think she's going to do? Would she *dare*?

Yes, I would dare. Watching his face all the time, I reach inside his jacket, undo his belt and his trousers and slowly unzip him. I glance down to see what's going on down there. Yes, there is action. Gently I take his slowly awakening cock, still encased in his underpants, in my hand. I give it a little squeeze. I hear an intake of breath. Otherwise, there's not a sound in the room, nobody is moving.

I ease his trousers down, tuck my fingers inside the waistband of his underpants and pull them to the ground. Everybody in the room is watching me – my God, are they watching me. Now I'm kneeling down in front of him, his cock is half erect an inch from my face, I put out my tongue and lick it gently on the very tip. It rises to meet my mouth so I take hold of it between my forefinger and thumb, very gently push the foreskin back and start to suck him.

Somewhere in the distance I hear the faint buzz of a car alarm.

My mouth is loose, my tongue is working its way up and down his cock, flicking around the base, licking into the crack at the tip. Then I start squeezing him with my lips and pulling him in and out of my mouth, steadily, controlling the pace, aware of the muscles of his body contracting, hearing his breath quicken. I'm really sucking him hard now and he's starting to groan. How I love his cock, the baby-smooth skin, the way it grows and grows still, inside my mouth, filling it, until I can barely breathe.

I'm sucking him so hard I know he's going to come at any moment so I take him from me, reach up and push my mouth onto his and feel his tongue down my throat. At the same time, with my arms around his neck, I jump up and straddle him with my legs so he's carrying me, and he turns and places me gently down onto the boardroom table. Now I'm lying on my back on the table, my arms stretched above my head, my legs apart and my cunt reaching up towards him, and he's immediately on top of me and in me and thrusting away deep, deep inside me, and the table is starting to shake and I'm clutching onto it for fear of I don't know what, and then I'm crying out and so is he and then with the most almighty shudder he comes.

And we lie there, together, for some time.

Eventually, slowly, he slides out of me. I look up at him. Those impenetrable eyes. He's watching me to see what I'll do next. He knows I will do something next. I've got to do something about the others.

The car alarm starts to buzz again.

Only it isn't a car alarm, it's my alarm clock.

'Good morning!' sounds the chirpy radio voice. Good morning indeed. I have a good stretch and reach across the far side of the bed. It's as bare and as cold as Alaska. That's the price you pay for being a bad girl, I guess.

I lie there, drifting as slowly as I possibly can back to reality. Morning. Weekday. Work. Up.

Up.

Work doesn't mean a lot to me, I have to say. To me, it's a way of passing eight hours a day and paying the rent. Mine is a mundane job that 'has to be done', insofar as any job has to be done, and only has to be done because such is the structure of life, and work, that jobs, work, get created to keep us all happy and fulfilled. Well, keep us occupied anyway. Like, for instance, Nick wouldn't have a job if it weren't for computers. Or rather, if computers *worked* in the way they should Nick would be out of a job. If cars *worked* the way they should we'd have no need for mechanics. Think how many people make a living out of things – cars, computers, washing machines, people – breaking down.

If life is about killing time, which in a way I suppose it is, then why not kill it in the most imaginative way possible. That's my view. Which is why every so often, like now, I slip off into fantasy land.

All this I'm thinking as I heave my body out of bed, stagger zombielike to the shower and stand there, naked, gazing at myself.

The shower is made of mirrors. This is not my vanity, I have to say; it's the way it was when I moved in. But I like to look at myself naked, it gives me a strange kind of a buzz. I like my body. It's taken me 25 years, and it's only now that I've really learned to stop worrying about my lack of boobs/hips/stomach/general *voluptuousness*. I think after all these years I'm done with wishing to be what I'm not and I've grown to quite like my slightly bony shoulders, my angular little hips, my long, straight legs with their perfect little blobby knees – I'm particularly fond of my knees. I've even learned to live with these cool, pale eyes, the overfull lips, the pointy chin and the uncontrollable, bouncing mass of curly, golden-blonde hair that I've wasted so many painstaking hours trying to straighten. OK, so it's not a conventionally pretty face, but it is a sensual face, so I'm told; it transmits sensual messages apparently. And that's just fine by me.

I stand there in the shower, stretch my arms above my head, close my eyes and bask in the sensation of the soft, lukewarm water raining down on me, caressing me, like a man's fingers – 'his' fingers. Everything in my life is a sensual, sexual experience. It's sex – doing it, thinking about it, fantasising about it – that keeps me going. It is my number one favourite hobby – far healthier and a lot more fun than going to the gym. It's also about the only thing I'm good at, which is perhaps why I find it so endlessly interesting.

Time skids by. And before you know it there I am, standing on a packed Central Line, crushed up against the suits and loving it, loving the proximity to those strange bodies, to the peculiar mix of body smells (more fragrant now than they will be later in the day), gazing around me and wondering about the sex lives of these blank-faced men and women, wondering if they are getting any and, if so, why they are looking so glum.

I expect it's because they're eaten up with guilt. That's the trouble with sex – for every ounce of sheer joy contained in one glorious moment of sexual conjugation there is an avalanche of shame, deceit, secrecy and doubt. The most joy you can give in the world is to a lover. The most harm you can do in the world is to a lover. And it's all down to the greatest failed experiment of the modern world: monogamy. That, at least, is my view.

My mother was a case in point.

My mother was a good woman. She was a good socialist and a good mother and a good wife. She brought us up strictly but fairly. She was not a Christian, but she might as well have been. She had impeccable morals and she would do anything for anyone. She was a paragon.

She met my father on a CND march in the 70s. He was tailor-made for her. He too was young and idealistic – they attended meetings together, argued till the small hours of the morning about the Cold War, the bomb, imperialist aggression (American) and socialist utopia (Russia). The wonder was they found things to argue *about*, so similar were they in their views.

My mother worked for the Housing Department of

the local council. Even after my brother and I were born she continued to work, part time, but still was always there to pick us up from school, and to be a leading light in the parent teacher association. She had boundless energy and always seemed serenely happy. Which just goes to show how little you can know about someone who's so close to you.

'You're putting it in the wrong way, love.'

I look around for the speaker. A yellow-jacketed London Underground worker is leaning up against the barrier into whose slot, apparently, in my abstraction, I've been trying to shove my ticket upside down. He grins at me and I smile icily back as I emerge into the grey daylight of Holborn and set off down Southampton Row.

I am back in the boardroom, lying on the table. Naked among the blotters and the jugs of water and the sheaves of paper. Naked and empty, wetter than ever.

I sit up and look around.

The other suits – two of them anyway – have their hands inside their trousers and are working away at themselves. They watch me expectantly. I'm calling the shots here, clearly.

One of them is not watching me. His eyes are fixed on the floor and his hands, in his trouser pockets, nervously jangle his keys.

'Come here,' I say to him.

Tentatively, he comes to me. He's still looking at the floor as I undo his trousers and reveal his massive erection. 'Come inside me,' I whisper to him.

Sitting on the edge of the table, I open my legs, take hold of him and guide him gently into me. I pause for a moment to register the sensation of a strange but wonderful new cock, and I wriggle slightly, easing my shy new friend deeper into me.

Then I beckon to the other suits, and like well-trained lapdogs they surround me, one on either side, and one by my head. Now I'm lying back on the table again, with floor-gazer inside me. I reach out with both hands and immediately there's a cock in each of them, and number four is straddling my head and sliding his cock into my mouth. Four of them to service simultaneously – we'd better get the right rhythm going, because we're all going to have to work together here.

I dictate the pace. With my hands I begin gently kneading, and at the same time I start slowly circling with my pelvis and sucking with my mouth. They immediately get the idea and soon we're all moving as one, like one great erotic machine, but *very* slowly – an orchestra, playing the overture.

After a while I feel it's time to up the tempo, just a bit, so with the hands and the pelvis and the mouth all working in unison we begin to move a little faster. Every so often when I feel one section of the orchestra running out of control, I relax my grip on it, because I want this one to last, boys. But my own needs are beginning to run away with me by now and soon – now – we're into *accelerando*, the five of us, and now I know there's no turning back and there's no stopping, we're *crescendoing* together, faster, ever faster towards the most glorious, powerful and perfect mass-climax; and then somehow I manage to cry out, it's like a clash of cymbals, and there's a glorious, suspended moment when my hands and my cunt and my mouth all squeeze simultaneously and they come, and come, and come, and come – one after the other after the other. I feel their juices spurt into one hand, into the other, into my mouth and then, best of all, into my cunt. They cry out – we all cry out together – and there's a long, frozen moment as the conductor (that's me) holds the moment, baton aloft ... and then relaxes, to the deafening sound of (metaphorical) applause.

Oh, bliss.

Am I a sex goddess or what?

'Good morning, Hazel.'

'Morning, Barbara.'

I have arrived at work. Such is the power of my imagination that I have allowed my boardroom musings to propel me all the way up Southampton Row, right round Russell Square, through the entrance hall of our building and up the lift to the second floor, totally oblivious to anything or anyone around me. Until now, that is. Thank you, Barbara.

I am not late. Nor am I early. I am not looking particularly dishevelled. But such is the disapproval on Barbara's face I immediately feel guilty and wonder – horror of horrors – if perhaps she is able to read my mind.

Barbara Osborne is our department's part-time accountant. We have worked in the same place together for goodness knows how long, but it's always been an uneasy relationship.

Barbara is in her fifties and, truth to tell, I know very little about her. She has a tendency to talk in code, as if direct address was something alien to her. For instance, I know she is highly curious about what's going on between me and Nick – Nick from IT, that is. I suspect she'd like to know all the gory details of what we got up to that time right here in the office when we thought she wasn't there; and more, what we got up to the next time when we knew she *was* there – *because* she was there. But because it is to do with sex – or because she *suspects* it is to do with sex – she hasn't managed to get round to asking me direct questions. She prefers the elliptical approach, as in:

'So, do you have plans for the weekend, Hazel?'

'Not really.'

'You'll be going clubbing, I expect.'

'Clubbing? You've got to be kidding.'

'Isn't that what young people like to do at weekends?'

'Young people maybe. As in teenagers.'

'Well then.'

A meaningful nod.

'Well what?' I'd snap, irritably.

'I thought you liked young people. I thought you preferred the company of people . . . younger than yourself, let's say.'

'What makes you say that?'

And there would be no reply. She'd just stare at me over those wretched glasses of hers and then down would go her head and she'd be absorbed, or pretend to be absorbed, in her figures again.

The phone is ringing as I reach my desk.

'Hi, it's me.'

Talk of the devil.

'Nick. How are you?'

'Fine. Just wondered how your new hard drive was coming along.'

'It's pulsating. How's yours?'

He laughs, feebly.

'You don't, er, want me to drop by and check it out?' he asks.

'No need. Thanks all the same.'

'I could come by at lunchtime. Are you busy lunchtime?'

'I'll – I don't know. Yes, I think I am. I'll call you.'

'Or there's now. I could come now if you like.'

'I'm busy right now, Nick.'

'Oh. OK.'

'I'll call you later, OK?'

'Righto.'

That was Nick.

Nick is very young and very clever. He looks after all the electronic gadgetry in our department. He looks about nineteen, and he's tall and skinny and walks in that slightly stooped way young things do when they've been taken by surprise at the rate of their own growth. He is brilliant with computers, he communes with them, he gets transported on beams of delight with them; he probably dreams about them the way I dream about sex.

He arrived in the department a year ago, fresh out of college. Like a lot of young men of his age, his eagerness to look older than he is made him seem that much younger. He had the word 'virgin' printed all over him.

Now that's something I can't resist. Fresh fruit. Unplucked. So I targeted him from the word go:

'Hello. Is that Nick?'

'Yes it is.'

'It's Hazel here, we met –'

'I remember you.'

'Good. Well, the thing is, my computer is doing some very strange things.'

'What, er, sort of things?'

'It keeps telling me I'm performing "an illegal operation".'

'Oh, yes. That could mean anything. What have you been –'

'I haven't been doing anything, illegal or otherwise. Could you drop by and have a look at it?'

'Sure,' he says.

'One o'clock would be just fine,' I say.

I would be alone in the office, you see.

'Er, right, OK. See you then.'

It would be wonderful. I thought I would be ever so gentle with him. He would knock at my door very quietly, and he'd stand there not looking at me, in the way he had, his hands in his pockets, as awkward as hell.

But I'd put him at his ease. I'd invite him in and stand behind him as he sat down at my desk and communed with my computer. I would let my hand rest lightly on his shoulder as he worked and when he'd fixed the problem, which should take him no time at all because there really wasn't a problem, I'd sit down next to him and we'd chat, about ROMs and RAMs and megathingies, and I'd ask him a bit about himself. Not too much – I'm not actually particularly interested – and then I'd probably say something like:

'You are incredibly clever for somebody so young.'

'Er, thanks.'

'You just love computers, I can see.'

'Well actually, yes.'

'Are you self-taught?'

'In a way, yes.'

'I thought so. You can't learn passion, can you? It's not a subject that anyone can teach anyone else, is it?'

He'd probably look a bit alarmed at this.

'I suppose.'

'And you know what? It's a real turn-on.'

I'd have my hand on his shoulder again, to stop him from bolting.

'Tell me something, Nick – no, no, relax, there's nothing to be concerned about. I really want to know. What is it about computers that gets your blood up and running?'

And he would tell me. Once I'd opened the floodgates it would all come pouring out and he'd be so bound up in what he was saying that he'd hardly notice me fingering the buttons on his shirt, and before he could say hypertext transfer protocol I'd have his shirt off and I'd be rubbing my hands all over his luscious young torso. Round about now he'd be starting to protest, feebly, at which time I'd be putting my lips very close to his ear and whispering, 'It's all right, relax, just relax and let it happen.'

And then slowly, or as fast as I could get away with, which probably wouldn't be fast at all, I would remove his clothes, item by item. All the time whispering reassurances, telling him, 'Go on, tell me more about file transfers and data sources.' I'm in no hurry, I've got two whole hours. And then, eventually, he'd be naked, and he'd have this whopping erection, naturally, and I'd be looking at him in amazement and saying, 'Wow! Look at *you*!' and he would be looking back at me, totally helpless, utterly confused, but above all excited as hell, and I would say:

'Is this your first time?'

At which he would probably nod, and he'd still be looking at me in that terrified sort of puppy-dog way, wondering what on earth this woman was going to do next. And I would then very gently take his cock in my hand and hold it, and I would feel it throbbing, and I would see his body tense with terror and excitement, and all the time, as I'm gently caressing his cock with my thumb, I'd be saying, 'Relax. Relax, Nick, I'm not going to do anything you don't want me to do.' Which wouldn't necessarily be strictly true.

And when I thought he was beginning to calm down a bit I would swiftly remove my clothes, smiling all the while in a reassuring manner – just kids playing a game together. And then I would press my naked body against his naked body and say something like, 'How does that feel?' to which he would respond, 'Er ... wonderful.' Then I would take one of his hands and place it softly on parts of me – on my mouth, my breasts, my belly, explaining 'These are the erogenous zones' – and then I would take his still-rampant cock in my hand and guide it very gently in the direction of my pussy, where I would introduce it to my clit. 'And this,' I would continue, softly rubbing the tip of his cock against it, 'is the part of the body the woman loves the most, but *the* most. This is the seat of her greatest pleasure. Feel how wet it is. When a woman is wet it means she is truly aroused.' And then with one firm movement I'd push him inside me.

Then, locked together, I would ease us down onto the (softly carpeted) floor. I'd be on top of him, guiding him in and out of me, swaying my pelvis this way and that, in rapture, sighing stuff like, 'Yes, oh yes, that's so, *so* good,' and all the while I'd be asking him, 'How does it feel, am I too heavy? Tell me if I'm hurting you,' but he would be speechless, he would be transported, he would simply not believe what was happening to him, he would be pumping away fit to bust and soon – far too soon – he would come, with a shout, his body jerking, his face contorted. And then he'd lie there breathing hard, and I'd feel him subsiding and slipping out of me (just when I was really getting going – oh well, never mind) and he'd be saying things like, 'That was, that was, er – oh God, I think I love you,' and stuff.

Yes, it would be exciting. He would never forget that experience.

Except, of course, that it didn't happen like that.

But that's another story.

* * *

I turn on my computer.

As I wait for it to boot up, a face, a half-familiar face, drifts into my mind.

I'm lying once again on the boardroom table, panting, exhausted, gazing up at the beautiful corniced ceiling. Slowly, gently, one by one, I feel the cocks, the four wonderful, new cocks, slipping gently out of me. I am satisfied. But not sated.

Four plus one plus one equals six. There was a sixth person in the room, I'm thinking as I'm lying there. What happened to him?

I sit up and turn around and there he is. Sitting quietly in the corner, watching me. Brown hair flopping over ice-blue eyes, eyes that are fixed on me. Legs, elegant, grey-suited legs, casually crossed. He stares at me. He's waiting for me to do something.

The wretched phone rings again.

'Hi, it's Nick here again.'

'Nick. For God's sake.'

'Sorry. Was I interrupting something?'

'What did you want?'

'I've just found this really hilarious joke site on the Web. I can give you the address, it's www dot . . .'

The awful thing is, I know he's been sitting there probably for hours dreaming up an excuse to call me. And I couldn't give a damn. That's the trouble with younger men. They get sex all out of proportion. They muddle it with love. I blame the parents.

'Did you get that? Take a look at it when you've got a moment and . . . Hello? Are you still there?'

I give a tiny sigh. Not audible.

'Nick.'

'Yes?'

'What did you really call me up for?'

There's a bit of a silence.

'I'm sorry, I'm interrupting you.'

'I didn't say that, I said what did you want to say to me? Really?'

'I need to talk to you.'

'What about?'

'I can't, er, say it here.'

The problem is, it didn't happen quite as I imagined it would, with Nick, that first encounter. Not at all. For a start, he was not a virgin. Not by a long chalk. I don't know how many sexual experiences he had had, but boy did he know what he was doing. And the problem is, he wants more. And I ... Yes, I want more too. As a matter of fact I want an awful lot more. As lovers go, he is one of the best. But it's so complicated with younger men. They keep saying things like:

'I love you.'

'You don't love me, Nick. You just fancy me. You want me. It's different.'

'Not in this case.'

'If it comes to that, I want you too.'

'You do?'

'Of course. You're a highly sexed, highly sexy man. Of course I want you. But it doesn't mean I love you.'

'I want to fuck you. I want to come over to your office right now and fuck you.'

There's a pause. Am I considering this?

'The office is full of people, Nick, there's no way.'

'That didn't stop you before.'

He's absolutely right.

'Look, don't be ridiculous. I've got work to do. You've got work to do.'

'OK.'

He's gone all hurt on me.

'Another time, Nick.'

'Yeah. Maybe.'

Oh, God. Now he's got me all hot and bothered.

There are a lot of foolish things we find ourselves doing in this life of ours. Not the least of them is arguing with a lover who tells you it's all over – as if arguing is going to make the slightest difference. They've fallen out of love with you, they don't fancy you any more, they don't want you any more, they're revolted by the thought of you – how is anything you say to them going to make them change their minds? And yet we still do it.

It's foolish of me to meddle with Nick. He's a sweet boy and I've corrupted him in the worst way imaginable. And the real problem is I can't let him alone. Even though I know how desperate he gets, how much in love he thinks he is. I shouldn't encourage him, but I can't help myself. Which is why I find myself putting him through this ridiculous humiliation on a fairly regular basis.

It certainly is complicated with younger men.

'Photocopying for you, Hazel. If you wouldn't mind.'

'Thank you, Barbara.'

Plop! Onto my desk lands a hefty bundle of papers, all tied together with Barbara's unique green ribbon.

She thinks I mind. I don't think she does it deliberately because of that; I think her reasons are somehow more complicated, more devious. I think she thinks I ought to protest at being asked to do such mundane tasks as photocopying, but the truth is ...

The truth is, as I'm standing over the machine waiting for it to warm up, I am strangely attracted to mundane jobs. There is something about the whirr and the clunk of a (laboriously slow, hopelessly out of date) copying machine that I find infinitely soothing. The way the copied sheets float out of the machine, down to the receiving tray, resting so neatly, lightly, gently on top of the paper beneath. Whirr, clunk, whirr, clunk. Demanding just enough of my attention but not too much. Whirr, clunk. Leaving my mind just free enough for my thoughts – my random, unfinished thoughts.

Why does he seem familiar – the guy with the floppy brown hair? Number Six. I can't place him and it spooks me slightly.

I climb off the boardroom table and go to stand, naked, right in front of him. He waits, unmoving. For lack of any other ideas I begin to touch myself. I gently rub the palms of my hands over my breasts, tease my nipples and feel them harden. Then I move them slowly down my body. His eyes are following them, following the movement of my hands. He sees them hovering over my pussy. He watches me insert a finger inside myself and start to stroke back and forth. I watch him watching me. I want him to keep watching me. I am very close to coming and he knows it, he must know it from the way I'm breathing.

Whirr, click. The machine stops and blinks at me. Renew paper.

Give me a minute. I lean against the machine, push my crotch against the hard metal.

My breath is shortening now and I know I've gone beyond the point of no return. I look at Number Six and there's a flash of something in his eyes, he hasn't taken them off me for one second, but his body is still relaxed, he's still sitting there, unaroused, but watchful. And now I'm on the verge, I am really on the verge, but the next thing I do will really shock him.

I stop.

I didn't think I could do it, to be honest. Bring myself to the very edge and then stop, completely. Believe me, it's not an easy thing to do. I'm in agony but I'm damned if I'm going to show it.

I bend down, take a handful of paper from the shelf and refill the tray. Whirr, clunk! goes the machine gratefully.

I turn back to Number Six. He is smiling slightly. His very stillness taunts me, and I realise I want him. I want him powerfully. It's all I can do not to go to him and tear off his sober grey suit and fuck him, watch his expressionless face writhe in ecstasy, feel his stiff businessman's body soften, arch and contort, hear him scream as he climaxes as he's never done before in his life.

I have to find a way to do this.

I turn and walk away from him. I walk slowly towards the door. The robe is still lying there on the floor. I pick it up and, as I slide my arms inside the sleeves, one after the other, wrap it around myself, pull the belt around me and tie it, giving it a little tug, I turn back to Number Six.

'One day,' I whisper. 'I'll have you one day, Number Six.'

'What?'

'Oh, sorry, Barbara, I wasn't talking to you.'

'Ah.'

She looks at me nervously, as you do with a mad person.

'How are you doing?'

'Done.'

'Done already?'

'Done but not quite dusted.'

'Good. Thank you, Hazel.'

'My pleasure,' I say.

And it will be. Oh yes, it definitely will be, one day.

2

One night a long time ago, when I was about ten years old, I couldn't sleep, so I went downstairs to rifle the fridge and I saw my mother sitting there doing two things I'd never seen her do before except at weddings: drinking whisky and crying.

I was so embarrassed I hastened back up the stairs before she could see me. I guess that proves that while we were a 'happy' family we weren't that intimate. To witness one's mother crying seemed, even at ten, to be a violation of privacy.

I didn't think a great deal of it at the time. Ten is pretty young and, since my mother seemed to carry on in her usual cheerful – or *stalwart* – manner, I soon forgot all about it.

Eight years later my parents split up. I was eighteen and I'd just finished A levels, my brother was twenty-two and had just left university. It was all done very properly – they spoke to us separately and seriously, explaining that 'these things happen', that it was nothing to do with us, that they still loved us very much. Though it was a shock – neither my brother nor I had seen it coming – it was all handled in the best way possible and I carried on my life as I remember with barely a pause.

But I found my attitude to my mother changing. I carried on living with her, in the house I'd been brought up in, which my father left to her. And I don't know if it was teenage bolshiness, but suddenly I started to find her stoicism, her smiling-in-the-face-of-adversity irritating. It seemed to me she'd had a pretty shitty life, or that's how I saw it. She'd lived decently, modestly and above all unselfishly. She was loved and admired – admired more than loved I think – by everyone who knew her.

But she'd never had any *fun*. I suddenly wanted to take her by the shoulders and shake her and say, Mum, why the hell don't you go out and have some *fun* for a change? Well actually, that's pretty much what I did. She looked at me in mild, amused surprise.

'What do you mean, "fun"?'

'Go out on the town! Find yourself a lover! Come with us to a club one night – you often see old people there!'

'"Old"? As in over forty?' She was highly amused by this.

'You know what I mean. Let your hair down! Stop worrying about Third World debt for once and come on out and boogie!'

'Thanks, darling, but I think I've had all the fun I'm going to have.'

That silenced me. I misunderstood it of course – I thought she was pining for my dad. Wrong again.

She died not long after that conversation, when I was twenty. It happened quite quickly and, as one would expect, she took it *stoically* – both the cancer itself and the treatment she went through. It was less than six months between diagnosis and death and it was all a bit chaotic; there never seemed to be time to stop and think, there were always appointments to be kept and decisions to be made, and then suddenly she was dead.

There followed a period of what I can only call numbness. Her absence, the lack of her, was in many ways stronger than her presence had been. Or so it seemed. I remember wanting to cry and being unable to. There didn't seem to be the time. There was so much to do, so much sorting to be done.

It was while we were going through her stuff, my brother and I, that we came across her diaries. And yes, I did read them. It didn't occur to me not to. That was when I realised her comment, 'I think I've had all the fun I'm going to have,' had nothing to do with my dad, or with the cancer. My adoring, adorable, sweet and selfless mum had, in my eyes at least, thrown her life away.

It's eight o'clock on the dot and Alistair is ringing the doorbell. You could set Greenwich Mean Time by him.

He's taking me to dinner at one of those quiet, understated restaurants that most people don't realise are there. That only the cognoscenti know exist because there's absolutely nothing on the outside of the building to indicate there's a restaurant inside – is that exclusive or what? Inside, the decor is tasteful and calm, the lighting so subtle you can barely read the menu. It's the sort of place the politician takes his secretary, the married man his lover, and so on.

I've known Alistair for almost a year now. We meet every other Thursday, twice a month. I'm not quite sure how this regular arrangement originated (doubtless with Alistair, being the regular sort of person he is).

He holds my chair for me like an old-fashioned gent and enquires after my health and well-being as if it was weeks since I'd seen him. Which, of course, in a sense it is. There's no mention of the boardroom. But then perhaps that never happened.

I'm gazing at him and thinking what an utterly gorgeous specimen he is. And how I love his inscrutability, his well-cut grey suit, the slate-grey tie with the subtle motif, the pale yellow shirt with just the right amount of cuff showing; his hands, long, delicate fingers, fingernails trimmed rather than manicured; and his hair, conservatively, exquisitely cut, but not over-groomed. No hair oil, just loosely brushed back from his beautiful face. He is, I realise, perfect.

'What sort of a week have you had?' I ask him politely.

Yes, I can do the small talk when I have to. I can do the weather even, and the latest political chitchat, even a bit of foreign stuff. I can give him a little dollop of gossip – gleaned from *Hello* or invented – which I don't think he finds remotely interesting. In fact, I really don't think he has the faintest clue what or indeed who I'm going on about most of the time. But he is so polite, he listens, he *really* listens; he even makes the odd comment. What a sweetheart. What a catch.

He orders the wine – always French, don't ask me what – and he usually orders fish of some kind for himself and the most expensive item on the menu for me. His idea, by the way.

If you watched us you'd think we were two old friends sharing a quiet evening out together. We talk, we listen, we don't flirt, there's none of that gazing into each other's eyes over the wine glass stuff, or toying with each other's fingers. There's always plenty to talk about – he has a PhD in conversation and knows how to keep the banter light and the tone upbeat. He would make the most wonderful gigolo because he has a natural ability, in his quiet, understated, noncommittal way, to make anyone on earth feel at ease.

There is also something rather impersonal about him. Our conversations are not intimate, they're not even particularly warm, they're the sort of conversations he might have with – who? – an acquaintance of some kind, a distant aunt even. You would never guess. You would never guess from his mild, easy-going, light-weight manner that in bed he is a wild beast.

And he's delightful – in a genial, noncondescending way – with the waiters. He knows them, they know him back, but he doesn't pretend to be interested in their private lives, he doesn't patronise them with personal questions, he just says hello and how are you and leaves it at that. And they love him for it.

And me? You wouldn't recognise me. On my absolute best behaviour. Dressed to the nines, but in the best possible taste. Ravishing, ready to be ravished but not showing it. Chatting away politely like the little Lady Muck I can be when I try. And how is his mother? Better? Got over that awful cold or whatever it was? Oh, that's good news.

His parents are aristocracy, I believe. Minor, very minor. You wouldn't have heard of them, nobody has. Very 'old school', whatever that means. They live in a cottage in Suffolk – at least he calls it a cottage but I've no doubt it's a mansion with wings and so on – with a summer house and a large and slightly unruly garden that is his mother's pride and joy. They are impatient, no doubt, to see their son decently married to a young woman with a pedigree, living in Chelsea and bringing up two perfect children called Tristram and Tamsin and living a scandal-free, respectable, slightly boring life.

What they don't know, or probably don't know, because they have never seen their son in that situation – at least I hope they have never seen their son in that situation – is that he is one of the most rampant, inventive and enduring lovers that ever walked this earth.

Take off the Savile Row suit (personally, I can't wait), the shirt, the tie, the embossed underpants, the Austin

Reed socks – and there is the biggest and the liveliest cock you ever saw in your life. Always active, always ready for you, it can go on all night if needed, never repeating itself, always thinking of something different – a new position, a new rhythm, a new movement. Inside that cool, perfect exterior is the wildest and most athletic lover it has ever been my most intense pleasure to meet. I am a lucky girl.

No, Lord and Lady Alistair, or whatever your name is (and I don't suppose I'll ever get to meet you so what the hell), you have no idea what your son is capable of.

We've finished our meal, we're into the coffee. His dark brown eyes are gazing into mine and he's taking one of my hands in his, lifting it and brushing his lips against it. Can you imagine? I feel like a queen. Yes, that's the effect he has on me.

'Have you had enough? Would you like more coffee or shall we hit the road?' he asks.

Yes, hit it, hit it.

He has the capacity to pay a bill without you noticing. I swear I never saw the glimmer of a credit card – perhaps it all goes down onto some discreet, high-class chitty and the money is electronically and quietly extracted at a later date without anyone actually having to *look at* a bill or, God forbid, *check* it.

I swan out of that place like royalty, I swear it. Friendly nods – goodnight, miss, sir – I love it, I love it. I am the whore who's been wined and dined by the prince. Under this black jersey frock I am wearing nothing but a pair of satin panties, beneath which I am moist and pulsating, but my smile would shatter glass.

Into the car, glide through the street, up the stairs and into his flat, then the ritual begins.

'Would you like to use the bathroom first?' he asks politely.

Of course. So while he checks his answer machine, clears up the non-mess in the kitchen, double-locks the doors, turns out the lights, I'm there in his beautiful, Italian-tiled bathroom, having a shower in something sweet-smelling, rubbing my skin all over with an essential oil of some exotic substance, and I mean all over. Brushing my hair, cleaning my teeth, clutching his dressing gown around my naked body and then taking it off again – oh yes, this will do, this will definitely do.

I make my naked entrance into the bedroom, where he is sitting on the bed, also naked, his glorious body inclined towards the alarm clock, which he is setting; looking up at me and smiling. Reaching out his hands to touch me, to hold my face and kiss me gently on the mouth. Whispering, 'Won't be a moment,' and disappearing into the bathroom.

He emerges moments later, face scrubbed, teeth gleaming.

'Do you want the light on or off?' he asks.

I like it on.

I like to see his wonderful body. I like to see his powerful shoulders hovering over me as he gently lowers his body onto mine, kisses my shoulders, my neck, my face, hair, eyes, you name it. He sits back and looks down at me and I look at him. I can't look at him enough. For a man who does not work out – he would not be so vain – his body is in fine, fine shape. Powerful without being muscular, lean but not skinny. His stomach flat as a pancake, his long, long legs stretched out either side of me.

I watch his cock. I love this. It's soft, as it usually is at this moment in the proceedings. There are many ways of getting it up. Sometimes I caress it, with my hands or my mouth. Sometimes I rub myself against him. Sometimes I talk it up, like now.

'You want to know what I did today?' I say.

'What?'

'I went to your boardroom.'

'Oh?' He's running his hands over my body.

'There were six of you, all dressed in suits. I was wearing your towelling robe. With nothing underneath it.'

'Tell me.'

'I took off the robe and, with them all watching me, I walked towards you. You were watching me too.'

'I expect I was. What happened then?'

'I undid your belt and took off your trousers and your underpants.'

'Did you now?' He's working his hands over me, moving down my body. 'What was I doing at the time?'

'You were semihard.'

'Only semi?'

'I licked you. Licked your cock. Then I took you into my mouth and worked on you.'

'Sounds nice.'

His fingers brush against my pussy. I spread my legs.

'Then, before you were able to come, I took you out of my mouth and I kissed you and you lifted me up and you put me on the table.'

'On the boardroom table?'

'Among all the blotters and jugs of water and stuff.'

'Uncomfortable.'

'And then you entered me.'

He is straddling me now, legs splayed, and his cock, which is stiffening, is brushing against my cunt.

'In front of all the others,' he says.

'Oh, yes.'

'And what were they doing meanwhile?'

He leans over me and licks my navel. He toys with it with his tongue. I see his great cock start to move. I'm not going to touch it. I'm not allowed to until he tells me to.

'They were watching,' I say.

'They were watching you and me fucking.'

He's moving his lips down my stomach towards my cunt. He starts to lick me and I spread my legs wider.

'And did I fuck you well?' he mumbles, half-audibly.

'Well and truly.'

'And then what happened?'

'Then I . . .'

'Yes?'

'I – oh Christ – I fucked them.'

'What, all of them?'

'Yes.'

'One after the other? Or all together?'

'All together. Oh, God.'

'How?'

'One in each hand, one in my mouth and the other –'

'Inside you.'

'Yes.'

'Hold me.'

He places his huge throbbing cock in my hand. It feels – what can I say – it feels alive.

'All at once, all moving together and fucking together?'

'Yes.'

'And all coming together?'

'Yes. Oh, yes!'

'Describe it.'

'It was overpowering.'

'It must have been.'

I'm stroking his cock with my hands. It tenses and turns and throbs.

'It was like being part of one great machine, an unstoppable, moving machine,' I say.

'All the different parts working together.'

'Yes. And I was the master of the machine, or the mistress rather, dictating the pace.'

'In charge.'

'Oh, yes.'

'What a star you are. Were they grateful?'

'Who?'

His cock is still growing. It's huge. I rub it against my belly.

'The men in suits.'

'Yes, they were grateful.'

'I love your fantasies,' he says.

'So do I.'

'I'm going to enter you now.'

'Yes. Please.'

It takes my breath away. It truly takes my breath away, every time, every single time.

He is so huge. He is gentle, because he knows he is huge. I had forgotten. Believe it or not, in my fantasies, some things I forget.

Very slowly. His body curved over mine. Filling me. He clasps my bum and presses me tightly, tightly against him. He moves in and out, in slow motion. Then, after a while, with one movement he lifts my back right off the bed so my bottom half is vertical, and he's still in me, deep, deep in me, moving all the while in long, slow strokes; my legs are wrapped around his head and he's virtually standing on the bed now and I am almost inverted, and we stay like that for a while, his hands on my hips, steadying me, before he lowers me back down again. My legs are still around his neck, and in that position he is very deep in me, but he's going gently, slowly still, watching me, watching my face, murmuring 'How's this? Am I hurting you?'

'No. It's perfect. Keep going. Harder.'

He responds, and now our bodies are writhing together and he is really starting to fuck me hard now, so hard it should hurt he is so big, but it doesn't hurt – and then at last he comes, his body jammed against mine, his arms clamped around me like a vice.

Hold it like that. Just hold it. That's good. That satisfied you. That was good.

Then, after a while.

'Thank you.'

'My pleasure.'

'No, mine.'

Oh, he is so polite. If I didn't know myself better I could fall in love with this guy.

We lie there for a long, long while. I can feel his thumping heart slowly, gradually steadying.

Then, after some time, I feel him softly sliding out of me. He kisses my bum and he pulls the sheets over me and I turn over and cuddle him and we fall asleep, like babes in the wood.

And I never did get round to telling him about the mysterious Number Six.

I never dream of Alistair when I'm with him. No need, I suppose. But there's that warm and lovely feeling, knowing I'm going to be waking up next to him. That the alarm is going to go off 45 minutes before either of us has to get up.

That I am going to enter the waking world with his hand on my chest, at first like a dead weight, but then his fingers coming to and slowly tracing the circle of my breasts. And so we wake into the morning and into sex, slowly, gently, courteously.

He starts by running his hand softly down my body, caressing my breasts and smoothing over the hollow of my belly. I'm pretending to be asleep still, lying there like a sack of potatoes, prone, immobile, while my insides are beginning to burn up and I can feel the wetness between my legs. All my concentration and my efforts go into keeping my muscles from contracting and my body from showing anything at all. It's a game I find myself playing – see how far I can let him go without responding. All the time pretending I'm asleep.

Now he's stroking my legs. I can't see because I've got my eyes closed, but I think his face is very near my pussy. I want, I so want to part my legs but, of course, I'm asleep. I can feel his breath on my pubic hair – he's blowing it, for God's sake.

Then a hand reaches around the inside of my thigh and gently pulls my legs apart. He lowers his face towards my cunt and I'm really fighting now, fighting the urge to let my body respond. I can feel his tongue entering me and starting to suck me. Then it moves to my clit.

And then, suddenly, everything stops.

Yes, he's good at this.

I'm waiting. Lying there like a sack and waiting. I feel the bed move slightly – is he getting up? He can't be getting up. I hear a sound that could be a waking-up-and-stretching type of yawn. Then he starts to hum.

Oh no, this is not on at all.

I do one of those turning-over-in-bed-without-being-really-awake numbers, during which I sort of stretch out my arm to see if there is anything occupying his side of the bed, which there is.

'I thought you were asleep.'

I don't reply. Well, I'm still asleep, aren't I?

He leans over and kisses me on the cheek. He's about to climb out of bed dammit, so I have to reach out and grab him.

Only I'm too slow – he's out of the room and in the bathroom, leaving me high and – high and wet, actually.

Curses. What a bad start. Still, no point hanging around in bed while he showers and so forth. I'll get up and make the coffee.

I'm standing by the dressing table trying to summon my coffee-making faculties when – and I swear I didn't hear the door open – he's behind me. He wraps his arms around me so hard I can barely breathe. He presses his naked body against me and I gasp as he enters me from behind. He pushes my torso so I'm leaning over the dressing table while he thrusts into me. There's no foreplay this time, it's straight fucking, he can be an animal at times. And then, quite suddenly, he's out of me and he's spun me round till I'm sitting on the dressing table and all the stuff on it's flying onto the floor, and now he's pushing my legs apart and thrusting into me again – and while he's fucking me I watch his face and there's a look of total, but total abandonment that is so utterly different from the Alistair in the pinstripe suit. And then he's lifting me, lifting me bodily, still inside me, and carrying me over to the bed, laying me down on my back, and I'm clutching the bedstead as he continues to thrust harder and harder and I think, God, how long can he keep going at this wild, wild rate? At which point he withdraws, again without warning. And I look at him and he's crouching there looking down at me, sweating, panting, his cock still fully erect, a kind of scary, uncontrolled look in his eye, and I'm thinking, what the hell's going on now?

He stays there for some time – or so it seems. And I'm beginning to feel almost scared. His cock is still hard.

Then he whispers, 'Look at me.'

'I am looking.'

'Look at me all the time.'

This said while he very slowly starts to enter me again.

'I'm looking.'

'Your face.'

'What about it?'

As he eases in and out, in and out.

'So sexy. Christ, the expression on your face.'

'What?'

'You should see it.'

Deep into me.

'If I could paint –'

'Just keep going.'

'I'd like to take photos.'

The pace quickening.

'Photos of your face as you make love.'

His voice coming in gasps.

'Yours too.'

Faster now. On the home stretch, I think.

And we're watching one another's faces closely. His is getting red, his eyes are popping, his mouth is open.

And he shouts as he comes.

He lies there fully on top me, length to length. His body is heaving. I can feel the dampness of his sweat on me.

To tell the truth, I've never actually known him be quite this fierce before. Quite this animalistic. Wild, yes, but usually behind the wildness there's a certain – not restraint exactly, more of a sort of gentlemanly control.

He realises this.

He sits up, still inside me, but he's soft now. I clench my pelvic muscles, trying to keep him in there, and I sigh as he slithers out of me.

'I'm sorry,' he says.

'What for?'

'I think I kind of lost it there.'

'I think you did.'

'You haven't come.'

'No.'

'Do you . . .?'

'No.'

'I'm so sorry.'

What can a girl say? When she's seen a guy like this – a guy normally so butter-wouldn't-melt – lose himself so totally and utterly. It's a sure form of flattery, at least that's how I see it. No apologies needed.

And an even more amazing thing. More than 45 minutes have passed since the alarm went off. Alistair is going to be late for work.

By now, normally – and every other time has been normally – I, or maybe he, will have made the coffee and the toast and we'll be tucking into breakfast together. And then, together on the dot of 8.30 a.m. (which is far too early for me), we will leave his flat together. He will offer to give me a lift which I will decline, my office being in a different direction from his, and besides, why should I want to get there so early? And he will give me a little hug and a peck on the cheek as he climbs into his car and glides off, and I'll head off, walking a tad stiffly perhaps, towards the tube station.

But not this morning.

This morning he rolls off me and lies there, on his back in bed, staring at the ceiling. There's a long pause. I say something cheesy like, 'A penny for them.'

He says nothing. He just turns to look at me and reaches out a hand and plays with my nipple.

I suddenly want to tell him about Number Six. I'm not sure why – not specifically to get him aroused again,

I think that might give him a heart attack – but because ... I don't know. Because just thinking about Number Six makes me excited, I can feel myself trembling.

'A penny for yours,' says he.

Well, if that's not an invitation.

'There was someone else in the boardroom,' I say.

'Yes?'

'There were six of you altogether, if you remember. There was you, and the four suits –'

'And another suit.'

'Yes.'

'And? What was the other suit doing during all the fun and games?'

'Nothing. That's the point. He was just sitting there. Sitting there and watching, with great interest. But he wasn't joining in.'

'Poor guy. Why not?'

'He didn't ... I don't know. He wasn't even playing with himself, he didn't even look aroused. So I went to him.'

'You went down on him.'

'No. I didn't dare. He had this kind of keep-away look in his eyes. Not hostile, not at all. Just a bit detached. I didn't know what to do, so I started to touch myself.'

Alistair's hand starts moving down my body towards my cunt.

'You're going to be late for work,' I tell him.

'Go on.'

'I don't want you to get excited again.'

'I'm not. I'm just interested. You were touching yourself.'

He starts to stroke my clit. It's nice, very nice, but ...

'By now I'm getting very close to coming. But I don't want to. I'm desperate for him to touch me, to fuck me, but he's just sitting there, watching me, and smiling slightly. By now I'm almost bursting, and I'm getting slightly pissed off at his non-reaction.'

'I'm not surprised.'

Alistair kisses my breast. Takes the whole thing in his mouth. Meanwhile his hand quickens on my clit and I want to take over, to show him where to touch, but I can't.

'So I do the only thing I can think of,' I continue.

'You come.'

'I stop.'

'You stop?'

'Yes. Believe me, it wasn't easy.'

He's kissing my other breast now.

'And what does he do?'

'Nothing.'

'Nothing at all?'

'Absolutely zilch. He's not even aroused.'

By now his hand is moving very fast, and I'm responding, or my body is trying to respond – twisting and heaving and wanting, but somehow ...

'Unbelievable. Who is this guy?'

'I don't know. I just know he has the iciest blue eyes.'

I cry out. It's what's called faking orgasm.

We lie there for a moment.

'Thank you,' I say.

He lies still, gazing at the ceiling. His hand moves softly over my belly.

'So, what happened next?'

'Nothing. I just got dressed, back in my robe, and left.'

'Interesting.' He turns to look at me. 'And what did he look like, this guy with ice-blue eyes?'

'He had brown hair that flopped over his eyes a bit.'

His hand stops moving on me.

'Did he have a slight European accent?'

'Yes, I think he did.' Now how do I know that? He never –

'I know him,' says Alistair. He turns away from me.

'You *know* him?'

'He's my boss. He's on secondment from Head Office in The Hague, his name's –'

'Don't tell me his name.'

I don't know want to know it. I really don't.

'You know him too. You met him once in the pub, where we were having a drink together.'

'I thought he seemed familiar.'

'He couldn't take his eyes off you.'

I don't remember that bit.

'And now you're fantasising about him.'

Now that is weird.

There's a silence. Alistair is staring at the ceiling.

He is preoccupied, which is not like him. Alistair has that irresistible ability to make you feel he is always in the moment, always totally with you, that you are the centre of his universe when he is with you.

But as he lies there, and I lie there looking at him, suddenly he looks distant. Slightly troubled. With anyone else I wouldn't give it a second thought. But with Alistair, I find it slightly unnerving.

But he quickly breaks the spell. He glances at his watch, exclaims 'My God!' ruffles my hair briefly, jumps out of bed and goes into the bathroom.

And half an hour later we're stood on the street, and he's offering me a lift and I'm saying no thanks, and we're giving each other a hug and a peck on the cheek and 'see you in a fortnight', and he's off.

And I'm left standing there for what seems like ages. Watching his disappearing car and feeling ever so slightly puzzled.

3

I remember Frank very well. I was only around eight years old at the time so I didn't think to question why he spent so much time round at our place. He was a friend of Mum's, that was enough.

He was wonderful. We adored him, my brother and I. He was everything our dad wasn't. He was huge, but *huge*, and grizzly, like a bear, and incredibly clumsy. He made our perfectly normal-sized house look tiny. He hit his head on the door frame *every single time* he walked through it, and somehow the furniture and all the things on them would go flying whenever he went near them.

He was a bit clumsy in his behaviour too – or perhaps I should say indiscreet. He told us risqué stories and rude jokes that we didn't begin to understand but laughed at anyway. And oddly enough my mother, who was normally such a puritan, didn't seem to mind too much – she made half-hearted attempts to tell him off but she was laughing as she did it. If that didn't arouse my suspicions, nothing would.

But an eight-year-old doesn't have suspicions. At least, this eight-year-old didn't. Not even when Frank used to exit the house invariably half an hour before my father entered it. Had I thought about it I would have realised that he and my father were never in the house at the same time. But I didn't think about it.

But I did wonder – we both did, my brother and I – why he disappeared off the scene so suddenly, and without explanation. My mother was rather vague about it, she didn't seem to want to talk about Frank then, which was odd, because she always used to love talking about him before. But from the moment he wasn't there any more it was as if he'd never been there, had never existed.

It was not long after this that I caught my mother crying and drinking whisky. But I didn't connect the two events, not then.

When I came across her diaries, all those years later, it really did not occur to me I was doing wrong by reading them. She could have – she would have – destroyed them before she died if she hadn't wanted them read, at least that's how I saw it.

They had been written retrospectively, that's to say some years after the events described. And they only covered a few years in her life. Strictly speaking they were not diaries so much as the story of a part of her life. I like to think she had written them partly as a way of trying to make sense of an intensely emotional period in her life, and partly to convey something to us. Or to me at any rate.

She loved Frank with a love she had never experienced before. She loved him passionately, deeply and uncontrollably. She loved him in a way she did not believe existed: with her entire body, her mind, and her life.

You have to picture, if you can, my mild-mannered, pure-thinking, rather easily shocked mother. Everything in her life was ordered. She never overslept, she was never late, she never forgot anything, she never made a fuss, and she rarely raised her voice. I never saw her row with my father, not even after he ... When she told us off it was calmly, firmly and, of course, fairly. She was neither impulsive nor impetuous, yet she was tolerant with those who were. I know she loved us deeply – my brother and myself – and she was always there for us, with the right words of reassurance or comfort or whatever was required at the time. But I never had the faintest idea what was going on inside her head. She never told me anything remotely personal, or surprising. I think perhaps as a child I assumed that grown-ups' emotional lives stopped when they got married, or had kids. Actually I don't think I really gave the whole thing much thought at all, not until I saw those diaries.

So for my restrained, self-controlled mother to have given herself so totally and so dangerously to someone else, to a man who was not her husband, was a double shock. And not only to have given herself so completely, but to have *described*, in graphic detail, everything that happened between them. Now that's a lot to take on board.

It was March, I remember that because the magnolia was in full bloom. The house was empty, the children were at school, David was at work, and there was just Frank and me, sitting there. He had stopped talking, which was unusual for him, and there was a particular kind of silence hanging in the room between us.

He took my hand and sat there holding it in his and studying it as if he was reading my palm. Then, without, looking up he said:

'You know I'm totally and completely crazy about you.'

Yes, I did know. I think I had been waiting for this moment for weeks.

'Yes,' I said to him. 'I love you too.'

As I said it, I felt a great weight lift off me.

We went into the bedroom and without saying anything at all he took all my clothes off. I thought I would feel unbearably shy but I didn't. I could feel myself trembling all over because I so wanted him to make love to me. It's a shocking thing to admit, but the feeling was overwhelming.

We lay down on the bed together and he placed his hands on my body, all over it. His touch was so gentle, and the look on his face so tender that I had to kiss him. I kissed him deeply, and for a long time. I didn't want to stop kissing him.

I knew he was going to make love to me, and I don't know why but I didn't feel in the least bit guilty because it felt so completely right. The love I felt for him at that moment was so total I knew that what was happening was inevitable. There was no choice to be made, no decision. It felt like the most normal thing in the world.

Then he started to make love to me, with great tenderness and great gentleness. He kept his eyes open, all the time, and I remember his face looking down on mine with such a soft expression, such a look of joy, of delight. I knew above all that he didn't want to hurt me, either physically or emotionally.

I felt a need, a physical need, that I had never felt before. God forgive me for saying this, but I never ever felt this with David. With David, making love had always been a bit of a routine, a duty I suppose, which I performed without discomfort but without much pleasure either. But here, with Frank, it was an act of the purest joy I had ever felt in my life.

We made love all afternoon. As time passed I began to feel quite abandoned. It was as if all the restraints inside my body, that I had never before realised were there, had been suddenly released. I basked it in. I wallowed in it. I laughed out loud. I shouted his name. There was nothing else, nothing else in the room, in the house, in the entire world but him. I didn't care about anything else but loving, loving, loving him and being loved by him. I wanted the moment to go on forever, to never stop. I wanted him to be within me and to grow within me and never ever leave me.

Needless to say this took my breath away. Literally. I think I went into a kind of shock as I sat there. It felt for a moment as if my bodily functions had closed down. This was my mother talking. My quiet, sensible, contained, restrained mother.

First there was the shock of realising my mother had sex. Mothers don't. All children are immaculate conceptions, in their own minds, at least.

Moreover it was good sex. Glorious sex. Sex that gave her more pleasure than she'd ever experienced – than she'd ever imagined possible. And it was not sex with my father.

This is not what shocked me. I was surprised, not shocked, to hear she'd had a lover. What was shocking was how successfully she had managed to keep it from us. How she had stopped herself from shouting it from the rooftops, from grabbing me, and my brother, the moment we came home from school and crying out, 'Guess what, I've found happiness! Happiness beyond my wildest dreams! I have a lover! Look at me! Look at my joy!'

What a delight, what a pleasure that would have been, to have seen my mother so supremely happy. To have been allowed to witness, to share some of her joy.

The diaries went on. And on. They made love on a

regular basis after that, she and Frank, though she didn't go into such detail about it. I suppose that first time was kind of special for her, because it was a first time in so many different ways. It's astonishing to think that as I was sitting in a classroom struggling with my seven-times table and my Roman history that my ancient mother – actually she was in her forties at the time – was fucking herself into oblivion.

The next section came around a year later.

I told him we would have to end it. There was no alternative.

He was married, with children, and I was married, with children. We both had partners who loved us and children who depended on us. There was absolutely no question of separating from our families, it would have destroyed the lives of so many innocent people. I could not have lived with myself and nor I believe could he. There was nothing else we could do.

He cried. This great big man actually broke down and cried like a baby. It broke my heart to see it.

But I do not regret one moment. I thank God for having known him, for having spent time with him, and above all for having loved him in a way I have never loved before and will never love again.

I am not a bad woman. I know I am far from perfect but I have tried in my life to do the right thing by the people I love most. No doubt I have sinned from time to time, but to have continued with this deception would have made all my past mistakes fade into nothing. There is no greater harm I could have done to those closest to me. The guilt was overpowering, it was killing me, it would have killed me.

There was more – to do with knowing she would never be happy again and so on. Hence the remark she made to me that day about all her fun days being behind her.

After it was all over she told my father all about it, like the saint that she was. And she didn't complain at all when he declared he never wanted to touch her again, that they would remain married, in name only, until the kids – us – were older, and then they'd go their separate ways.

After the divorce she tried to find Frank again. But he'd vanished off the face of the earth and she never saw him again.

And my reaction to those diaries?

I guess above all else I was angry. My mother had loved like few people have ever loved, with the kind of overpowering, all-consuming passion you usually only read about in books. That is not something that comes along every day and wags its tail at you. To be honest, it's not a feeling that has ever entered my experience, but that's another matter.

What I'm clumsily trying to say is that – to my mother at least – the love she felt for Frank was clearly something precious, and good. Above all it was good. It's good to love someone like that, it is, clearly, the most wonderful feeling in the entire world, at least she obviously thought so. And what did she do? She put it in an old dustbin and threw it out. And all because of her family.

We would have survived, my brother and me. My father too.

So yes, I was angry. Angry at my sweet, long-suffering mother, who was so right about so many things and so utterly, self-deceivingly, tragically wrong about this.

I suppose most of us end up either like our mothers or the complete antithesis of them. No prizes for guessing which way I went.

We are all products of our antecedents, like it or not. I'm not trying to make excuses for my way of life – far from it – but I think what happened to my mother had some bearing on the way I view things. I don't suppose she was the only saint to have produced a sinner like me.

The news about Alistair's boss, the man from The Hague, Number Six, has tantalised me, to put it mildly.

I've never obsessed about a man before, it's not my style; it's counterproductive in my view. But now that I know that this man that I invented (or thought I had invented) actually *exists*, well . . .

I have to find him. I have to find him and yes, I have to have him.

I start at the only place I know. I wait for him outside the office, lurking in the shadows of nearby buildings, like a mugger.

After forever he appears, on his own, thank God. I cross the road so I'm standing on the pavement in front of him and, wonder of wonders, he doesn't seem that surprised to see me. He's smiling, slightly, in recognition.

'Hi,' I say.

'Hello,' he says.

'I'm Hazel.'

'I remember you. It's good to see you again.' He shakes my hand.

You cannot imagine how odd it is to be standing on a pavement, politely shaking the hand of someone you have, in your fantasy, stood naked in front of, masturbating. I'm struggling to remind myself he knows nothing about having starred in my little dream and at the same time I'm wondering what the hell I'm doing here and what the hell is going to happen next.

'What can I do for you? Or were you waiting for someone else?' he asks. A very good question.

'I was waiting for you.'

'Indeed?'

His expressions are almost imperceptible. A very slightly raised eyebrow denotes his surprise.

There's a little pause.

'Can I give you a lift somewhere?' he asks.

'Sure.'

He has a car. Parked in the company car park.

We walk to it in silence, climb in together, and for a moment we sit there, going nowhere. I think he's still waiting for something. I've no idea what happens next.

'Where do you live?' he asks.

'Battersea.'

'Battersea. That's south of the river, I think.'

'I'll direct you.'

'Please.'

As we go, he chats to me about London, like a tourist.

'It's a very pleasant city,' he says.

'You think so?'

'So many parks and green spaces.'

'That's true.'

'For such a large and bustling city this is amazing. I love it here. You are very lucky, you people, to live and work in the most vibrating city in the world. Everything is here – high culture, low culture –'

'Vibrant.'

'I beg your pardon?'

'I think the word you mean is vibrant,' I say. 'Vibrating means, well, you know ...' I shake and shimmy my body, by way of illustration. He looks at me and laughs. I find myself blushing slightly, for God's sake.

'Your English is very good,' I continue, like a tour guide. 'Where did you learn?'

'All over the place. You cannot help it, if you are Dutch. If you expect the rest of the world to speak your language then you will find yourself talking to nobody but yourself for the rest of your life. Am I on the right track?'

'What do you mean?'

'I am going straight until you tell me otherwise.'

'Oh, yes, er ... next left at the lights.'

'Ah, the river, the beautiful river. "Earth hath not anything to show more fair," and so on. Magnificent. Did you see the seal?'

'What seal?'

'There was a seal who came visiting right up as far as your Houses of Parliament, so I read in the papers.'

'Was there? I didn't know that.'

'He was probably a secret agent. Spying on your government.'

'It's next left here, over the bridge.'

'Very pretty. Battersea, you say. I don't know Battersea at all. Is it nice living in Battersea?'

'It's OK. A bit out of the way.'

'Victorian, by the look of the buildings. Very imposing. These are, what do you call them, palace blocks?'

'Palace blocks?'

'These flats. They are called palace flats, I believe.'

'Mansion flats.'

Despite myself, I burst out laughing. I don't know, but I have a strong suspicion he's taking the piss.

'Well.'

He pulls up outside my place, jerks on the handbrake and turns to look at me.

'Everything a person could want, he or she will find it here, in London,' he says, meaningfully.

Now what.

He lets me out of the car and follows me to my front door.

This is going to be easier than I thought, I tell myself.

'Would you like to come in?' I ask.

'Thank you.'

And he does.

Wordlessly we climb the stairs and we're into my flat.

What now? Straight to the bedroom? Do I just take my clothes off? Do I just take *his* clothes off?

Or do we do what people normally do, and talk a bit first?

'Can I get you anything?' I ask.

He doesn't answer this. He plonks himself down on a chair and casually drapes one elegantly trousered leg over the other.

He watches me, smiling, waiting.

He looks exactly as he did in my dream, sorry, *fantasy*: his brown floppy hair belies his pale-blue eyes; his expression is calm and watchful; his demeanour is relaxed and, I think, this is not a man to mess with. This is a man who likes to be in control, who is in control, who has to be handled carefully.

And as I stand there looking down at him I realise how much I want him. I can't account for it really, how powerful this feeling is. So powerful I can't afford to make the wrong move, say the wrong thing. I'm treading on eggshells.

'Would you like to . . . to take your jacket off?'

He chuckles slightly at this. He's wrong-footing me I realise. But this is a challenge I'm going to meet, and enjoy and, somehow, conquer. Exactly how remains to be seen.

'So? Tea? Coffee? A drink? What can I offer you?' I accentuate the innuendo. He looks coolly back at me.

'Nothing, thank you. Sit down. Relax.'

Thanks so much for the suggestion. I do.

Something has gone awry here. Here we are, in my flat, he is my guest, my visitor, and he is the one telling me what to do. Ah well, we'll see how it pans out.

We sit there in silence for a while. His eyes rest on my thighs – my uncovered thighs. My skirt has unaccountably ridden up my legs, exposing several inches of flesh. I stroke myself, idly, absent-mindedly.

Touch me, says my hand, silently. Please, touch me, touch my thighs, feel how my skin loves to be touched.

'It is an interesting flat. You live here alone?' he ventures after a while.

'I do as it happens, yes. It's a housing association. I'm very lucky to be able to afford it.'

'So you are a single girl?'

'Yes.' A single girl crying out to be touched.

'Self-supporting?'

'Oh, yes.' I shift back in my seat, pull my skirt down over my thighs, cross my legs and fix him with an unambiguous stare.

He stares back at me.

Suddenly he gets up and starts walking around the room. Now and again he pauses, leans down to gaze at a photo in a frame, squints closely at a painting on the wall, stares out of the window. 'Ah,' he goes from time to time. 'Mmmm. Interesting.'

I look at his hands as he moves them over my things, touching them, fingering them, getting the feel of them. I like to study a man's hands. I like to imagine them on me, in me, stroking me, taking me.

Number Six's hands are soft, white, almost feminine hands, with long delicate fingers that look as if they have never done a day's manual labour. They are inquisitive hands, searching, prying into the clutter on my shelves. They flutter sideways along my bookshelf, pausing, touching, tapping thoughtfully on the books' spines. He pulls out a book, opens it at random and stands there, making an appearance of reading with total concentration. He chuckles. It's a *Malory Towers* book. Enid Blyton.

'So. What are you doing here, in London?' I ask after a while.

'I'm on secondment,' he replies. 'I think that's what you call it. I'm here for a few months, just seeing how the UK end of things operates, you could say.'

He snaps the book shut and replaces it on the shelf, exactly where it was before.

'On your own?'

'I'm sorry?'

I'm asking are you attached, you idiot.

'Well, I mean, you know, your family, I mean –'

'My family?' He smiles, raises both eyebrows this time. 'Oh, you mean – ah, no. I mean, yes, I am on my own.'

He's worked his way around the room so he is behind me now. I lean back in the chair. If he tries – if he wants to – he could lean over and see right down my cleavage.

I want to feel those soft, delicate hands. I want them to touch my neck, reach down inside my shirt to my breasts.

'You have beautiful hair.'

His tone is matter-of-fact. But his voice is quiet suddenly. He is standing very close to me.

'Thank you.'

I lean my head back and close my eyes. His face is so close to mine I can feel his breath on my cheek.

Touch me. Kiss me. For God's sake!

His hand rests on my hair, briefly, lightly. It sends an electrical charge right through my body.

'So many beautiful women here in London,' he whispers, softly. 'I don't think I have ever seen so many.'

What is he telling me?

I open my eyes slowly and look up at him. He smiles down at me, upside down.

'You wouldn't think this was one of the most polluted cities in the world.'

'It's not.'

'Looking at you, looking at the wonderful, healthy gloss on your hair.' He strokes my hair again, lightly, blows on it. 'On your lovely, vibrating – *vibrant* – skin.'

I sit up. It's giving me a crick in the neck, this upside-down conversation.

'It isn't polluted,' I say, turning to look at him. 'Well, of course it's polluted, it's a city. But it's nothing like as polluted as, as, say Paris, or Madrid, or . . .' I'm burbling now. God knows why I've suddenly become so defensive about London. 'And the river – we wouldn't have seals coming all this way to check out the Houses of Parliament if the river was that polluted. Anyway, what makes you say that, I thought you liked London?'

He moves so he's standing right in front of me. His hands have escaped to hide themselves in his pockets, out of temptation's way. He looks down at me, seriously, concerned almost.

'I didn't mean to insult your city. Very far from it. I am its greatest fan, as I have said. I simply meant, how interesting it is that a city, a huge city like London, should have so many healthy, youthful, *vibrant* and,' he pauses, 'beautiful women in it.'

Oh, God. His eyes are boring into mine. Now. It has to be now.

I feel unaccountably paralysed. I don't know what to do. I want to grab him by the collar and drag him to me, just as I did in my fantasy – as I *wanted* to do in my fantasy – rip off his jacket, thrust my hand down his trousers, grab him, squeeze him . . .

But I don't. I sit there, returning his gaze, as cool as can be. Those pale eyes of mine? They can be as bland and expressionless as the next person's.

The pause goes on for what feels like an hour. His hands remain resolutely inside his pockets.

'Is that why you're really here?' I find myself saying at last, a tad lamely. 'Because of all the beautiful women?'

'Perhaps it is,' he says, perfectly seriously.

'Then . . .'

'Then?'

I stand up. We are standing so close to one another he has to take half a step backwards to keep his balance.

'I have to go,' he says, very quietly.

'Why?'

'Oh, you know. Things to do, people to see.'

'Really?'

'Thank you so much.'

'What for?'

'For letting me see your flat. For being such interesting company.'

'You must come again.'

'Thank you.'

Now we're smiling at one another like distant cousins.

Eventually he moves to the front door, opens it and pauses in the doorway.

'Alistair is a very lucky man,' he says, and he goes.

* * *

I stand there after he's gone, not quite knowing where to put myself. Believe it or not it's never happened to me before, this kind of thing.

I can usually read a man. Correction, I can always read a man. Or so I thought. I can tell within moments whether or not he is interested. If he is, the next step is usually predictable. It's a matter of judgment how and who makes the first move. Being an impatient sort I don't tend to wait around for long. If need be I'll jump right in with both feet, eyes wide open.

And if he isn't interested, well, let's move on; there's plenty more where he came from.

But in the case of Number Six, frankly I'm baffled. He's interested, I know he is. I know a sexual charge when I feel one. So why don't I do what I normally do, in my subtle fashion: rip off the clothes and get stuck in? Because there is something about him, something about the look in his eyes, the studied restraint of his movements, the careful casualness of his posture that says 'back off'. Not until I say so. I am the boss here.

Or perhaps he's just playing hard to get. Perhaps he's concerned that I'm Alistair's ... what? What exactly am I? Alistair's girl? Alistair's partner? He knows that's not the case, and even if it was ...

He was not actually there in the boardroom, Number Six. I have to keep reminding myself. He was only there in my mind's eye, he didn't know, he hasn't seen, he hasn't seen me, my naked body.

Enough. There's plenty more where he came from.

I pull out something from the fridge, stick it in the microwave, sit myself in front of the TV, watch something, eat the food. A couple of hours later and I couldn't tell you a thing about what I'd eaten or what I'd been watching, such is the state my mind is in.

This is ridiculous. This is obsessive.

I go to bed and dream about thick brown hair flopping over intense blue eyes, eyes as hard and pale as ice. I dive into the ice and the coldness freezes me, then burns me, and I realise it isn't cold at all; it's heat, it's fire. The fire consumes me, covers me, shrouds me, and I feel myself melting, dissolving, bursting into tiny fragments of nothing at all.

I wake in the morning expecting to find a heap of ash in the bed where my body used to be.

But there isn't one. It's me, Hazel Cunningham, waking naked and randy from a dream, like any other dream, like any other morning.

So life goes on.

4

As computers are to Nick and sex is to me, so are figures to Barbara.

They are her passion. They are what motivates her, what gets her up in the morning. Astonishing to think it, but it's true. You only have to see her, to watch her bent low over her balance sheets. Her eyes are alive, afire, her fingers dance like dervishes up and down the page. A tick there, an adjustment here, round and around they go, the point of her pencil (she always uses a pencil) poised a centimetre above the paper, ready to swoop like some predatory bird at a misplaced decimal point, an incomplete number, an incorrect total.

And she does it all in her head. The calculations, that is. I have to say that, in these days when computers can think for you, choose and organise your holidays for you, virtually eat your dinner for you, for people like Barbara not only to avoid using them altogether but to calculate *everything* in her head, eschewing all machines including calculators, is frankly perverse.

But, of course, she has never *ever* made a mistake. Not one. It pains her – it physically pains her – to have to hand her precious figures over to anyone else, because she knows that is where things will start to go wrong. It's not the machine's fault: even she, the technophobe, knows that. It's the fault of the machine operator, of the idiot whose job it is to input the data into the system. In short, me.

I'd have sacked myself long ago, to speak the truth. I

realise that to make one little slip-up with the figures is tantamount to stabbing Barbara with a knife. So it's a source of constant mystery to me why she doesn't report me. Maybe she has a soft spot for me. Maybe it's because I'm the only person who doesn't mind her checking and double-checking every single entry I make.

And now here she comes, walking purposefully over towards my desk, and you'll understand why she speaks to me as if she's addressing a five-year-old:

'These are the annual figures, Hazel.'

'Very good, Barbara.'

'Incomings on the left, outgoings on the right.'

'I understand.'

'They tally.'

And the Pope is Catholic.

'If, by any chance, once you get to total them up, they don't tally, then there's a mistake somewhere.'

'The computer does the tallying,' I suggest.

'I understand that. But even a computer can make a mistake if you enter the figures in wrong.'

'True. Oh!'

'So take extra care, will you?'

'Yes, I . . . Sorry.'

'Are you all right, Hazel?'

'Yes, I . . .'

For one crazy moment I think Barbara has brought her dog into work with her. I'm sure she's got a dog. A little yappy thing probably. But then I realise that this *thing* under the desk, which appears to be brushing against my leg, has fingers on it.

'When you've done that, let me know so I can check them,' she says.

'Yes – ah!'

'Because there's more where they came from.'

And she chatters on, and I'm not listening to a word.

The fingers that have been creeping up my thighs have now reached my crotch and are pawing rather clumsily at my knickers.

I ease my bum off my chair slightly so they can get a purchase, and the knickers are pulled rather roughly down my legs. I spread my legs wide to aerate my fanny – God, that's sexy! – and I wait for what I know is going to happen next.

But I never got round to the truth.

I never told the truth about Nick, about what *really* happened the day I decided to seduce him.

I share an open-plan office with two other people: Barbara and Janine, the junior. Barbara is part-time and usually comes in two mornings and two afternoons a week, and Janine never takes lunch breaks shorter than two hours. That's why I knew – or thought I knew – that we had two full hours on our own.

Nick came to the door much as I described. I sat him down at my computer and tried to describe the 'problem' I'd been having, at which he asked me some rather technical questions which I couldn't begin to answer.

I rested my hand on his shoulder, as I had intended, but he obviously thought that was hampering his progress as he kept sort of shrugging it off, like I was a rather irritating cat. But then, as he got into his work, I sat down beside him and watched his fingers dancing over the keys like a spider and I marvelled at his speed.

'You are so *fast*,' I said.

'I think I see the problem,' he muttered.

'Where did you learn about computers?' I asked.

'Home. Taught myself.'

'I thought as much.'

I leaned over towards him as close as I dared. He was

completely oblivious to anything but the beloved computer.

'I envy the computer,' I murmured.

An odd thing to say, perhaps. He hesitated for a nanosecond.

'Sorry?'

'All that love and care and attention you lavish on it.'

'Oh.'

'Lucky old computer, I say.'

I only knew he'd heard me because those flying fingers suddenly started typing gobbledygook. And I only knew it was gobbledygook because he cursed mildly, wiped the screen and started again.

By now I was beginning to get a bit bored. He didn't have to be that thorough.

'How's it going?' I asked.

'Fine. There's nothing wrong with the software that I can see. Have you downloaded anything from the Net recently?'

'I've no idea.'

'You would know,' he said nervously. 'You can't have done it without knowing.'

'You'd be surprised what I can do without knowing.'

He flashed me an odd look.

'OK. Well, that's, er, all looking fine. I'll just run a scandisk.'

Oh, fly me to the moon, for God's sake, I thought.

'You don't have to do that. I can do that.'

'Won't take a sec.'

While he was doing this I got up and, as casually as I knew how, wandered about the room, quietly closing the shutters of the Venetian blinds, blanking out the outside world.

'Tell me something, Nick,' I said, coming back to sit beside him. 'What is it about computers that gets your blood going?'

'Er, it's ... what, sorry, what did you say?' he stammered.

'Never mind.'

He turned towards me suddenly and I was so close to him we practically bumped noses. He jumped slightly, which gave me the excuse to reach out a hand to steady him. Then, my hand still resting on his chest, and in my sexiest voice, I said:

'You know what? I've had enough of computers for the time being.'

'It's nearly done,' he reassured me.

He tried to turn back to his true beloved but I wasn't having it. I wasn't going to compete with a machine. I boldly rubbed my hand on his chest and very lightly toyed with his shirt buttons.

He was looking at me, mesmerised. Mesmerised or maybe terrified.

'You know what?' I began. Two buttons undone already and he wasn't trying to stop me. 'Watching you working on that machine is really, how can I say this, it's a real turn-on.'

His eyes widened and he started breathing rather heavily.

'Do you know what I was thinking, as I was watching you?' – almost all undone now – 'I was thinking how I would love to be that machine and have your fingers playing over me.'

I looked him squarely in the eye as I said this. He was still staring at me. For someone whose favourite centre of focus was usually the floor, he was doing well.

I had his shirt undone by now and I was slipping it

off his shoulders. He was absolutely still, neither stopping me nor helping me.

'Nice,' I said appreciatively.

I started running my hands over his bare chest. Still he didn't move a muscle.

'Tell me,' I said as I reached for his trouser button, 'is this –'

And then the most amazing thing. He brushed my hand aside, reached for his own button and, before you could say 'twenty gigabyte hard drive,' he had his trousers off, then his underpants. Before I could gasp with amazement at what I saw underneath he was grabbing me and, with what I can only call some expertise, he was pulling my top over my head and tearing off my bra and tugging at my skirt until in no time at all I was as naked as he.

And we stood there, Adam and Eve, facing each other, his cock rampant. Then, before I could say, 'Wow look at *you!*' he'd grabbed my hand and placed it on his throbbing cock, and was rubbing it up and down and breathing so hard I thought he would come in an instant. Then he took hold of me, lifted me bodily from the ground and, roughly shoving aside the keyboard and the mouse and a pile of other stuff, he plonked me down onto the desk so my back was against the computer. To get a grip on the desk I bent my knees so my legs were spread-eagled, and this made it all the easier for him to thrust himself into me. I cried out – it was rough, but it was good – and as he thrust away I grabbed at anything I could to stop myself from crashing off the desk and bringing him with me. He was getting more and more frantic and then he was on top of the desk too, at which time I managed somehow to get my toes caught in a bundle of cables and I think part of me must have been pushing against the keyboard, because I was aware of all sorts of extraordinary things coming up on the computer screen.

Then he turned me over in such a fashion that the cables pinned my body to the desk. And while I'm normally not into bondage and all that stuff this constriction in some extraordinary way quadrupled my excitement. By now he was fucking me from behind, and there was something about his total lack of finesse and control that fired my loins something terrible and I was crying out in a mixture of pain and delight, and he was crying out too, and then with a crash the computer toppled off the desk, but still he kept going – I thought he was never going to stop. I thought this might be my first experience of the infinite fuck and it was wonderful and dreadful all at the same time and then, with a great heave, and shudder, and a groan, he came, and everything went completely still.

So there we were, sprawled across the desk, me pinioned by the cables, computer on the floor, him lying on top of me panting hard; and I could feel his sperm trickling down my legs and for some reason I found that the sexiest thing.

As soon as he allowed himself to shift his weight off me I stood up and carefully extricated myself from the mess of cables. He sat back down on the chair, still panting away as if he'd done the marathon – which in some ways he had, let's face it. And never a thought or a glance towards his beloved computer.

'Christ, that was knackering,' he said.

So romantic, the young. I gazed at him.

'You've done this before,' I said.

'No.'

'Oh, come on now!'

'Never on a desk. Never with . . . computers and stuff.'

He was still struggling to get his breath back.

'What about that?' I looked down at the poor fallen computer. Nothing looked broken, but still. 'Shouldn't we...?'

But I looked back at him and, blow me, he was coming at me again, and his trembling cock was slowly edging upwards all over again, and this time he reached towards me, roughly grabbed my face and thrust his mouth onto mine.

'Yesss.' And he kissed me again. And pulled me down with him onto the floor.

Which is just as well as at that moment Barbara walked in.

We were hidden from her by the desk and the computer, thank God. Nick, needless to say, didn't notice her at all.

He was too busy kissing me. I thought his tongue was going to crush my windpipe, and his mouth was attacking my lips with such force I thought my face would split in two. He had no control at all; it was thrilling, and terrifying.

Then I felt him trying to push himself inside me all over again. I whispered in his ear, 'Barbara's here,' but either he didn't hear or he didn't want to, because he just carried on pushing himself into me, rather roughly, and I had a terrible urge to giggle.

He obviously sensed this. Still inside me, he pulled himself up onto his elbows and glared at me. 'Barbara,' I whispered again.

'What?' he mouthed.

'Here. In the room,' I mouthed back.

There was a pause. And then, more gently this time, he carried on thrusting.

I couldn't believe it. I thought I had had it – had enough, exciting though it was. But there was something about hearing someone else in the room – the sound of papers being shuffled, the odd cough – that excited me all over again. And him too. His eyes, which never left mine while he was fucking me, were afire. Unfortunately we were lying on a creaky floorboard so there was a squeak as he thrust away, at which Barbara called out:

'Is there anybody there?'

Nick roughly shifted my body a few feet to a safer bit of ground. I could hear Barbara's footsteps approaching and both our naked bodies went completely rigid. And then her phone rang. I heard her irritated sigh, and her retreating footsteps.

'Hello, Barbara Osborne speaking.'

And on he went, thrust, thrust.

'Yes, I have all that in order. I'm preparing the accounts right now.'

He desperately tried to stop himself from groaning.

'They should be ready in a couple of weeks.'

'Christ!'

'Sorry, what did you say?'

And his body stiffened as he fought not to cry out, as he carried on thrusting.

'No, sorry, I thought you said . . . Anyway, if you'd like to give me a call in a week or two, I will have some figures for you.'

'Aaaah!' Unmistakable.

'Did you? No, no, I will have them. Absolutely, you can.' Poor woman, she was dying to get the conversation over with so she could come and investigate.

'Rest assured. Rest assured. In two weeks. Yes, and . . . what?'

He withdrew from me, then reached over, grabbed my mouth again and kissed me.

'Yes. Oh, yes, I haven't forgotten.'

I was trying to scramble away from him and grabbing at my clothes.

'All right. I will do. All right. Well, thank you and good –'

And he was still trying to reach out for me, while I was pulling on my top and my skirt, hunting around for my knickers.

'Yes. I understand. That won't be a problem, thank you, Mr, er . . .'

And still he was trying to reach for me and, dammit, his cock . . .

'Thank you, Mr Simpson. Will do. Promise. Thank you. Goodbye.'

'Hello, Barbara. What are you doing here today?' This was me, advancing towards the enemy, better attack than retreat.

'I could ask you the same thing,' she said, with ice.

'I work here, remember?'

'What were you doing just now?'

'I was trying to see what had happened to the computer. It just, I don't know how it happened, it just fell off the desk.'

She was staring at me.

'Just like that,' I said.

'Really?'

'I just hope it's not broken. I don't know how it happened. I guess I must have pulled at the cables or something, got the mouse caught up with the printer. Or something.'

'Well, I don't know how you're going to account for it if it is broken.'

Never a truer word.

And what was Nick doing meanwhile? How long was I going to have to keep up this inane conversation?

'All right, then. You'd better get on and see that it's OK.'

'Right.'

So I wandered back to my corner of the office and dammit if he wasn't still lying there, under the desk, stark naked, making no attempt to dress, and grabbing me by the ankle as I walked by.

I cried out.

'Now what?'

'Stubbed my toe.'

She was looking at the chaos around my desk.

'What *have* you been up to? It looks as if a hurricane has hit it!'

Oh, Barbara. Little do you know.

As a result of that I realised that not only was Nick the nervous computer nerd rampant and insatiable, but that nothing gave him greater joy than doing it right there in the office among the computers and the cables and so forth. Which, if you think about it, is not so surprising.

And so we did. Regularly. Fucked in the office.

And then I realised something else. Knowing that other people were in the room, or likely at any moment to walk in, was an added turn-on for Nick. And because it turned him on it turned me on. There was something about his animal behaviour, his total lack of control, that did something for me. I knew that once he'd got the idea in his head, nothing – hosepipes, nuclear bombs, collapse of buildings – nothing would stop him. Which was kind of glorious.

So here he is again, under the desk, while Barbara is trying to hold an important conversation with me.

'Ow!'

'What was that?'

That was Nick bumping his head on the underside of the desk.

'I just bumped my knee. Stupid me.'

His tongue is on my pussy now. Licking and sucking me like I'm an ice lolly.

'We need to get the accounts sorted out by Friday week, do you think that's too much to ask?' says Barbara.

'Not at all.'

And his tongue is thrusting into my cunt and he's chewing my lips, my pussy lips, that is. It's painful but . . .

'Ah!' I go.

. . . nice too.

'Are you sure you're all right?'

I kind of wish he would stop, actually.

'Yes, thanks.'

Because I'm beginning to slide down in my seat and, any moment now, despite myself . . .

Barbara is standing there staring at me. She's good at that.

I fall off the chair.

'Extraordinary,' she mutters.

And she's gone.

She must think I'm stark staring bonkers. Not just an inefficient data inputter, but mad as a hatter to boot.

It's been a long day.

I've knocked myself out on those figures. Went through them line by line, decimal point by decimal point, checking and rechecking. Barbara will be amazed. I thought I owed it to her. I don't want her having me put away, or getting me sacked come to that.

I'll drop into a bar on the way home, have one quick one and retire early.

It's a bar I've not been to before. But I know it's a place where you can just sit in a corner on your own and look on and nobody minds much. Believe it or not, that is what I like to do. I'm not always on the make.

This bar is full of suits. Business people, City people rewarding themselves after a hard day making all those millions.

Perhaps he will be here. Number Six. I idly wonder what he does with himself of an evening.

He's standing there by the bar, one foot resting on the strut of a bar stool, talking to two other suits. One hand is on his drink, the other in his pocket. Relaxed, serious, smiling occasionally.

He listens to the other two. He listens more than he talks and, as he listens, his eyes on occasion dart briefly but swiftly around the room. Something tells me he is the leader of this little group. The other two seem to hang on his every word, laughing so very heartily at his jokes, listening, nodding so eagerly at everything he says. Maybe they're just humouring the boss.

His eyes dart in my direction and he sees me. He gives no sign of recognition, just stares at me for a long while before returning his attention to his companions.

OK, it's not coincidence. I lied – I have been to this bar before. This is where I met him all those weeks ago, whenever it was, with Alistair. It's a City bar, hence the suits.

He's making no move to come over to me. Why should he? He's not even glancing in my direction. Clearly it's of no importance to him whether I'm here or not.

I get up and make my way over to the bar for another drink. One or two of the suits are looking at me now –

not him, nor his companions – and I know I could score here if I wanted to.

But I don't do that. I am not, believe me, a whore; not that kind of whore at any rate. I don't pick up people in bars, I'm not (yet) that desperate. But I do like to be looked at.

I'm standing next to him now, at the bar. Our bodies are touching. It's busy, and the guys behind the bar are taking no notice of me.

'We meet again,' he says.

'We do.'

'And how are you today?' he asks.

'Tired,' say I.

'Oh? How come?'

'I've had a very long day. Annual accounts.'

'How exciting. Did you show a profit?'

'More or less.'

'It's good when the numbers balance.'

'But it didn't half take a long time.'

'Anything that's worthwhile takes a long time,' he says, without looking at me.

'Does it?' I reply, without looking at him.

'You have to be very patient when it comes to figures. But in the end, when they all balance up as you hope, then it is very satisfying.'

'"Satisfying"?'

'Yes. Patience is rewarded finally.'

'You reckon.'

'Always.'

'I want you to fuck me,' I blurt out suddenly.

There's a silence.

'Did you hear what I said?' I ask.

'I did, yes.'

'I'm sorry, I thought I was making it obvious the other day. When you came to my place.'

Still he says nothing. He turns to look at me. His ice-blue eyes are expressionless.

'Well?' I persist.

'I'm flattered,' he says, courteously.

'You're flattered? I don't want to flatter you, I want to fuck you.'

Why can't I learn restraint? I ask myself.

'As I said, I'm flattered.' He's smiling now. 'What are you drinking?'

And then, cool as you like, after what I have just said, he introduces me to his companions. I'm vaguely aware of one thin pale one and one florid fat one and I smile at them without really taking them in, or their names. I have other things on my mind.

Number Six orders drinks and finds the four of us a table and sits down next to me.

With the drinks comes a cornucopia of snacks and nuts, crisps and dips of exotic textures and colours. The fat guy's eyes are bulging.

'Geoffrey here works for a rival bank,' says Number Six. 'So we talk about everything other than business. All the time he is double-talking me, hoping to pick up something, but I am too clever for him.'

'That's what he thinks,' mocks Geoffrey, who has a braying laugh. He dips a crisp into a bowl, piles it high with goo, and stuffs it into his face.

'Tim here, on the other hand, is a stockbroker. He's in a different line of business, quite. We were talking about tourism.'

Tim's smile is watery and vague and his eyes don't join in.

Number Six's hand, underneath the table, rests lightly on my thigh. I feel my nerve endings go into red alert.

'Geoffrey says all cities are the same nowadays. He says they are all full of Starbucks and McDonald's and tourists, and you cannot tell one town from the next. I am saying that is not true of London, not at all,' he says.

His hand is working its way slowly along my thigh, the naked thigh beneath my skirt, towards my crotch. I have to remind myself to breathe.

'London has a charm all of its own,' he goes on. 'I think it has to do with its history and the way in which it evolved.'

His hand is inside my knickers now and slowly, slowly and gently, with those long, delicate fingers, he begins to tease my pussy.

'London grew up as a series of villages, isn't that correct? Each one separate from the others, which is why there is so much diversity.'

'Yes, but you wouldn't know it now. Now they've all got the Starbucks and the McDonald's.' Geoffrey talks with his mouth full. He is a bore and a glutton, I realise.

Number Six's fingers, with their extraordinary light touch, are beginning to work their magic on me. How does he know, I ask myself silently, how does he know so precisely what to do?

'Moreover, there are still many parts of London where the tourists simply do not visit. The East End. The Mile End Road. Brick Lane,' he goes on.

Geoffrey snorts and sprays the table with guacamole. 'Who'd want to go there in the first place?'

Number Six has two fingers inside me now, deep inside me, and with his thumb he teases my clit. Such is his dexterity nobody seems to notice a thing.

'Where do you live, er . . .?'

'Hazel. Battersea.'

I smile coolly at Geoffrey and graciously offer round the nuts. Butter would not melt in my mouth and this time I am certainly not going to fall off my chair.

Underneath the table, meanwhile, I'm spreading my

legs. Wider and wider. Come into me, say my legs and my cunt.

'I used to live in Battersea,' says Geoffrey.

'Did you?' I ask with apparent interest. 'When was that?'

Suddenly Number Six withdraws his hand. The bastard.

'Fifteen years ago. Very different it was then.'

He brings his hand to his mouth and, slowly and with great delicacy, he licks his fingers, one by one, as if he was tasting caviar. I catch my breath. Geoffrey watches him with interest.

'You could pick up a nice bit of property then,' Geoffrey drones on, his eyes still on Number Six. 'For next to nothing.'

'And did you?' asks Six.

'Did I what?'

'Pick up a nice piece of property in Battersea?'

'I – oh!' Geoffrey's attention has drifted somewhat. 'Is that the end of the dips?' he complains.

Six's hand is back again. His fingers flutter lightly on my clit.

'No, as it happens. Didn't have the readies then. But it was true nonetheless. Ask anyone if you don't believe me,' Geoffrey adds, a touch belligerently. He's onto the nuts now. Shovelling them in.

'I'm sure you're right,' say I.

I lean back from the table, ostensibly in an attitude of calm relaxation but, in fact, to ease Number Six's fingers deeper inside me. The strain of keeping the two halves of myself separate – the growing surge inside and the sphinx-like smile on the outside – is intense and glorious.

'Do you own your own place?' mumbles Geoffrey through the nuts.

'No, I don't as a matter of fact.'

'Silly girl. You're missing a trick, wasting your money on rent.'

'I'm sure you're right,' I say again, with a gracious and, I hope, patronising smile.

My body stretches as my pussy leans and strains against Six's fingers.

'Should have bought while the going was good. Property. Property's the thing at the moment, what with the way the stock market is today, ain't that right, Tim?'

'Oh yes. Absolutely. Property, yes.' Tim dips his wraith-like fingers into the nearly empty bowl of nuts and scrapes them hopelessly back and forth.

I lean my head back and touch my neck. Six's fingers are working fast now, tiny little circular movements on my clit.

'Mind you what's true of today ain't necessarily so tomorrow,' Geoffrey ploughs on. 'Housing market's too damn volatile for my liking. We're fast running out of options. Have I scoffed all the nuts? Terribly sorry.'

My body shudders imperceptibly as I come.

'Have you considered buying property abroad?' says Tim.

'In the sun, you mean. Buy to rent. Now you're talking.'

And again.

I close my eyes and give a tiny gasp. I can't stop the orgasm.

My cunt grips his fingers. Number Six looks at me in surprise.

'Free holidays into the bargain,' Geoffrey goes on. 'And all that foreign food – mind you, France is OK, I could handle the Froggy food.'

Still he looks at me, Number Six. Still my cunt

clenches and unclenches around his fingers in multiple, endless orgasm.

No one ever made me come like this.

'What do you think?'

The two men are looking in his direction.

'You people are obsessed with property,' says Number Six with a lazy smile.

I've clamped his fingers inside me.

'In Holland we rent,' he goes on. 'It's not a big deal.'

Holding them there with sheer willpower. And well-toned muscles, naturally.

'It is a mystery to me how you people can afford to live here,' says Six, gently sliding his fingers from me.

'Good God, is that all the dips finished?' Geoffrey's eyes bulge with disappointment. 'Do you think we could order up some more?'

'Try this.'

Number Six is proffering his fingers. Waving them gently in front of Geoffrey's face.

'Why? What you got there?'

'No!' I try to grab his hand back, but he moves it out of my reach.

Geoffrey's eyes are boggling.

'The sweetest thing you ever tasted. Go on, try it.'

Geoffrey sniffs the fingers.

'Don't recognise it. Was it something we had before?'

'I don't think so.'

Geoffrey's tongue flicks out and licks the finger suspiciously.

'Mmm.'

'Good, isn't it?' says Six, gently pressing his knee against mine.

Geoffrey licks the fingers again. I am fighting the giggles.

'There's something ... familiar.'

. Now Geoffrey is sucking Number Six's fingers like a small child with a dummy. I don't think I have ever seen anything so bizarre in my whole life.

'Mmm. Can't put my finger on...'

He swallows. And realises.

He looks at Number Six, and then he looks at me.

'What?' say I.

'Am I right in thinking...?'

Number Six pulls out a handkerchief and delicately wipes his fingers. 'Well,' he says.

He is still staring at us, is Geoffrey, as Number Six stands up.

'If you will excuse us, gentlemen, we have to go.'

He puts his handkerchief back inside his pocket and stands behind my chair, ready to help me to my feet.

And before Geoffrey can clamp shut that gargantuan mouth of his we are out of there and standing on the pavement.

'That was outrageous!' I say.

'It was quite amusing, wasn't it?'

He smiles at me as he shakes my hand.

'It was delightful to see you again,' he says.

'And you.'

'Such a surprise.'

'You can say that again.'

'Forgive me, but I have to rush off. An appointment.'

'That's a shame.'

'Till the next time.'

'Yes.'

'Until the next tasting. I shall look forward to it.'

You'd think we were business partners or something, arranging our next meeting. With a little bow of the head he turns and walks rapidly away from me along the pavement.

I close my eyes and start to laugh.

Reality stranger than fiction? You can say that again. That little scene certainly knocked spots off the wildest fantasy I have ever invented.

Number Six, you are a miracle.

5

Alistair has invited me to the opera. It's called *Dido and Aeneas*. Actually it's opera plus. It's taking place at a stately home somewhere in the country, dinner on the lawn beforehand, all that stuff.

As you can imagine, opera is not my bag. The prospect of spending an English summer's evening – i.e. in the freezing cold and possibly the driving rain – sitting on a hard bench watching fat singers trilling away in a language I don't understand doesn't fill me with delight.

Still, this is Alistair. He is genuinely cultured, that's to say he truly loves opera and music and theatre and all the grand arts, he isn't posing, and I'm hoping against hope that some of this culture might just rub off on me, you never know.

For practical reasons I'm tempted to go in jeans, sweater, parka and wellies. But such is the English way of doing things I'm putting on this almost totally diaphanous pale yellow silk number, because I know it will excite Alistair; and much as I'd love to forget the underwear, I don't want to embarrass him as well, so I'm getting out my best lacy stuff and I'm just hoping he appreciates how much I am sacrificing comfort in order to please him.

He's wearing an Austin Reed shirt – I think that's what it is, he's not exactly at the cutting edge of men's fashion, bless him – and a sports jacket for God's sake. If he wasn't so gorgeous he would look positively middle-aged. So off we drive down through London to this village somewhere in ... somewhere. Park among the Bentleys and the Aston Martins and squelch our way – it constantly amazes me how much, the more classy you are in this country of ours, the more moneyed you are, the more sheer, unnecessary discomfort you are expected to put up with – squelch our way through the muddy car park to a vast tent where we are treated to a three-course dinner.

I've brought a pashmina, which I've been hugging about myself to stave off hypothermia. Once inside the tent – sorry, the marquee – I shed it, and there I am, in my diaphanous glory, sitting down opposite Alistair, whose eyes are boggling.

'You are truly outrageous,' he murmurs.

'What do you mean?'

'Your dress. It's completely see-through.'

'So what? I'm wearing undies.'

He smiles. He loves this. He loves to think he's dating a tart. He's a conventional lad, deep down.

Salmon mousse; followed by saddle of lamb and raspberry sorbet. All helped down the gullet by Sauvignon followed by a gentle Beaujolais – at least, I think that's what it is.

We are seated at a table for six, so we make polite conversation with total strangers, which is tedious. But I'm enjoying the tremulous feeling of anticipation. Knowing I've got to get through what's bound to be a long and rather tough evening before I can grab hold of Alistair and fuck him senseless all night kind of adds to the excitement.

The gentleman opposite – they are all 'gentlemen' – never takes his eyes off my breasts throughout the dinner. I think he's trying to see my nipples. His wife/ girlfriend/date/tart quivers with badly suppressed irritation. I smile at her warmly, knowing it'll irritate her even more. She bares her teeth back at me. Alistair looks on, amused. So far the evening is going rather well, I think to myself. There's just the wretched opera to get through.

However, perhaps it's the wine or the food or I'm just feeling relaxed, but as we find our seats – canvas, a touch up on wooden benches but not much – I'm feeling both a lot warmer and a lot less ill-disposed towards the evening's entertainment. Moreover, Alistair tells me it's quite short.

He's very solicitous, offering to lend me his jacket, which I decline. There are blankets, which I accept.

Is there any other country in the world, any other nationality, that deliberately chooses to spend a Saturday summer's evening driving through the traffic in order to spend a small fortune (as I suspect it is) to sit on a rickety canvas chair whose legs as the evening progresses are going to sink slowly but inexorably into the mud, in the freezing cold, with a heavy risk of rain, knowing that the only chance of survival – since we have all of us chosen to wear our most elegant yet unsuitable floaty numbers – is to shroud ourselves in army blankets, to watch fat singers who can't act trilling silly stories in ridiculous languages? I love the Brits, I do, but really . . .

So here we go, overture and beginners.

It's a very small band, which is a shame, because opera can sometimes be redeemed by sheer volume of noise, in my view. Just a few strings and a keyboard that Alistair informs me later is a harpsichord.

And true to form the singers are fat, and wearing unsuitable clothing (unsuitable for their size I mean), and their acting is – well – *not*, really. But.

Actually, some of the music is rather fun. There are one or two songs – or whatever you call them in opera

– especially the choral ones, that fairly rip along. There's a fun chorus of witches wearing black and green masks and singing in this kind of unearthly way, all of which is quite effective. And it's in English.

And then, just when I'm beginning to think, well that was quite a short evening – in other words towards the end of the show – something amazing happens.

Aeneas, Dido's lover, has just weighed anchor and pissed off back to wherever it was he came from, Troy I think, leaving Dido alone and longing for death. As the (fat) soprano playing Dido sings this mournful song (aria) to her handmaiden Belinda, I feel something welling up in my eyes and, to my horror, great globules of tears come plopping down my cheeks and dropping onto my lap like water bombs.

I don't know why this is. It's not because I'm feeling sympathy for Dido, who had it coming to her. I can only think it is the music itself. She sings it very slow, very soulful, notes sung high and clear in semitones one after the other in a minor key (I'm told later), all with the simplest accompaniment.

> When I am laid, am laid in earth,
> May my wrongs create
> No trouble, no trouble in thy breast.
> Remember me. Remember me.
> But forget my fate.

I tell you, I am sobbing. I am sobbing so hard my shoulders are shaking. Alistair reaches out a hand and lays it on mine and I clutch it hard.

What *is* this? It's such a silly story after all. Dido does nothing but complain – first when she hasn't got her man, then later when she loses her man – and he, Aeneas, well if he can be so easily diverted from the path of true love by a bunch of dubious-looking witches pretending to be gods then he's certainly not worth shedding tears over.

I'm feeling above all *embarrassed*, and I'm hoping the moment will pass before the show ends and the lights come up. But it doesn't. I'm still sitting there slightly stunned several minutes after it's all over.

We squelch back to the car park in silence. Alistair has an arm around my shoulder, a comforting arm. Once inside the car he turns to me.

'Are you all right?'

'Yes, I think so, thanks.' I'm dabbing at my eyes and hoping my mascara hasn't run. 'I don't know what happened, it just ... they just ... I just couldn't help ...'

'It's the music. It does that to you. It does it to me, every time.'

'I didn't see you crying.'

'No, I don't cry. But that doesn't mean it doesn't get to me.'

I look at him curiously. Men aren't usually so eager to admit to being affected by emotional music. Not the men I've known.

He starts up the car. Soon we're joining the queue to the exit and, what feels like several hours later, we're on the road.

'That particular piece of music, "Dido's Lament", has got to be one of the most soulful pieces of music ever written. And it's over four hundred years old,' says Alistair, after quite a long silence.

'It's gratifying, don't you agree?' he goes on.

'In what way?'

'To be moved – to be able to be moved – by something as simple as a piece of music. It's a sign we've not completely lost our senses, that we are still civilised.'

I don't know if I'm quite following this.

'I cried when Bambi lost her mum,' I offer.

'Everyone cries when Bambi loses her mum.'

'I cry at soap operas.'

'No doubt that's what they want you to do.'

'Even commercials.'

He shrugs and smiles slightly. I realise he might think I've been taking the piss, which I regret.

'Still, who'd have thought it – me, crying at an opera?'

And as I think about it the tears start welling and, before you know it, I'm off again. Once again Alistair reaches out a reassuring hand.

'You're lovely when you cry.'

'Oh yeah. Blotchy cheeks and smudged mascara.'

'It shows your vulnerability.'

'It shows my stupidity.'

There, I've done it again. Thrown his sweet remarks back in his face.

'I'm sorry,' I say. 'Sometimes I think I should sew my mouth up.'

We are staying overnight at a nearby hotel. It is, as you would expect, one of those small and completely out-of-the-way places set back from the road down a driveway you would never find if you didn't know it. It is old, wood-beamed, and covered from top to toe in ivy.

Our room has a four-poster. I give a tiny squeal of delight when I see this. I have always wanted to sleep in a four-poster, and I guess I've said as much to Alistair in the past and he's remembered, bless him.

It's a real one too, ancient, oak probably, with white lace curtains and what look for all the world like satin sheets. It is too, too much.

All the furniture is oak, or at least some dark, heavy wood that looks as if it's been there for centuries. There are beams in the ceilings, real ones, and lush, crimson and gold rugs on the floor.

I run my hand down the carved wood on the posts of the bed. It's like something out of a museum. You could just see Henry VIII – or perhaps someone a tad more glamorous – lying there in the bed, among the goose-feather pillows and the satin sheets.

'I'll just use the bathroom,' says Alistair.

I'm completely lost in reverie. I am the mistress of a sixteenth-century nobleman and we've escaped for an illicit weekend to this ancient, hidden inn, where no one could possibly find us. My lover's wife is rich and ugly and I work for them as a kitchen maid in their mansion in London.

My lover is on the run from the authorities because he is a Catholic in this newly reformed Protestant country, where Roman Catholicism is illegal. If they find him they will probably imprison him – in the Tower quite possibly – and torture him until he reveals the names of fellow dissenters. He knows that one day, sooner or later, they will catch up with him, and that his days therefore are numbered, which is why we are here.

I am standing there hugging the post of the bed and, barely knowingly, pressing my body against the hard knobbly bits. I didn't hear the door behind me open but suddenly I feel the weight of Alistair's naked body as he crushes it against mine. I am squashed between him and the post, a knobbly bit of which, fortuitously and deliciously, protrudes against my crotch. I can barely breathe.

He runs his hands down my body. I'm not sure if he's just doing it for the pleasure of it or to find out how to get my dress off.

'What do you want me to do for you, my lord?'

He laughs. 'I beg your pardon?'

I help him by undoing the buttons down the front of my dress.

'We don't have long. Your wife doesn't know where you are, but if the authorities find you –'

'Authorities?'

He reaches into my dress and, without removing the dress itself, with some manoeuvring he takes off my bra.

'They will torture you, won't they? Lock you up and torture you until you give them the names of your friends, your fellow Catholics.'

'I would never do that.'

He lifts up my skirt and takes off my panties. I am now naked under my see-through dress.

'I know you would never betray anyone, sir,' I say. 'You are a man of honour.'

'Except my wife, or so you say.'

'That is not betrayal.'

'Turn round,' he says, quietly. I do.

'Christ, you are sexy,' he says.

'Your wife does not care for you, she only married you for your money.'

'And you are? Remind me.'

'My name is Sara, sir. I am your kitchen maid.'

'And what do kitchen maids do, Sara?'

'They can do anything you want them to, sir.'

Once again I am rubbing my crotch, naked under my dress, against one of the knobs on the bed. I'm wondering when they designed these beds whether they realised what useful sex aids the decorative bits would turn out to be.

'Turn around again, Sara. Please.'

I turn my back on him again.

Holding me by the waist with one hand, the other lifts my skirt and he leans into me. I feel the touch of the tip of his cock against my cunt. I open my legs in readiness.

Then, gently, he pushes me so I am bent forwards over the bed. I can still feel his cock, but it's still only the tip, the very tip.

'Are you big, sir?'

'I am pretty big, Sara. I don't want to hurt you.'

'I can barely feel you. You don't feel very big to me.'

'I'm not in you yet.'

'Oh.'

Now he's in me. Just. Again just the tip, and only an inch of it.

'That's not big, sir.'

He begins to fuck me, with tiny movements. Each time he thrusts, a bit more of him goes inside me. But I'm still only feeling half of him.

'Is that it then, sir?'

'No, Sara. That's barely half of me. Are you ready for more?'

'I should say so, sir. I can't hardly feel anything.'

She's a liar, this Sara.

Still he's only giving me half of himself. I'm squirming, pushing back to press him into me.

'Are you a virgin, Sara?'

'Oh yes, sir.'

'You feel very tight.'

'Is that a good thing, sir?'

'It's a very good thing.'

Now he's about two-thirds in.

'Can you feel that now?' he asks.

'Yes, I can just about feel that.'

'Am I big, Sara?'

'You're not bad. I've known bigger.'

'I thought you said you were a virgin.'

'Only in a manner of speaking, sir.'

'How's this?'

'Oh!'

'Or this?'

'Yes!'

'There's more.'

'I should hope there is, sir.'

'Do you want it?'

'Yes!'

'Are you sure?'

'All of it!'

And he gives it to me.

'Oh, sir.'

'You can feel that, I hope.'

'Christ, sir!'

'And that.'

'Yes, sir.'

'How's that, Sara?'

'It's . . . oh, sir!'

'Do you like it, Sara?'

'I do!'

'Hard?'

'Harder.'

'Like this?'

'As hard as you like. Oh!'

'Tell me how it feels.'

'It feels like you're splitting me in two, sir.'

'Would you do something for me, Sara?'

'Sir.'

'Kneel up for me.'

He grabs my waist, climbs onto the bed and pulls me until my body is upright, still with him inside me. Then he pushes me forwards so I am on all fours, doggy-fashion as they call it, and pushes deep into me.

'Can you feel that, Sara?'

'Christ, sir!'

'What?'

'You're so deep, sir.'

'I can feel the edges of you, Sara!'

'You're filling me, sir.'

'Am I big enough for you?'

'You're . . .'

'What?'

'Bigger.'

'Bigger than what?'

'Bigger than I've ever known, sir.'

'Oh, Sara!'

'Yes?'

'I'm going to come!'

'Go for it, sir.'

'Oh, Christ.'

'Yes!'

'My God!'

'Yes.'

'YES!!'

There's a long, frozen moment as he releases himself into me. His body rigid, on me and in me.

Then, slowly, and still inside me, he lowers my body onto the bed and lays his gently on top of me and we lie there together, gasping for breath.

'How was that for you, Sara?'

'Not bad, sir. For a first try.'

He spanks my bottom lightly and whips me over onto my back. I cry out as his cock leaves me.

'But you could do with a bit more practice,' says Sara, the cheeky tart.

'I'm sure that can be arranged.'

He leans forward and gives me a deep kiss.

* * *

When I wake the following morning Alistair is standing there, naked, his back turned to me. He is gazing out of the window.

I reach out a hand and run it lightly down his back. He turns, smiles.

'Sleep well?' he says, as he climbs back onto the bed.

'Hardly.'

'No?'

'Not with all that commotion going on, I don't think so. Sir.'

'What commotion?'

'The commotion last night. Don't tell me you've forgotten all about it.'

'I don't remember any commotion.'

'Bloody hellfire, sir, you've got a short memory.'

'Then you'd better remind me, er, Sara.'

'They came for you in the night, sir.'

'Did they? Who?'

'The secret police, or whoever they are. You could tell they were secret police because of their, their ... Anyway, three of them, there were. Built like tanks.'

'Really? Go on.'

He pulls the sheets down, exposing my naked body.

'They came clattering up the stairs, making enough noise to wake the dead. Well, to wake everybody but you apparently, sir.'

'And?'

He rests a hand lightly on my chest.

'They barged their way into the room without so much as a by-your-leave.'

'Outrageous.'

'Demanded you go with them, sir, immediately. To the Tower. For a spot of torture.'

'Well, fancy that. And did I?'

'Did you what?'

'Go with them.'

'Well hardly, sir. Seeing as how you're still here.'

'And you're telling me I slept through all this?'

'Well, not exactly, sir. It seems to have slipped your memory somehow.'

'Tell me. Tell me what happened, Sara.'

His hand begins to move slowly down my body.

'I saw them off, sir.'

'You saw them off? Single-handedly?'

'You could say.'

'How?'

'I tell you what, sir. You owe me.'

I slither down the bed slightly.

'I'm sure I do,' he murmurs, stroking my belly. 'Tell me what you did, and then tell me how I can make it up to you.'

'I gave myself to them, sir.'

His hand stops moving for a moment.

'What, all of them?'

'One after the other after the other.'

I give him a sly smile and wriggle my body from side to side. The feeling of the satin on my skin is deeply sexy.

'That is way outside the duty of any kitchen maid, Sara,' he says, as his hand travels on down to my pussy.

'Anything to be of service, sir.'

'And tell me what, er, what was I doing, meanwhile?' he asks.

'While they were fucking me?'

'Yes.'

'You were watching, sir.'

'Just watching?'

'Yes. I believe you quite enjoyed it, sir. I believe it got you quite worked up, sir, least that's the way it looked to me.'

His fingers are on my pussy, searching. I part my legs.

'You like to watch me fuck other men, don't you? Least you did last night. Specially when they were all at it together, all three of them.'

'All three of them together, were they?'

'At one point, yes.' I touch my breasts, lightly. His fingers move on my clit. On my wet eager clit.

'You like to think of me as your whore, don't you?' I say.

'What makes you say that?'

'And you like it too when other men ogle me. Especially when I'm wearing some tarty see-through number. You liked it when the guy at our table last night stared at me. It excited you.'

His fingers, his searching, questing fingers, cease moving.

'What are we talking about now?' he asks.

'You love it when I tell you about my fantasies. It turns you on to hear about other men fucking me. Especially when it's someone you know. Someone who exists. Isn't that right?'

He doesn't reply. He moves his hand away from me, away from my reaching, needy pussy.

I reach out for his cock, which is resting right there on the bed in front of me. It's not moving. I want to touch it with my tongue, to taste it, to wake it up. But he turns away from me.

'Say something, Alistair.'

'I'm sorry if that's how you think I think of you,' he says, eventually.

'I don't mind at all. Let's all be given credit for what we're good at.'

He reaches over to me and, with unexpected tenderness, he strokes my cheek.

'You want to hear more?' I ask him.

'Who and what are we talking about now?'

'This is me, Hazel. This is the real thing.'

'Right.'

'I saw him again.'

'Who?'

'Your Dutch friend. Number Six.'

'Ah, him.'

'Twice, as a matter of fact. Once he came to my flat.'

'Did he?'

'The next time I met him in a bar. In that bar, you know the one. You want to know what happened?'

He's just looking at me.

'He was with friends. We sat down at a table together, the four of us. We had drinks, and bits to eat, and we chatted, about this, that and the other. About the price of houses and all sorts of fascinating stuff. Very civilised it was. And all the while, while this conversation was going on between the four of us, he was masturbating me.'

I pause, for dramatic effect.

'Right there, under the table. With his fingers. While he was chatting on about what a wonderful place London was he was making me come, over and over and over. And you know what? He knew exactly what to do. It was as if he'd known me all my life, it was mind-blowing.'

There's a pause.

Something has gone horribly wrong. I don't know what it is – he's listening, he's not trying to stop me. But this isn't doing anything for him, there's no movement in his cock, none at all. Suddenly I feel like a prize idiot.

'You don't want to hear about it, do you?'

'Not really, no,' he says, looking away from me.

'Right.'

There's a bit of a pause.

'So what's happening here?' I say eventually, touching his cock lightly. 'Not a lot by the look of it.'

'I don't like you thinking I only want you for sex,' he says quietly. 'That's not right.'

'There's no need to be ashamed of that. I love it, you know I do. I like being your whore.'

'You are not my whore.'

'What else am I, then?'

He's starting to grimace. I still have his cock in my hand and I am lightly stroking it.

'Please don't do that,' he says, with an effort.

'Why not? Don't you want me?'

'You know I want you. I want you all the time.'

'Well then.'

'And yes, it does excite me to watch other men watching you. And to see your naked body through your dress. It excites me to think of your body, at whatever time of the day or the night it is. And to hear about your fantasies, it excites me more than you can imagine.'

'Then what's the problem?'

His cock is beginning to twitch slightly.

'I can't really explain. Please.'

'What?'

'Stop doing that.'

I do.

He gets up suddenly, stands back from the bed and looks at me.

'What?'

He stands there gazing at me for what feels like a fortnight. But it's an odd sort of a gaze and after a while I find myself slowly pulling the sheets right up to my chin.

Then, quite abruptly, he turns and exits into the bathroom.

Well, I don't know what the hell was going on there. And it was all going so well.

It's a shame, I think as I lie back in the bed, because the sensation of the satin sheets against my skin is gloriously sensuous. As I slither back and forth I feel the weight of the fabric falling in folds into the crevices of my body, and the coolness of the satin – or whatever it is – against the hotness between my legs is sexy beyond belief. I stretch an arm above my head and my hand encounters the headboard and, on it, what feels for all the world like a phallus. I stroke the phallus with one hand while moving my body from side to side, wallowing in the sensation of the sheets against my pussy and thinking, oh God, he should be here, with me, enjoying this, enjoying me.

But he's not. He's in the bathroom. I hear the shower starting up. The shower? OK, so that means no sex this morning.

I am so turned on. I am so hot I could scream. With one hand on the wooden phallus and the other on my pussy I rub myself, lightly, quickly. It's all over in a moment, my body writhing, my mouth open in a silent scream of ecstasy – of self-induced, empty ecstasy.

I get up and throw on some clothes. By the time he emerges from the bathroom I'm sitting cross-legged on the bed, immersed from head to foot in jeans and sensible, opaque knitwear with barely an inch of flesh showing.

He takes one look at me and laughs.

'What?'

'You.'

'*What?*'

He kisses me. It's a brotherly kiss. But the look on his face is not like a brother at all.

I used to think Alistair was such a straightforward

person. A bit repressed perhaps, like all products of public school. But I always used to think I knew where I was with him, until now.

A while later he drives me back to London, chatting idly as if nothing had happened. Which I suppose in one sense it hasn't.

He talks about all sorts of things: the surrounding countryside, what the weather's doing to the poor farmers, the terrible state of English cricket. He describes in great detail the rules of some sport he calls 'real tennis' – a favourite hobby of his. If he senses I'm not really listening, and therefore not really interested, he switches topics seamlessly, almost without you noticing.

But of him and me? Of the conversation we had this morning? Nothing. All of a sudden I'm beginning to wonder if I'm losing my touch. Perhaps, I'm thinking, I ought to get used to knowing it was fun while it lasted.

Relationships – who'd have 'em?

And eventually he delivers me to my door.

'Are you coming in?' I ask, as I always do.

'Not this time, thanks,' he replies, as he always does.

'See you in a couple of weeks then,' he says.

'I hope so.'

'I'll call you.'

He kisses me on the cheek, jumps out of the car, lopes around the front of it to open the passenger door, and watches me as I climb my steps, enter my front door. With a smile.

6

It's time I paid another visit to my dad.

I don't see much of my dad nowadays. To be honest it's become a bit of a duty now, like going to confession.

He works for the Home Office in the Immigration Department, where I'm sure he does noble and fine things and helps to improve the lot of countless dispossessed people. But as a person, himself, frankly he's become a bit sad.

If my mother was a Stoic my father is a Spartan. He lives on his own in a flat in Hackney which, each time I visit, looks more and more bare. Each time there is less furniture and fewer 'things' – the sort of things, useless things as often as not, that go to make a place a home. It's as if he's trying to strip his life down to the absolute minimum, in order to get at something, something intangible. As if ridding himself of material things is suddenly going to reveal the secret of life or something.

He's in his sixties now and due to retire in a few years, and I worry about him. Along with the Spartan lifestyle, he's gradually reducing his diet. First he gave up on red meat, then he became a vegetarian, then a vegan, and lately he's turned to macrobiotics, so all he ever seems to eat now is brown rice with the odd pulse thrown in and perhaps an organic tomato for special occasions.

We never talked much about anything important, in the past. We never discussed the divorce, or Frank. We never really talked about my mother's death in any depth. After the divorce there was one of those ridiculous, unnecessary family schisms, where my father assumed – because my brother Ed and I stayed with my mother, not because we chose to but because that was the obvious and practical thing to do – that my brother and I had 'taken her side'. The result of this was that we were never able to have anything resembling a decent relationship with him, and by the time my mother died it was really too late.

And I regret this. I don't like having a father who's a stranger, and besides, he was – and probably still is – a decent man. Each time I see him I resolve to get to grips with it, to get him to talk about all these things. But somehow it never happens.

On this occasion, however, I'm clutching a couple of bottles of wine and a lot of determination.

'Hello there, Sox, how are you?' he greets me on the doorstep.

'Hi Dad, good to see you.'

I've no idea where the nickname Sox came from, but I imagine it probably originated in some catch phrase like 'Bless her cotton socks' that my parents used to use in the days when they still made jokes.

I look around in dread, as I enter his place, to see if there's any furniture left at all. Soon we'll be sitting on cushions on the floor, or even on bare floorboards. But no, there's still a sofa and a couple of chairs left. Bare wooden ones, the plainest and hardest ones imaginable.

'You've still got some furniture left, then,' I say as I look around his living room.

'Of course,' he says.

'What are you trying to do, Dad? Are you trying to reach some kind of nirvana or something?'

'What are you talking about?'

'All this.' I wave vaguely at the nonexistent surroundings. 'What happened to all your stuff? You know, your knick-knacks, photos and stuff?'

'I got rid of them.'

'Why?'

'It's clutter.'

'It's the past.'

He doesn't reply to this.

'I brought these.' I plonk the two bottles down on the table.

'You drink them,' he says. 'You know I don't.'

'You're going to have a glass,' I insist. 'Or two. On this occasion.'

'What occasion is this?'

'It's my birthday.'

'Is it?'

'In a couple of months it is, yes.'

He laughs at this.

'Oh, all right then.'

Well, that was surprisingly easy.

So I open up the first bottle and we drink a toast to one another. I look at him closely; I can't help feeling he looks more than his sixty-something years. I don't know that macrobiotics have done much for him, but he's definitely got smaller over the years, as if he's trying to gradually shrink and eventually disappear from life altogether through a crack in the floorboards.

We eat our way through the meal he has lovingly prepared for us. God knows what it is; it's all vaguely brown and grey in colour and nutty-textured. It's a bit like eating shredded cardboard with nuggets of grit in it. He's matching my drinking glass for glass and beginning to glow a bit, and even to laugh out loud, so I'm beginning to feel really quite relaxed. And then:

'So how are things with you, Sox?' he asks me, genially. 'What are you doing with your life? Something useful I hope.'

'Useful? Ah, well now.'

'How's the job?'

'The job is a job.'

'Is that all it is?'

'Don't make me feel guilty, Dad.'

'I don't want to do that, sweetheart. I just want to know that you're – you know, making good use of your life. In some way that your mother would have been proud of, that's what I'm saying.' He smiles at me.

'I don't know how to answer that.'

'You're not in love or anything, are you?'

'No. Why?'

'Just don't fall in love, whatever you do.'

'Why do you say that?'

I think he's regretting saying it, already. But he has said it, and I want to know why.

'Dad? Why did you say that?'

I refill his glass.

'Because it'll destroy you,' he says simply. He's still smiling, but in an odd sort of a way now.

'What *are* you talking about?'

'Like it destroyed me. Like your mother destroyed me.'

This is more than I reckoned on, and now it's happening I'm not at all sure I'm ready for it.

'Explain, Dad.'

He takes a swig of wine.

'There is – you know this already – there is only one person in the world for each of us, one person for us to fall in love with, as you know.'

'I know no such thing.'

'Well, it's true. That is why we have marriage. One man for one woman, and vice versa. No, don't interrupt.

'If you're lucky enough to meet that person, and if you're lucky enough to discover that that person loves you in return, then ... then you are the luckiest person alive. On the other hand, if – and when – that person betrays you, then you are destroyed. Totally and utterly.'

There is a stunned pause.

'I never heard so much garbage in my life,' I say.

'It's true, Sox. Otherwise we would not have marriages, we would not have one husband to one wife, for better for worse, in sickness and in health. That is the way it is, you can't argue with that.'

He speaks quietly, with measured confidence, as if what he's saying is the most obvious thing in the world.

'You make it sound like it's some kind of ... something to do with nature,' I say, trying hard to keep my temper under control. 'But it's us who invented marriage, one man to one woman and all that stuff. We, people, invented it; it wasn't some divine intervention.'

'We invented it for a purpose,' he goes on, in his calm, infuriating way. 'For the purpose of breeding, of having children, of nurturing children in a loving environment. It's lasted centuries and it will go on lasting, no matter how much we change our moral thinking. People are still getting married, still searching for that One Single Person, and they always will.'

'They may search for them, but that doesn't mean they exist.'

'I'm telling you they do exist. She, she did exist. I know, because I was lucky enough to meet her, and to love her, and to spend some – a few – happy years with her.'

There's a silence.

'She hurt you,' I say, needlessly.

'She hurt me, yes.'

'I'm sorry. But that doesn't mean your life has to be over.'

'I didn't say my life is over.'

'Well, you're behaving like it.'

He's a bit taken aback by that. I am too. I'm taken aback by my own anger, my own burning fury.

'Sox, you misunderstand –'

'All this –' I gesture at the bare walls '– all this deprivation, this emptiness, this throwing out, throwing away – if that isn't giving up, I don't know what is.'

'You have absolutely no right to say that.'

'You know what you are, Dad? You're a coward.' My voice is shaking now.

'*What?*'

'All this masochistic nonsense, it's just a way of punishing yourself. You've given up. It – she – has given you the excuse to give up. First it was red meat, then it was –'

'Come on, Sox, now you're being ridiculous,' he butts in.

'Then it was good food, booze,' I continue, 'and now it's enjoyment. You've given up on enjoyment.'

'I don't know what makes you say that.'

'This – all this – makes me say that. There's no joy here, Dad, you've cut all the joy out of your life.'

'You know nothing.'

'But I know what I feel. Here. Christ, Dad, it's like a monastery here. And you've become a monk. That's what you are. You'll be shaving your head next.'

For some reason that makes him laugh.

He shakes his head, in that irritating 'You would never understand' sort of a way.

'It's true, Dad.'

I feel a little bit ashamed. I really had no right to have a go at him like that. But the truth is, apart from all the garbage he's been talking, there's nothing I hate – nothing that makes my blood boil – more than someone who's given up on life. There's no excuse for joylessness. Certainly not when it's deliberate.

He's worse than my mother.

There is a silence. He is looking into middle space.

I reach across the table and grab his hand and hold on to it tightly.

I do love him. It's a funny thing, to love someone you're supposed to love, like your dad. I wasn't ever good at doing what I was supposed to do. But there is something about a blood relationship I guess.

The truth is, I don't understand what he's been going on about. This one man to one woman thing – it seems to me that is precisely where we've always gone wrong. To be led to expect the unreasonable, the impossible even, and then to feel guilty and let down and disappointed when it doesn't happen. It's Adam and Eve all over again, only worse, because it's real and it's here and now.

And my poor deluded dad. He really did believe the fairy tales, and look where it got him. An intelligent man like he is, and what a fucked-up life he's had.

He strokes my hand. I have this awful ghastly feeling that we're going to cry.

'I'm sorry, Dad,' I say.

He shakes his head and squeezes my hand tightly. I think he'd like to say something but he can't quite find the words.

So I open up the second bottle and we sit drinking and watching rubbish television together, and I fall asleep on the sofa and wake up in the morning with a crashing headache to find he's already gone to work.

Such is life.

* * *

Meanwhile, back at the farm:

Barbara has begun to take a bit of a shine to me. After all my efforts on her behalf the other day, when for the first time ever I presented her with sheaves of accounts *without one mistake in them*, she's decided I am not, after all, a total waste of space. Her reward has been to give me more accounts to input, lucky me.

So I am toiling over these when, for absolutely no reason whatsoever, my computer freezes. Perhaps it's overworked. It's certainly not used to having to do quite so much in a day.

I'm on the phone to Nick. As I'm dialling his extension number it occurs to me I haven't seen much of him lately, more's the pity.

'Hi, Nick, it's Hazel.'

'Hi.'

Oh, freeze me out, why don't you?

'How are you?'

'OK. You?'

'I haven't seen you for a while,' I say. 'What's up?'

Silence.

'Nick, speak to me.'

'It's nothing.'

'You're sulking again.'

'What do you want?' he finally asks.

'My computer's bust.'

'Are you sure?'

'Well, put it this way, it's not doing anything, it's frozen, petrified, on strike.'

'I'll be right over.'

He greets me noncommittally and sits right down and gets on with it.

I know what's wrong – I'm talking about Nick here, not the machine – and I know it's going to take a while to talk him round. It kind of amuses me, this sulky behaviour of his. I shall enjoy this.

He sits there in total silence, doing weird and wonderful things with the computer. I'm standing there right behind him, shifting from one foot to the other impatiently, resisting the urge to run my fingers through his hair, grab hold of it, twist his neck around and plant a smacking French kiss on his mouth.

'So? You see I'm not making it up this time,' I say.

'Mm. This machine definitely needs an overhaul.'

Don't we all, I'm thinking.

'It's your hard drive,' he says. 'I'll have to take it to pieces, I think. Have you backed up all your data onto floppies?' he asks.

'Yes, sir.'

'Good. In that case I'll take this one away with me and find you another, temporarily, while we get it seen to.'

He's starting to unplug things and move stuff about.

'Nick.'

'What?'

'What's up?' I ask.

'Nothing. What do you mean?'

'If there's nothing up then why are you talking to me like I'm a worm?'

He stops for a moment to glare at me. 'You should know,' he mutters.

'I've absolutely no idea.'

He resumes the dismantling. I have to grab his hands and physically stop him.

'Nick! Freezing me out will get us nowhere.'

'It's . . .'

'Go on, tell me.'

He goes quiet.

'Coffee?' I ask.

He doesn't respond immediately.

'Come.' I grab his hand and start to pull him out of the room.

'What's going on?' he says, as I drag him down the corridor and round the corner and along a bit, then up a few steps and then round another corner to the meeting room.

The meeting room is a rarely used room. Most meetings tend to take place in people's offices. The only pretext I have for dragging Nick there is that it has a coffee machine. It is a rarely used coffee machine. Most offices (except ours, of course) have their own, so the only person who regularly uses this one is me. I know this for a fact.

I have another reason for luring Nick away from my rather open-plan office. The excitement of messing around with Nick while Barbara is in there – which, as I have already mentioned, is something we have done from time to time – is actually beginning to pall. Also, I can see there is a need here for a Serious Talk, followed by . . . well, let's see.

As I suspected, the meeting room is empty. I pull Nick into the room and gently close the door behind us.

He stands there silently watching as I pour two paper cups of steaming, frothing cat's pee.

'Thanks,' he says, as I hand him one.

I manoeuvre us over to the table.

'So,' I say. 'Tell me all.'

I sit down on a chair. He perches his bum on the table next to me.

'You think I'm an idiot, don't you?' he mumbles, eventually, into his coffee.

'What do you mean?'

'You just think I'm a good for a laugh kind of thing.'

'Of course I don't! What makes you think ... ah, I know. You're thinking of that time with Barbara.'

I'm thinking of the time when I was trying to hold a conversation with Barbara while he had his tongue up my pussy.

It finished with me falling off my chair, you may remember. Barbara just gave a deep sigh, as if to say 'This child will never grow up', and walked away. And there I was, once again, down on the floor with Nick all over me like a puppy.

His tongue went from my pussy to my mouth, or rather down my throat. And he was pawing at my clothes like a frantic thing – he obviously wanted it, had to have it, right then and there, Barbara in the room or not.

But I did something unforgivable. I got the giggles.

It wasn't him, it was the situation. And you know what it's like when you get the giggles, nothing in the world will make you stop – the Archbishop of Canterbury walking in on us would have done nothing to stem my ridiculous, childish giggling. And sex and uncontrollable giggling do not go together.

'It's not that,' Nick is saying. 'Not just that.'

'Nick, you've got it completely wrong. That time with Barbara –'

'You don't need to explain.'

'It was just such a funny situation, I'm sorry, I wasn't laughing at you, it was Barbara's face, and the whole situation.'

'It isn't only that.'

'Nick, lighten up.'

'No. The point is you don't ...'

'I don't what?'

'You don't love me.'

There's a pause. He won't look me in the eye.

'Nick.'

'What?'

'I don't do love. You know that.'

'What does that mean?'

'I do sex. Not love. Uncomplicated, unfettered sex. That's what I do, I've never made a secret of it.'

'But I love you,' he says to his coffee.

'I don't know that you do,' I say, as nicely as I know how. 'But even if that's the case, you like to make love to me. Don't you?'

'Of course I do.'

I reach up and start stroking his face.

'Then what's the problem?' I say huskily. 'You enjoy being with me, you enjoy fucking me, and you know I enjoy fucking you.'

I get up and move to him so I am standing between his legs as he sits there, glumly, still on the edge of the table.

'So I don't see the problem,' I whisper.

I start to press myself against him. I can feel his growing bulge. He closes his eyes.

'Of course there's a problem,' he says. 'Ah!' he exclaims, as I grind my groin against his.

'I can't bear to think of you ... Oh! ... with other people, it –'

'Give me your cup.'

I take the coffee cup from him and place it carefully down some distance away on the table. He watches me as my hand goes to his flies. He doesn't try to move away.

I'm a bitch, I know. But some people make things too complicated.

I undo his trousers, reach inside and grab the bulge.

'Oh, God,' he croaks.

And then, afraid that he might come there and then, I move back a pace and pull off my knickers, and then I push him back onto the desk and pull down his trousers so he's lying there, with his cock rampant. I climb up onto the desk till I'm crouching over him like a cat, pull up my skirt and allow the tip of his cock to brush against my bare stomach. I sway my body from left to right so I can feel his cock stroking my skin. His face is starting to contort.

'For God's sake, let me inside you,' he gasps.

'Not yet. You've got to make it last.'

I move slightly so his cock is touching the entrance to my fanny. It isn't easy, what I'm doing here. Believe me, it isn't. It's torture actually.

I take his cock between two of my fingers and stroke it slowly back and forth against my clitoris. I close my eyes and the room disappears and there's just the sensation of cock on clit, of suspended animation.

Then, thank goodness, while his cock twitches and moves in my hand, his body relaxes and he lies there, no longer contorting and writhing, allowing me to play with him, play with his cock against my clit, gently squeezing the end of it and wafting it back and forth, round in circles.

'Ah,' he murmurs.

'You like that?'

'Ah.'

'I do, too.'

'I want to –'

'Not yet.'

'Not –'

'Not until you can't bear it any longer. And I can't bear it any longer.'

I move down his body and take the tip of his cock into my mouth. It is wet. I toy with it with my tongue.

'Oh. Oh. Oh.'

It's starting to leap around a bit. I suck it, gently.

'Oh,' he says again.

'OK,' I murmur. 'I'm just about ready for you now.'

Then, holding the trembling thing between my fingers, as I lean over and very gently guide it towards the edge of my threshold, I look up and see a face.

Not his face, you understand.

'Don't stop!' he cries. 'Oh, Hazel!'

'Hello, Janine,' I say.

Why is it that this room – this room that for days, weeks on end nobody ever, *ever* goes into – has suddenly become a mecca?

More to the point, what the hell is Janine – Janine of all people, of the two-hour lunches – what is she doing here, in the meeting room, in a room that, as likely as not, she did not know the existence of?

Nick sits up with a jerk and I practically fall off the table.

'Janine! Jesus!'

He grabs at his trousers, frantically, untidily, like a schoolboy who's been caught at it in the classroom; while, with what I hope is a little more decorum, I jump lightly down from the table, smooth my skirt with my hands and turn to smile graciously at the intruder.

She stands there, staring at us, embarrassed and slightly baffled.

'What are you doing here, Janine?' I ask her.

'I was actually looking for you,' she stammers. 'I'm sorry, there was a phone call, I couldn't find . . .'

Janine, by the way, whom you haven't met, is very young and very pretty. She has long, dark, dead-straight hair that falls rather boringly around a perfect oval face containing two huge but slightly blank eyes. Those are

the eyes that are still gazing at us in – well, embarrass-
ment, to say the least.

It occurs to me that perhaps, just *perhaps*, she doesn't
know what we were up to. She might just think we
were larking about. She's that innocent.

'Sorry,' she says, and turns to go.

'Don't go, Janine.'

An evil thought has wormed its way into my head.

'Come here,' I say.

She does. She stands there looking from me to Nick
and back again, awaiting instructions.

'Do you fancy Nick?' I ask her.

I happen to know that she does, because she has
made it fairly obvious in a roundabout sort of a way, to
me at least.

She blushes. Nick is looking at me in disbelief.

'Because I have it on good authority he's a fantastic
lover,' I say.

She doesn't say anything. He doesn't say anything.

I walk over to the door and, with two pairs of eyes on
me, I turn the key in the lock.

I walk back to them, take them both by a hand and
draw them away from the table to a corner of the room
where there is no furniture.

'Why don't you touch him, Janine?' I say. 'Go on. He'd
like it.'

Nick is still breathing rather heavily, and his trousers
are still bulging.

Janine turns to face Nick and hesitates. Then Nick
does something quite surprising. He gives her a whopping great kiss that looks as if it could go on for
minutes.

After a while I gently pull them apart. 'Make love to
her,' I say to Nick. 'Go on. You want to.'

He's up for it, my God is he up for it. But Janine looks as if she needs some encouragement.

So I go to her and very gently, as gently as it is possible to do, I start to take off her top. For a moment I can feel a resistance, but then, shyly, she lifts her arms above her head to help me.

I'm looking at her deep in her pale, blank eyes. She looks back at me with what looks suspiciously like total trust.

'And now your bra,' I whisper in her ear as I reach around and unsnap the fastening.

I've never done anything like this before. I've never fancied women, more's the pity I sometimes think, but there's something about this scenario that is truly turning me on.

She has sweet breasts. Small, pert and expectant. And irresistible. Unable to stop myself, I reach out and touch them gently, and then, to my amazement, I lean down and kiss them, on the nipple, one after the other. They are unbelievably soft.

I pull back and she is looking at me, wide-eyed and, I sense, terrified.

'Your turn,' I suggest to Nick.

Tentatively he puts out a hand and touches her breast. I hear her intake of breath. I move round behind her, undo the fastening of her skirt and pull it gently to the ground. Then her knickers.

She has a lovely body. I let my hands slide down it from her shoulders to her tiny waist, brushing slightly against her breasts on the way. I follow the contours of her hips and her thighs. Her skin is flawless.

Over her shoulder I see Nick's face as he bends to kiss her again. I'm holding her by the waist and I can feel her muscles contract as his mouth reaches for hers.

He undoes his trousers and, still with his mouth on

hers and with some difficulty, he takes them off. Very gently, with my hands on her thighs, I ease her legs apart. Her body is shaking very slightly.

I kneel down so I am between them, and from that position I have a perfect viewpoint of Nick's rampant and quivering cock. I reach out and take hold of it and guide it in the direction of Janine's pussy.

I don't know who's the most excited of the three of us. Janine is looking at him, staring at him. She is shaking visibly now. I put my spare hand on her buttocks, for reassurance. My other hand still has hold of Nick's cock. I feel it run through my fingers as, very gently, he enters her.

I keep my hand there for a few more moments, between them, thrilling in the feel of him as he thrusts into her. Then I remove it and, as he pushes himself totally into her, she gives a great sigh.

Now I'm standing behind her again and my hands are once again on her waist, and as he pushes into her I feel the movement of her body against mine, her bum pushing against my pussy, and it's as exciting as anything I can remember. I tighten my grip on her and now it feels as if he's fucking the both of us together.

Then Janine bends her knees and I move away as they lower themselves onto the ground. Nick is on top of her now, his body moving, moving remarkably slowly on her. She lies still. Her eyes are open and they stare into space.

Then Nick shifts position slightly so he can go deeper into her and it's as if he's pressed a button. Janine's eyes close softly and she starts to move her body, imperceptibly at first and then, gradually, as if she's slowly come alive, she begins to arch her body, to push herself into him. She lifts her arms above her head so her lovely body is stretched. She moans, twists her pelvis, abandoning herself to him. She lifts her legs to wrap them around his neck and their eyes lock as they fuck the life out of one another, with no thought for anything but each other.

I can't help thinking as I watch them humping away that he, that Nick, never ever lasted this long with me. This is a different Nick, a controlled Nick, a Nick who looks as if he could go on and on. There must be something about this slip of a girl because now – my God – now he's lifting her bodily off the floor, still with her legs wrapped around his neck, still with his cock inside her, and he's carrying her over to the table. He puts her down, on the edge of it, and now he's thrusting so deeply into her that her bum is lifting right off it. They're beginning to speed up now. I can see Nick's eyes starting to bulge and I know – I've been there, remember – I know this is it, he's about to come.

And so he does, with a jerk and a shudder and a sigh, as if all the breath has left his body.

I want to be a part of it. I have the feeling, the dreadful feeling, that they have forgotten my existence. I walk up them, to their unmoving, gently heaving bodies.

She, Janine, lies back on the table, eyes closed. He, Nick, half-lies on top of her, eyes closed. I place a hand on each of them – a reassuring, 'remember-me?' kind of a hand. There is no reaction at all.

That's fine. I turn and walk quietly over to the door. Soundlessly I unlock it and, as I make to go, I turn back to look at them and, to my surprise and slight consternation, Nick is staring straight at me.

I feel both slightly left out and at the same time smugly proud at being the instigator of it all. There aren't many new sexual experiences left for me, or so I had thought, but this was something I'd never done, or even fantasised about, before.

It is an odd sensation, being a voyeur. It's not just that you are watching two other people indulging in the most private of activities, it is watching someone you've fucked fucking someone else. Inevitably you look for comparisons, and in this case the most obvious difference is the way Nick seemed able to pace himself, to keep going. With me he has always been a bit quick, apart from the first time, and I haven't minded that much because I know the moment he's got the first lot over with there'll be another one following right behind, and that given the right mood and opportunity my friend Nick can probably keep going ad infinitum.

But with Janine ... Maybe it's because she's more passive. Or maybe – and I think I prefer this one – maybe it's because after all this time I've managed to teach Nick a thing or two.

I have to admit it, watching two people coupling is, in a purely visual sense, frankly hilarious: all those naked heaving buttocks, the groans and the squelches, the gasps and the heavy breathing. It's the imagination that makes it so erotic.

They make a lovely couple, Nick and Janine. Much better suited than Nick and me. I realise with a tinge of regret that that's probably it as far as Nick and I are concerned. So be it. I hope they'll be extremely happy together.

I know something else. I know there is no other activity that reveals more about a person than the act of making love. There is something about seeing a man completely lose himself, and lose himself in you, that gets right to the heart and soul of him. How many arrogant bastards are tender, unselfish lovers? How many quiet, gentle souls are animals in bed? There is something about a man with his guard down and his clothes off and his inhibitions gone and his most precious organ inside you that is the true man, man at his most open and vulnerable. That's how I see it anyway.

I'm just sorry I can't make it with women so I could get to know some of them in the same way.

Enough idle thinking. I shall take myself out for a spot of fresh air and maybe a cappuccino – give the two lovebirds a bit more time on their own.

As I trip down the stairs I remember the look on Nick's face as I left the room and idly wonder what that was all about.

7

It's now a couple of days since the Nicky and Janine event, and Janine has been avoiding me. At least, I think she has. There has usually been someone else around, like Barbara, so it's hard to tell. I suppose it's not surprising. She probably thinks I'm planning to leap on her and drag her behind the filing cabinet.

But this avoidance – avoidance of looking at me, that is – gives me the opportunity to look at her. While I'm not a lesbian – I haven't the energy or the time – that doesn't mean I cannot appreciate a beautiful girl when I see one, and Janine is, now I look at her, a beautiful girl.

She is everything I am not, which is partly why I think she is so beautiful. She is delicate and graceful and moves – almost dances – swiftly and lightly, like a gazelle; her eyes are huge and innocent and her skin looks as if it might be translucent; and she carries all this without self-consciousness.

I'm watching her now as she works on her computer. She is the junior in the office, which means she gets to do all the things no one else wants to do, including me. She does it all quietly and efficiently, and without complaint. As for her home life, her private, social life, I've no idea. She doesn't talk much; she never did.

I am, of course, absolutely bursting to know, and I realise she isn't going to volunteer anything, so:

'How's Nick?' I ask her.

'Sorry?'

'I said, how's Nick?'

She is staring at me now with her gazelle's eyes, big grey things they are.

'He's fine.'

And that is all she is prepared to say, evidently. I know better than to probe, so my curiosity must remain unsatisfied.

I haven't seen Nick at all since That Day. He exchanged my computer for a new one in my absence. Otherwise, there's been neither sight nor sound of him. That, I suppose, is not surprising either. But it's damned frustrating.

And now I come to think of it, it's well over two weeks since I saw Alistair. I know we didn't exactly have a contract stating 'thou shalt see one another every two weeks', but that's the way it's always been, one way or another. For whatever reason.

That's the trouble with routines. It matters when they get broken. It matters if you have expectations that aren't lived up to, which is why it's best not to have expectations in the first place.

Of course, being a not-so-shy sort of a girl, you'd think it's not beyond my ability to pick up a phone and find out what's going on. I don't really know what stops me. I just know that when – if – I ever see Alistair again I'm going to Get My Own Back.

Then, a surprise: Number Six calls to ask me out on a date.

'Date' perhaps is not the right word. As a fan of ancient architecture, particularly ancient English architecture, he wants to visit a place called Syon House, and wonders if I would care to accompany him.

Normally I'd have passed on an opportunity like that. Old houses and I don't really have much in common.

However, this is Number Six, and Number Six is, well, Number Six: the Great and as yet Unconquered.

So I set about deciding what I am going to wear.

I'm not usually the sort of girl who makes a fuss about a thing like this. Clothes usually dictate themselves, so to speak. I have enough different outfits for more or less any occasion I am likely to encounter. I have several 'come and get me' numbers, one or two pricey items that say 'take me seriously, I'm a modern, working girl' (they don't tend to leave the wardrobe very often), a couple of outfits I could wear to the local church fete, should I be so inclined, and, of course, rackfuls of slob-abouts.

When it comes to choosing what to wear on this occasion, however, I am in a bit of a quandary.

I am going to have Number Six. Sooner or later, it will happen. Whether or not it will happen while we are perusing the charms of 'one of the finest examples of eighteenth-century English architecture' (his quote), however, is another matter. Still, it's important to send the right signals.

In the end I find the perfect solution. It's a floaty number, made out of a lawn-type fabric with images of flowers in various shades of blue and green and all colours in between. At first glance it looks perfectly respectable: it is loose-fitting, with a modestly scooped neck and short sleeves, and it ends at knee-level.

The joy of it, however, is that in certain lights – that's to say with the light behind me – I know it is almost completely transparent. Moreover, when I move my body in a certain way it swings and clings to it so closely it can give the impression I'm wearing nothing at all. All this of course is only noticeable to the close observer and the whole effect could be lost on Number Six. But the most important thing is, knowing what this frock is capable of makes me feel both sexy and full of the most glorious anticipation.

'Very nice,' murmurs Number Six, looking me slowly up and down.

He, for his part, is dressed in an expensive off-white shirt, elegantly cut dark grey trousers and a leather jacket. It is the first time I have seen him wearing anything other than a suit and the effect is, in an odd sort of a way, faintly shocking.

Syon House is one of those rectangular-shaped symmetrically designed mansions set around a courtyard, with neat little windows equally spaced, all set in a neatly mown lawn surrounded by neat trees in the middle of a neat park. And it all looks as if it comes out of a children's book.

'Syon House is home to the Duke and Duchess of Northumberland. The original building, Syon Abbey, dates back to the early fifteenth century...'

We have joined a guided tour. Number Six seems quite serious about this. He is, I realise, rather a serious man. Then again, there is that perpetual, faint, slightly mocking smile. To describe him as enigmatic, or inscrutable, is a ridiculous understatement.

We are in a party of around fifteen people, not one of them under fifty years old. They are, of course, mostly American, with a smattering of Germans and a couple of English. Our guide is a fierce, tiny, middle-aged lady who speaks very rapidly and with total authority. I suspect she knows the complete history, not just of the building and everything in it, but precisely what the various Dukes and Duchesses of Northumberland (which, it only now occurs to me, is a long way from Twickenham) had for breakfast and the maiden names of every aunt and second cousin twice removed who ever set foot inside the place.

She's not too keen on interruptions. The Americans – one couple in particular – are doing their damnedest to distract her every time she gets into her flow, usually to ask, 'Is that real?' and her temper is wearing thin. At each interjection she glares at them over her specs in her most ferocious manner, but they, being Americans, are oblivious.

Number Six is completely absorbed. He is especially impressed by the Great Hall, which is the first room you set foot in and looks like something out of a Roman villa, with pillars and Roman statues and a chessboard for a floor. It's difficult not to be overawed. It is very grand, and very elegant, and symmetrical to the point of obsessiveness, which is why I find myself feeling distinctly uneasy.

There is something about things being carefully placed in perfect balance, the right side exactly like the left side, that makes me want to get up and smash something. Psychoanalyse that if you want, but to me symmetry represents something nonhuman. Humans aren't symmetrical. When did you ever see someone whose face was exactly the same on both sides? Or with identically sized feet? Human beings are, at their best, a bit haphazard. So symmetry to me represents nonhuman. The whole classical world is nonhuman, cold, unfeeling, restrained, unnatural.

So I'm standing there in the Great Hall and I'm beginning to get the shivers. Nobody notices, least of all Number Six. He's doing a good imitation of someone who is so engrossed in his surroundings he's forgotten there's anyone else there.

However, when we get to the Long Gallery I find I

can't contain myself any longer. The Long Gallery is, as you would expect, long and thin, with windows down the length of one side, and bookcases along the other. It's the bookcases that bother me.

'The Long Gallery was designed by Robert Adam expressly for the amusement of the ladies. It was to this room that they retired after dinner, for conversation and gossip and perhaps a game of cards,' intones our guide.

'Are the bookcases real?' This from one of the Americans. Our guide shoots them a withering look and declines to answer the (perfectly reasonable, in my view) question.

'On one side of the room eleven windows, equally spaced, give a view over the lawn. On the other, the wall is divided, as you can see, into five identical bays, three doors, and two fireplaces. Each bay comprises three bookshelves separated by groups of four Corinthian pilasters, totalling sixty-two in all. The busts . . .'

She hasn't mentioned the furniture. All the furniture is lined up against the wall. It goes, precisely: settee, tall table, chair, table, chair, table, fireplace, table, chair, table, chair, tall table, settee – you get the picture? It reminds me of a hospital waiting room.

I don't suppose those ladies, for whom this room was designed, gossiped or played cards sitting all in a line with their backs to the wall, it would have been impossible. The furniture has obviously been placed that way by some modern-day obsessive, and I resent that.

'The diagonal pattern in the ceiling, as you can see, echoes the pattern in the carpet, which – excuse me, what do you think you're doing?'

I can't help myself. I have moved some of the furniture about. I've pulled out some of the chairs and the odd table and placed them in such a way that one could imagine those eighteenth-century ladies in their crinolines, or whatever they wore in those days, playing cards and gossiping away and laughing at one another over their fans.

You might think this childish, but it's not a prank, I promise you.

'What do you think you're doing?' barks the guide again.

Well, I've got the attention of the room, that's for sure. 'I'm giving it some life. I'm trying to make it look as if someone lived here. Lives here, even,' I reply.

'You are not to touch the furniture.'

'But it's more interesting this way, don't you agree?'

The tourists are aghast. Especially the Germans. The talkative American couple are staring at me like owls. Only one person in the group is not horrified.

'You are not to touch the furniture,' she repeats.

It's her tone. I can't help myself. I plonk myself down on one of the chairs.

'I, please, would somebody . . .' She's looking around for a security guard.

I reach behind me into the bookshelves to grab a book and a panel of cardboard cutouts comes away in my hand.

'See? They ain't real, I told you, honey,' says the American with the owl eyes.

'Would you kindly replace that and go. Now.' The guide's eyes bore into me like a laser.

Number Six steps forward. It's brave of him to associate himself with me. He offers his arm like an eighteenth-century lord and, as gracefully as you like, as if we owned the place, I rise to my feet, link my arm in his and together we glide down the long narrow room, with eleven windows on one side and five identical, symmetrical bays on the other, as if we're off to the ballroom for a minuet. As we go, I sway my hips from side to side so that the dress, The Dress, can swing and cling and do its saucy business.

With a bit of luck, if the light is in the right place, what those wide-eyed tourists, and laser-eyes, are watching is a naked woman walking slowly out of the Long Gallery arm in arm with her beau.

In no time at all we're out of there, out of the house altogether, and into the grounds before any mythical security guard can get to us.

We walk together without saying a word across the manicured lawns and down to a lake, where we sit ourselves down on a bench.

'So. What was that about?' he asks eventually.

'I just wanted to see what it might have looked like when those ladies were playing cards after dinner. You know, real live flesh and blood people. The people she was so anxious to tell us about.'

'Fair enough,' he says.

'I don't know why they have to make these places look so much like museums. Dead places for tourists to gawp at. I hate the place, I hate the whole thing, it gives me the creeps, it's too . . .'

'Too what?'

'Clean. Lifeless. Symmetrical.'

'I see.'

'Now you're going to tell me you like it.'

'I do like it. Very much. I like the symmetry, the order, the cleanness, as you put it. It has a restraint, and a balance, that I find most exciting,' he says.

'"Exciting"?' I stare at him. 'It's not human. It's anti-human.'

'You don't like symmetry,' he says.

'And you don't like humans.'

'Does that follow?' He laughs lightly.

'So, restraint excites you, does it?'

'Very much. You should know that.'

There is a pause. This is turning into rather a weird conversation. But I'm beginning to get a bit of an insight, I think, into my strange companion's character.

'This house – to me it is nearly perfect,' he says.

'Only nearly?'

'Nothing, by definition, can be perfectly perfect.'

'Hmm,' I say, sulking slightly. 'You know, I don't think you and I have much in common.'

'On the contrary, I believe we do.'

He speaks quietly, steadily, addressing the air in front of him.

'Such as?'

'There is a tension between opposites. You like chaos.'

'I didn't say that.'

'Disorder then. I like balance. You like the mess of humanity. I like cleanness and order. You like passion. I like restraint.'

There's another silence.

'You don't ever feel passion, then?' I ask him.

'I feel very strong passion. I suspect I feel as strong a passion as you. The restraint, the control, adds to the tension of it. I rein it in, and it becomes all the more powerful.'

I turn to look at him. What an odd man he is. He glances at me, expressionless as always, with those pale blue eyes of his. I don't think he knows the meaning of the word passion.

'I don't think you know what passion means,' I say.

He looks away from me again, without responding.

'You're just a cold-blooded ... Dutchman.'

'If you want to think that.'

'I will fuck you one day,' he goes on, so quietly I'm not totally sure I heard him right.

'What did you say?'

'I said, one day, we will fuck. You and I. Perhaps.'

'Well, lucky old me.'

'And when we do, it will be with restraint. And you will experience sensations you have never experienced before.'

'What makes you so sure?'

He leans over and picks some grass from the ground by his feet.

'But we will not fuck until we can do so with control,' he says.

'Fucking isn't about control. It's about losing it, losing it completely.'

'When you lose control it means your mind is not functioning well, if at all.' He sorts the grass into three stems of equal length, discarding the rest.

'Fucking can never be truly pleasurable, truly satisfying,' he goes on, 'unless your mind is clear.'

'You make it sound like listening to a lecture.'

There is a pause. He begins to plait the three strands of grass together.

'You will have, I will give you, when and if I feel you are ready, when you can achieve restraint, the most astonishing mental experience of your life,' he says, as he twists the grass deftly between his fingers.

'I'm not sure mental experiences do it for me.'

'Then there is still something left for you to experience.'

'Well, maybe.'

There it is, in his hands. A perfect, symmetrical, neat little grass plait.

'For you,' he says, presenting it to me.

'Thank you,' I say. 'I shall treasure it.'

And there we sit, like two perfectly normal people, on a bench in a perfect park by a beautiful lake with ducks and things on it, having what I can only call one of the weirdest conversations of my life.

He drives us back to Battersea and bids me farewell (literally) outside my flat. I do not invite him up and he does not even obliquely suggest I should. Clearly I have some way to go, in his mind, before I can be regarded as ready for the fully fledged, controlled, restrained, Ultimate Fuck.

He watches me climb the stairs to my building. I'm swaying my hips fit to bust but who knows what effect, if any, the dress is having on him.

What with one thing and another, I think it's time to treat myself to An Evening On My Own.

First, I gather together all my tools. They comprise scented candles – scent of cloves this time, I think – essential aromatic oils, bath salts, vodka and tonic, a rather special video, and my trusty old vibrator.

I turn all the lights off and place my tiny scented, lighted candles all around my living room – on shelves, tables and on the windowsills and, of course, around the bath in my bathroom.

I strip off and run myself a hot bath, into which I place a few drops of essential oil of rosemary and a small handful of mixed-herb flavoured bath salts. Into this gorgeous mixture I lower my receptive body and I lie there, head back, eyes closed, allowing these wonderful smells to tickle my olfactory nerve endings in the most enticing way. The water, thick and pungent, laps gently over my body, caressing my belly, my breasts and, as I open my legs slightly, my sex. I rub myself all over with the oils and the salts, my fingers lingering on the more sensitive places.

After a while, as I feel the water cooling, I climb out and dry myself and tuck myself inside my thick, baby-soft towelling robe.

Thus attired I wander into the kitchen and pour myself a vodka and tonic. Strong, with a bit of ice and a slice of lemon. I take my drink, and the bottle for top-ups, next door into the candle-lit sitting room, slot the video in the player and pile up some cushions on the floor onto which I sink, drink in one hand, remote control in the other, vibrator within easy reach. The scent from the candles is strong and quite heady.

It is a true wonder of nature that, while it is impossible to tickle yourself satisfactorily, it is possible to pleasure yourself in the most delightful way, all on your own, without a man in sight or within touching distance. Sometimes, when I'm enjoying one of these Evenings On My Own, I wonder to myself why we bother with men at all. After all, no one quite knows how to do it as well as we do ourselves. No one quite knows exactly where, and how, and how fast and how hard and in what way those fingers should move on that tiny, shy little organ, in order to give maximum, mind-blowing pleasure.

And the ritual helps, of course. The ritual – Number Six would be impressed by this – involves a certain amount of restraint. Not allowing myself to touch myself until it becomes no longer bearable. Trying to spin it out, make things last longer and longer so when it comes, the climax, it comes with an explosive force that is greater than ever before. That is the ambition, anyway.

But I could not do it, or do it to satisfaction, without my friends the video and the vibrator, not to mention the vodka.

I lie back on the cushions and undo the belt of my

robe, partly exposing my naked self. I place the vibrator on my stomach and turn it on low, so I can feel it humming faintly against my skin, and I set the video running.

The film was made some time ago – in the 70s probably, judging by the haircuts – in a European language, probably Scandinavian of some sort, dubbed into English. The 'story', if you can call it that, concerns this well-to-do and very proper housewife who lives in this very tidy house with her nice husband and her nice furniture.

At the beginning of the film hubby is kissing his tidy little wife goodbye as he leaves for work, wearing his sensible business suit and carrying his briefcase. Wifey then goes to the dressing table and starts to put on her make-up – which she is wearing already, as it happens, so she's really just pretending. After this she decides to do a spot of housework. This entails delicately flicking a duster along the mantelpiece and the bookshelves until, after a very short space of time, she is interrupted by the doorbell.

She answers the door and it's the electrician. He's a young chap with a big smile and a tool bag and he's come to look at one of the light fittings in the dining room. She shows him where it is and is on her way to the kitchen to make him a cup of tea when the doorbell rings again.

This time it's the handyman. He's a young chap with a big smile and a tool bag, and he's come to fix the shelves. So she shows him where they are and heads off to the kitchen to make him a cup of tea as well.

In no time at all she's heading for the dining room again, holding a steaming mug of tea. The electrician is standing on a stepladder checking the light fitting, and it so happens that, when she walks up to him so she's standing by him, her eyeline is dead on a level with his crotch.

Her neat little eyes widen just a tad as she fixes them on his flies, beneath which there are signs of movement. She looks up at him in some puzzlement and he looks down at her and smiles, and before you can say 'Did you know you have a ferret down your trousers?' she's whipped his flies open and out pops this gigantic thing which is definitely not a ferret. She fixes this thing with those killer eyes again and, very, very delicately, out comes her little tongue and gives it the tiniest lick.

The electrician's body goes immediately into something like spasm. Then she wraps her neat little mouth around the end of his cock and, very slowly, she eases it further and further into her mouth until it's all but disappeared. (As has the cup of tea – continuity is not a priority here.)

Then she starts to suck him, well and truly. The electrician is so aroused he's about to fall off his stepladder, at which point the handyman comes in.

He clocks the scene and immediately he goes to stand behind the woman. He takes hold of her waist and starts to rotate his crotch against her. She likes this. He likes it too, and now the three of them are moving together in a highly erotic fashion.

Then the electrician comes. And he really does – I can see his sperm running down the corner of her mouth. As she releases his cock, the handyman lifts up her skirt (she's wearing no panties presumably) and immediately enters her from behind. The electrician continues to stand there on his ladder, his cock still exposed and dripping, looking on while the handyman thrusts away at little wifey's neat little body, shaking it back and forth like she's a rag doll while she hangs on to the stepladder for dear life. She gives a little cry – 'Ah!' – as she comes, and her eyes pop open very wide. Then, as the handyman comes, the electrician begins to get another erection and hubby walks in.

There is a wonderful moment as he, hubby, stands there in the doorway in his neat suit with his briefcase, muttering something about how he forgot his wallet, and gazes at the tableau: one man up a ladder with his erect cock poking out of his trousers looking on at man number two pressed up against his wife's body, cock lodged inside her, hands clenched on her breasts, frozen in climax.

What is hubby going to do? Will he punch the men in the face? And, if so, in what order? Or will he turn on his wife and send her packing, and sobbing, out onto the street? The tension is unbearable.

He does none of those things. He orders the electrician down from the stepladder and then he ushers both men, along with his wife, into the next room, where he points to the sofa. 'Take off her clothes,' he says.

Wifey stands there while the two men remove her clothes. They do it slowly, caressing her as they go.

The camera pans slowly down her naked body. It is a glorious body, naturally – small and neat with not a spare inch of flesh anywhere. Her breasts are surprisingly large but perfectly proportioned and she has the tidiest, curliest little navel I have ever seen.

At hubby's instruction the woman goes to lie on the sofa. She stretches out on it and opens her legs invitingly. The two tradesmen stand behind the sofa and look down at her.

Hubby draws up a chair and sits down nearby, crossing his legs rather primly and placing his briefcase on the floor right by him.

By this stage, on some Evenings On My Own, I have already come. On this occasion, however, I am exercising amazing restraint, and I have not yet touched myself at all.

The vibrator still hums on my stomach and I move it an inch or two lower so it now throbs against my fanny, creating the most delicious not-quite-on-the-spot sensation. I pause the video momentarily while I pour myself another drink, and settle back to see what happens next.

The men, who have removed their trousers and underpants by the way, present themselves, at hubby's instigation, at either end of the sofa. The handyman dangles his cock over the woman's face while the electrician climbs onto the sofa and, with some difficulty – on account of their respective sizes – pushes his massive cock inside her. The woman reaches back with her head and takes the handyman's cock in her mouth, and then they begin to move together, in and out, in perfect rhythm. (I think perhaps this is where my boardroom fantasy may have originated from.) By now the woman has her legs wrapped around the head of the electrician and her arms around the buttocks of the handyman and her body undulates and arches to match their movements.

I reach down my own body. The urge to touch myself is getting stronger and stronger, but I resist it. Number Six would be proud. I move the vibrator down a tad so it is now sitting on my pussy and the throbbing head of it is very close to my clit, but not quite close enough. I am aware of the wetness between my legs. I take my breasts in my hands and stroke them gently.

Meanwhile, the movements on the sofa have speeded up and they are pumping away fit to bust. At which point hubby, who up until now has been sitting there and looking on with nothing more than mild interest, suddenly stands up and pulls them apart.

He is shaking his finger at them. Clearly he is not impressed.

'Come,' he says to them. 'I will show you how it's done.'

Together they move towards the bedroom.

She, naked and gorgeous, leads. Hubby goes next, the others follow on.

The bed, naturally, is enormous and covered in elaborately embroidered quilts and silk sheets.

With one movement hubby whips back the quilts to reveal the open and empty bed. His wife lies down on it in her naked glory and watches while he removes his clothes. The two bystanders come to stand either side of the bed, in great anticipation.

And now – this is the master stroke – the camera goes into extreme close-up. This is usually the point, in the past, where I thrust the vibrator deep into me and begin masturbating. But not this time.

The entire screen is now taken up with hubby's cock, which is hard and visibly throbbing. Into frame comes the wife's face and we watch in close-up as the cock slides slowly into her mouth. Then the camera pulls back and we see they are lying on the bed in 'sixty-nine' position, his body crouched above hers. His mouth goes down onto her pussy and she opens her legs as he starts to suck her. For a while the camera stays like this, with their two bodies in frame, writhing away there on the bed. Then it pulls back to take in the two bystanders who are now miraculously naked and watching intently, hard, breathing heavily, aroused as hell.

The camera movements now change pace in tune with the activities on the bed. First he comes and then she does, and faster than you can imagine they have changed position, so now they are head to head and she is on top of him and she reaches down and, with more tenderness than you have a right to expect from a cheap dubbed video, she kisses him on the mouth, deep and long.

I don't know if these two really are a couple, but it's pretty obvious they know each other very well indeed. (That's 'know' in the Biblical sense, of course.) They know exactly what to do to one another, how to turn one another on, how to press each other's buttons. And I know it's only a cheap dubbed video but there is something about knowing that all this is for real – this is not Michael Douglas and Sharon Stone simulating sex in a Hollywood movie, this is real people with real erections really fucking one another, and looking like they're enjoying it – that is the biggest turn-on of all.

Now it's my turn. I'm on the verge now.

I push the robe off my shoulders and away from me so I can I feel the silk of the cushions against my bare skin. I take hold of the vibrator and I ease it very slowly inside me. It's one of those old-fashioned things made of cool metal and it feels miraculous against my hot, wet skin. I lie there for a moment, motionless, feeling the throb of the machine deep inside me. Then I start to ease the thing in and out of me, as slowly as I can, allowing the edge of it to brush against my clit, moaning with the sheer, glorious, indulgent pleasure of it all. Out of the corner of my eye I can see two heaving bodies on the screen, but they're irrelevant now, for all my senses, all my thoughts are focused on the feeling of the metal inside me and the tender, throbbing vibrations on my clitoris. I start to rub the vibrator harder, harder against my clit until I'm right on the edge – right on the edge of coming – and then I stop.

I wait. It's torture. My naked, quivering body lies

stretched out on the cushions. You should see this, Six. This is restraint of the highest order.

I can wait no longer. Turning up the speed of the vibrator to full, I touch the end of it on my clit and then plunge it deep inside me, fucking myself, my body twisting and writhing, and then my pelvis, slowly lifting, pushing towards the steel, towards the vibrations of the steel, holding itself there, suspended, motionless against the machine.

And I scream as I climax.

The vibrator is clamped inside me, still going, and the orgasms just keep coming, and coming, and...

I just hope the neighbours are out tonight.

Meanwhile, on the screen, they're still at it – all of them now, I believe, all of them together. And I lie there, on the cushions on the floor of my sitting room, in the dimness of the flickering candlelight, my cunt still throbbing and twitching from the recent activities.

I am keenly aware of my nerve endings. I can feel the slightest movement of air on the pores of my skin, the gentle settling of dust particles on my body. I lie there for ages, just feeling.

And I can feel another thing, suddenly and unsuspectingly: an empty space, a gap in the molecules of the air where another body should be, a man's body. As I feel my skin slowly returning to normal I have an urge to feel another skin, another body. I want to feel the weight of something other than air particles.

Masturbation, after all is said and done, is not enough.

8

Some days later Alistair calls me. There's a bank holiday weekend coming up, he says.

I am seriously annoyed with Alistair. Worse, I am particularly annoyed that he has given me cause to be annoyed at him. He says nothing about not having rung me before, and I am especially annoyed at myself that this seems to matter.

Before he has a chance to tell me why he's rung I suggest we do something I want to do for a change, not because I don't enjoy the sort of places he's taken me to, but because I want to see him on my territory, so to speak, doing the sort of things I do. I want to see what he's like when he's not on home ground.

So I suggest the Hampstead Heath fair.

There's a tiny pause.

I haven't been to Hampstead Heath fair since I was a child. We lived in north-west London then and Mum and Dad used to take us, my brother and myself, every time it was on, which was most bank holiday weekends. For some reason they believed it was old-fashioned and wholesome, and this appealed to their 1950s sensibilities. They were very much 1950s sort of people, Mum and Dad, they would have been at home in those days of innocence, rationing, deprivation and the 'didn't we do well to survive the war' feelings of endless gratitude for being alive, and free, and living in a democracy.

The fair certainly was old-fashioned, with its candy-floss and its ancient, creaky rides and generally run-down atmosphere. As for wholesome – we kept on going until Ed, my brother, got physically thrown out of the amusements for allegedly trying to fiddle with one of the machines, and that was it.

'OK,' says Alistair, eventually.

'Oh, and Alistair . . .'

'Yes?'

'Don't wear your sports jacket.'

He laughs.

He turns up wearing jeans, bless him, which I've never seen him wearing before. You can tell they haven't been out of the wardrobe for a while, if at all, because they look brand new and have creases down the front. I expect he gets them dry cleaned.

It's a cloudy day and it's been raining and there's mud everywhere, which is exactly how I remember it. As I stand there gazing around I am suddenly transported back however many years and I'm eight years old and clutching my dad's hand and jumping up and down in excitement and pestering him to take me on all the unsuitable rides.

I look across at this gigantic thing – I think they call it the waltzer – and there I am, sitting next to my big brother, trying hard not to look terrified because he's two years older than me and thinks his little sister is a girlie wimp. And I'm remembering looking down and seeing my mother's face smiling up at me with encouragement and a touch of anxiety and I realise – and I think I realised it at the time – that she knew exactly what I was feeling. And that look of encouragement meant more to me than the whole world. And dammit I'm starting to cry.

All this in the space of a couple of seconds. All those memories. I move away from Alistair before he notices what an idiot I'm being and I'm making straight for the waltzer, shouting to him over my shoulder, 'Are you coming?'

'Sure.'

I think I'm thinking, wrongly as it turns out, that reliving the whole thing will expunge all those memories. But if I hated the waltzer all those years ago that is nothing compared with my feelings now. How anyone who is not a lunatic can pretend that having your stomach disassembled and your centre of gravity realigned by some violently lurching machine is anything approaching pleasure is beyond me. It's no wonder my past life is flashing before me so vividly, I feel I'm going to die any moment. And to top it all the tears are still rolling down my cheeks. I tell Alistair it's the wind making my eyes water, which he seems to think is a reasonable enough explanation. I daren't be seen bursting into tears on a regular basis. That sort of thing can put a chap off.

Next we go on the big wheel – excellent views over London if you can keep your eyes open long enough – the dodgems, the thing that pins you to the walls while the floor disappears beneath you (something to do with centrifugal force), the ghost train, fishing for ducks, and the shooting gallery.

And I'm reminded of the time I won a goldfish and had to give it away to a family friend who had a pond in her garden because, for some reason, my parents didn't want it in the house. Some weeks later we made a family excursion down to the country to visit Captain Courageous, as I had called it, to find he'd been cannibalised by the other fish. By now I have successfully worked myself into a total state of nostalgic misery.

Anyway they don't give away goldfish any more, no

doubt for health and safety reasons. Instead we come away with a plastic bag full of tiny furry things and a teddy bear that I want to give away to Alistair's niece, until he points out that it would probably come to bits and choke her in twenty seconds.

Come early evening we decide we've had enough. It hasn't been a great success, not for me. As for Alistair, either he's doing a very good job of pretending to have a good time or, and I think this is more likely, he really is. It's hard to tell with someone who has made a career out of being genial and sporting and good natured to know whether their enjoyment is ever real or faked. I like to think that, in his own reserved way, Alistair has enjoyed being ten years old again.

So what happens next?

Most of the things we do together, Alistair and I, are to me at any rate preludes to the Real Thing, which is what happens at the end of the evening when we tumble into bed. Whatever takes place earlier – whether it's dinner, or a play, or opera – my mind frankly isn't completely on it, it's on what's going to happen next. The pre-event, so to speak, is a kind of delaying tactic, a way of building the anticipation, which is why I don't mind what we do – I don't even mind sitting in the freezing cold watching the opera – knowing what's to come.

But that, of course, was when Alistair was calling the shots. Today is my day, and everything feels rather different.

'Are you hungry?' he asks. 'Because I know a little place just round the c –'

'Absolutely not,' I tell him, and lead him firmly in the direction of the hot dog stand.

I don't like hot dogs. I never did. We always had hot

dogs when we went to the fair and I never let on how much I hated them. Sometimes I think, with alarm, that Something Else is in control of my life.

Alistair looks on in only vaguely disguised horror as the girl at the hot dog stand lifts the sizzling plastic phallus out of the rancid fat and places it in a bun, along with a glutinous dollop of fried onions and some violent yellow goo that she says is mustard.

'Well,' he says, 'thank you so much.' Very gingerly, he takes the greasy, dripping package from the girl's greasy, dripping hands and holds it safely some distance from his still immaculate jeans.

We walk away from the fair to a quieter spot near some water and plonk ourselves down on the grass. I notice for the first time that the clouds have miraculously disappeared and it's turning into a rather lovely evening.

'So. Now for the real challenge.' Alistair then produces from his pocket an impeccably laundered handkerchief, on which he meticulously wipes his fingers as he works his way determinedly yet delicately through the entire bun, hot dog, goo and onions included, for all the world as if he's dining at the Ritz.

I am suddenly filled with an overwhelming affection for him and for the way he's gone along with things today – pretending to enjoy the rides, gamely trying out the hot dogs – all with the best humour and without one word of complaint, not even about the food.

What I really want to do, right there and then, is place myself on his lap, take hold of him and stick my tongue right down his mustard-flavoured throat. Then I want to press down, hard, against his groin and grind myself into him until he starts to groan, and then I want to undo his flies and grab hold of his cock and rub it and rub it until it is hard and then push it inside me and fuck him – right there in the broad daylight, on the heath, with all the people around. And I want to carry on fucking him all evening and into the night, pausing occasionally for breath, until we are both too exhausted to move and we fall asleep in one another's arms under the stars.

Instead, I find myself wiping my hands on the grass and getting to my feet and saying 'Well, I ought to be going.'

'What? You're not coming back with me tonight?'

He's on his feet too and looking ... yes, looking surprised and disappointed.

'No, sorry, I've got other arrangements.'

'Oh. Well. In that case, let me drive you.'

I have absolutely no idea why I am saying this, or doing this. This was not premeditated. As I say, sometimes I think Something Else is in control of my actions.

As we walk to his car and he drives me home I'm waiting for one of us to say something – myself, hopefully – along the lines of, oh to hell with it let's go back to your place and fuck ourselves stupid like we always do because I've missed you and I want you really rather badly.

But I don't. And the worst of it all is that I think I know why I'm doing this and it isn't working. I think I'm trying to get my own back on Alistair for something or other and I don't like it, it's not like me. I don't know why I'm doing it and I'm going to end up feeling wretched.

The sins of the wicked remain with them for all time.

Those weren't the exact words my mother used, but they're a near approximation. She used to think, in her innocence, that sinners didn't need to be punished by official forces because their own consciences would do it for them better than any court of law or outside opinion.

That, of course, was assuming sinners have consciences in the first place.

I'm reminded of her words because right now I'm feeling like the biggest sinner who walked the earth. Either that or someone up there doesn't like me.

I've spent two whole days doing Barbara's figures, checking and rechecking them as I go with the finest of fine-toothed combs, and they've completely vanished from my computer. And all this after that semi-disastrous day at the funfair with Alistair, since when I haven't heard from him, not surprisingly. It's enough to make you want to sit down and cry.

Which is exactly what I find myself doing. Unfortunately, Barbara sees me.

'What's up?' she asks.

I daren't tell her, not about the figures. She wouldn't believe me anyway.

'I, er . . .'

For lack of anything else to say I tell her about my lousy weekend, or the gist of it anyway. Not so much about Alistair as about going to the fair and being reminded of childhood memories and oh but it's all too boring for words you don't want to hear about it.

On the contrary. She sits herself down next to me and puts an arm around my shoulder and dammit, that's all I need, sympathy, and I'm well away. Sobbing my heart out.

Barbara, it turns out, understands families. She has a complicated family set-up herself, with divorces and step- this, that and others, and children – particularly her son, who is Nick's age and has gone a bit haywire apparently – who she believes have suffered irrevocably because of family break-ups. I try to explain that my family wasn't like that, that we were never particularly close and never really experienced any deep family trauma, but she says there's no such thing as a family that hasn't experienced family trauma.

I think she's a bit of a drama queen on the quiet. So I'm not at all surprised when she tells me she has a bit of Russian blood in her – her great-great-grandfather I think it was – because there is something about the way her eyes light up at the mention of my rather odd (to me that is) reaction to the memories sparked off by my innocent visit to the funfair.

I am trying to make light of it, to dismiss it, because it's getting a bit out of hand here, but then, out of the blue, she says:

'You should not bottle these things up, you know, it does you no credit.'

No credit? That's an odd way to put it.

'You give the impression of someone who doesn't give a damn about anything or anybody, you know,' she goes on. 'It's not attractive.'

She does have a peculiar choice of words.

'You should let your vulnerable side show a bit more, Hazel. Men like it.'

That's quite enough of that.

'Moreover,' I say, to change the subject more than anything else, 'my computer's crashed and I've lost two whole days' work. Your work. You won't believe me but it's absolutely true. Two days' work down the sodding drain.' And to my eternal shame I burst into tears, again. Maybe I am bottling something up.

She gives me a great big bear hug and rocks me to and fro, shushing and tutting and patting my back as if she's a *babouschka* from a Russian play and I'm the poor, unloved daughter of a noble but impoverished farmer who hasn't a friend in the world she can confide in.

Eventually she pulls away, looks me straight in the eye and asks, 'Did you save it onto disk?'

'What? What are you talking about?'

'That work. Did you save it onto floppies?'

'Er, no, I don't think I did. There was no point. I was waiting till I'd finished the whole thing and . . .'

I stop.

There was something about . . .

One computer is like another, as far as I am concerned. Sometimes they have different screensavers, and slightly different layouts, but I'm stupid enough half the time not to notice, or if I do notice I automatically think I've imagined it because computers and I are, for the most part, not on intimate terms.

But this computer . . . And then I remember, a few days ago –

'Thanks, Barbara,' I say.

I pick up the phone and dial a number.

'Hello.'

'Nick, it's Hazel.'

'Hi.'

'How are you?'

'Fine, how are you?'

'I would be fine too if it wasn't for losing two whole days' work from my computer. It's vanished. Gone. Can't find it anywhere.'

There's a pause.

'Didn't you save it onto floppies?'

I sigh, very loudly.

'You told me you always saved your work onto floppies.'

'Well I do, as a general rule, but in this case I hadn't finished.'

'I'm really sorry,' he says, sounding more sheepish than usual.

'Don't tell me.' The light begins to dawn. 'You brought my old computer back, didn't you? When I wasn't looking. Took my old new computer away, with all my work on it, gave me back my new old computer, the one that crashed that time. And all without a word.'

It's gone very quiet his end.

'I think I can retrieve it for you,' he says eventually.

'You'd better.'

'I'm really sorry, Hazel.'

'Call me when you've found it.'

Ten minutes later he's standing in the doorway holding a floppy disk in his hand.

'I found it. I think you'll find it's all here,' he says.

I take the disk from him, trying not to look too relieved.

'Why have you been avoiding me?' I demand.

He doesn't reply.

I'm slotting the disk into the drive on the computer. Yes, there it is. Perhaps not everyone up there hates me after all.

'Well, that's the first good thing that's happened to me in days,' I say.

He smiles. He's got a sweet smile.

'So, all is not lost. Thanks.'

'OK. Sorry again,' he says.

'How's Janine?'

He shrugs. 'Haven't seen her.'

'Oh? And you looked as if you were getting on really well.'

He shrugs again. He's scratching at a bit of peeling paint on the door frame.

'What's up, Nick?'

'Nothing.'

'Please leave that paint alone or all I'll be left with is a bare door frame.'

'Sorry.'

There's a pause. He's still standing there, vaguely looking around for something else to fidget with.

'Do you fancy a drink after work?' I ask him.

'Er, yeah. Sure.'

'I'll see you later, then.'

'Right.'

We meet at the Crown and Anchor, around the corner, where Nick apparently is a regular. It is actually the first time we've met outside the office and I'm pondering on how I expect, or would like, this particular evening to end.

I adore Nick. He's like the younger brother I never had. No, that's rubbish, he's not like a brother at all.

I love his youth, I love his body, I love his rawness, I love his energy. I don't suppose he'll stay that way for long, more's the pity. I hope I'm not corrupting him – I did genuinely think he and Janine might have got it together, but apparently not. So now, frankly, I don't really know where Nick and I go from here. Something tells me not to try to visualise him in my flat, in my bed. Something tells me if he ever got that far I may never get him to leave.

He is about to buy the drinks when this guy walks up to our table with a beer in his hand. He's a friend of Nick's evidently; they're slapping each other on the shoulder and saying 'Hey man,' and that kind of thing – this is a Nick I haven't seen before – and he introduces his friend to me as Slide.

'Sly?' I say.

'Slyde,' he says.

'Slide? As in door?'

'With a y.'

'Right.'

Slyde sits himself down at our table. I'm not sure this is what Nick intended him to do but he, Nick, is already on his way to the bar to get the drinks.

Slyde is a smallish, wiry sort of a guy with very short, spiky, bleached hair and a lopsided grin. I think he's worked on that grin. He winks at me as he sits down, which is not a good start.

'So – you're Hazel.'

'Yes.'

He nods and smiles lopsidedly.

'I hear you've got the tightest cunt north of the river.' Then he chokes on his beer.

I don't know if Nick set him up for this – I don't suppose he did, I hope not. But, one way or another, Nick has obviously been talking to his friends about me, and after all those nice things I'd been thinking about him.

He obviously dared himself to do this, did Slyde. Perhaps they've spent merry evenings together, he and Nick and God knows who else, perhaps even in this very pub, having a jolly good laugh about Hazel-the-easy, who likes to do it in the office, pinioned by computer cables. Hazel-anybody's, she with the tightest cunt north of the river.

'You can try it for yourself if you like,' I find myself saying.

He appears not to have heard me. He's pretending to be busy wiping down the bits of himself he spat beer over. His cool has gone completely, I almost feel sorry for him.

'When Nick gets back with the drinks, after a moment,' I continue, 'I'll say I'm going to the ladies. Give it a couple of minutes and then come after me and I'll meet you by the toilets. Then you can see for yourself what I'm made of. And vice versa of course.'

It's all a stupid game. I don't know why I rose to the bait, but there is something about cocky young lads that brings out the tyrant in me.

Nick comes back with the drinks. He's obviously not that delighted to see Slyde sitting there. Nonetheless they go through the ritual that passes for conversation among young lads. How you going man? Yeah, great. Fantastic. Cool. And then they're on to football.

'Excuse me,' I mumble. 'Back in a moment.'

As I sit there in the ladies I wonder whether Slyde is repeating our conversation back to Nick. I tell myself I don't care. At the same time I think this has to be curtains as far as Nick and I are concerned. I am actually, now I come to examine myself a bit, bloody furious. Sex is a private thing, even when you do it in semi-public. I may be a tart, in his eyes, but I have rules.

I decide I'll get back to the bar and say my polite goodbyes and go. I haven't got the energy for explanations and recriminations and I don't feel like a public row, not right now. All this is vaguely whirling around inside my head when I emerge from the ladies and see Slyde standing there.

Well, you could have knocked me down with a feather. I had not anticipated this. He's looking at me, expectantly. He's not looking cocky any more, he's looking young. Very young. And quite enticing.

'Right,' I say. And with a quick look to right and left I grab his hand and pull him into the ladies.

It's empty, fortunately. It's one of those old-fashioned toilets with tiles on the walls and wooden seats and – as luck would have it – quite spacious cubicles. It's actually, as these places go, not bad.

I pull him into one of the cubicles. I put down the lid of the toilet seat and sit on it. He is standing, as he has to, very close to me.

'Your move,' I say to him.

He is rocking back and forth on his heels and I realise, to my surprise, that he is shaking slightly. His head is bowed but I can see that his face has gone a bright red. He's going to need some help here, obviously.

I undo the belt of his jeans and unzip his fly. I pull his trousers down and his underpants, and there he is, standing before me, head still bowed, arms limply at his sides, his cock dangling there like an abandoned sock. He is rocking quite hard now, and it occurs to me that, perhaps . . .

'Have you ever done this before?' I ask him. He shakes his head.

This is what I always dreamed of. And here he is, standing before me: a real live virgin.

I'm filled with a sudden sense of responsibility. I feel like one of those mature women, usually a distant cousin or someone, who are brought in by French families – they're usually French, aren't they? – to initiate the son of the family into manhood. It's all done discreetly, in dimly lit boudoirs, with great tenderness and patience, and if all goes well – as it should if she knows her business – she will set him up for life, to know that sex is a wonderful thing, an art form, full of endless possibilities and capable of providing deep and boundless joy. I think it's a marvellous idea – much better than the usual messy fumble in the back of a Nissan Micra.

I would have chosen a more obviously seductive place than the ladies toilet of the Crown and Anchor, but, here we are.

'Take off your clothes,' I whisper to him.

It isn't easy in a cubicle, but I'm not keen on part-clothed sex, not if it can be avoided, and not on this very special occasion. Soon, with some difficulty and banging of elbows, we are both naked. He looks up and his eyes lock on to my breasts.

He has a neat, taut, lean body. A touch on the puny side but quite sporty, I think. Not bad.

I sit back down on the toilet seat, take his cock in my hand and start stroking it gently.

'Is that nice?' I say.

He nods, politely.

I carry on stroking for a bit. Absolutely nothing is happening between my fingers.

'Do you have fantasies?' I ask him after a while. He nods. 'Who do you fantasise about? Britney Spears?' He shakes his head, 'Pamela Anderson?' He shakes again, more violently this time. 'Who then?'

'Sam –' he clears his throat. 'Samantha.'

'Who's Samantha?'

'From *Sex and the City*.'

'Right. OK, then. Let's imagine this: she, Samantha, has invited you round to her pad in Manhattan. You don't know why, but you've a pretty good idea. You are hopeful, let's say. Close your eyes and imagine.'

He does.

'You ring the doorbell,' I go on, 'and her voice says, huskily, "Come right up". She's left the door of her apartment open for you. You tentatively walk in, but you can't see anyone. Then, as you close the door behind you, she calls out from somewhere, "I'm in here".'

I'm still stroking his cock, still very gently, and he is beginning to relax a bit. At least he's no longer rocking back and forth on his heels.

'You follow the sound of her voice and there she is, in her bedroom,' I go on, in a low voice. 'She's lying back on the pillows of this enormous bed, dressed in nothing but a lace negligee. "Come in, darling," she says, "and close the door after you." Well now – if that isn't an invitation I don't know what is.'

I can feel the faintest twitch between my fingers. Or maybe I imagined it. This could be a long haul.

'Stroke my breasts,' I say to him.

He opens his eyes, reaches out a shy hand and does as he is told. As he's stroking me, at arm's length, I start rubbing his cock between my hands and I'm beginning, just beginning, to feel a slight stiffening.

'What does this Samantha look like?' I ask.

'She's blonde. And –'

'Is she curvaceous?'

'Curv–?'

'Curvy? Or boyish?'

'She's curvy.'

'With big boobs.'

'Fairly big.' The thing in my hands is definitely starting to grow.

'She's undoing her negligee so you can see them. Describe them to me.'

'They're gorgeous.' He closes his eyes and starts kneading my boobs, with both hands. 'Round, and not that big, but –'

'Now she's taking off her negligee completely so you can see her naked body. She is displaying herself to you. Tell me what her body is like.'

'It's curvy, and shapely, and, and she's got these long legs, and a little waist, and ...'

'She sounds lovely. What is she doing now?'

'She's ... sort of lying there.' He's rubbing my breasts quite hard now.

'She's inviting you. She's looking at you and she's spreading her legs, right?'

'Oh, yeah.'

'And she's watching you as you take off all your clothes, and she really likes what she sees.'

'She does?'

'Oh, yes. She wants it. You can tell from her face.'

He takes his hands from my boobs and waves them around a bit. I think he wants to place them somewhere – on his cock, on my cunt – somewhere stimulating, he doesn't quite know where.

'She wants you to come to her,' I say.

'Yes.' His breath is shortening.

'You're getting hard.'

'Yes.'

'But not quite hard enough to enter her.'

He's about as big as he's going to get I think, which isn't that big, but . . .

'So she's taking your cock in her hands. She really wants you inside her.'

'And I want, I want . . .'

He's rocking backwards and forwards on his feet, he's beginning to fuck my hands.

'Do you want to be in her?'

'Yeah, yes.'

'OK, she thinks you're ready now. In you go.'

And with my guidance, in he goes, sliding into me.

'Oh, wow,' he says.

'How does it feel?'

'Oh, yeah.'

'Just rest it there for a moment, so she can feel you, so she can feel how huge you are.'

'Am I?'

'You certainly are.'

It's only a white lie.

'And how does she feel?'

'Soft.'

'Can you feel that?'

'Oh, yes!'

'She's got strong muscles.'

'Yeah, yeah.'

'The tightest cunt in Manhattan.'

He doesn't get it.

'And now she wants you to start moving in her, making love to her, thrusting – yes, that's the way.'

He's beginning to pump so hard now my back is hitting against the toilet cistern. I shift my bum a bit to get more comfortable. I lift my legs and place my feet on his shoulders so he is deep in me and, more to the point, I can balance myself against him.

'Just keep going,' I say, rather jerkily. 'Yes ... Oh, yes, that's good ... she likes that. She's calling out all sorts of things ... my God, you're driving her wild, Slyde. Fuck me, Slyde, she's saying ... fuck me hard, fuck me harder ... oh, my lover, my stud, my stallion ... my God!'

It's all over.

He's sweating, and shaking. I clasp his clammy body to me, and as I'm sort of half-sitting, half-lying there, and as he draws himself out of me, I begin to be aware of what a hellishly uncomfortable position I'm in. I may never recover.

'Was that good?' I ask him.

'Oh, yeah.'

It was worth it, then.

I give him a tender kiss on the mouth. Something to remember me by.

By the time we get back to the bar – Slyde first, followed by myself, ridiculous really to pretend, but still – Nick, perhaps not surprisingly, is nowhere to be seen.

I say a quick and firm (but friendly) goodbye to Slyde outside the pub and, before he has a chance to say or do anything further, I've turned and walked away.

He won't forget that, I tell myself, with some satisfaction, as I travel home on the tube. You never forget your first time, do you? He may forget my name, what I looked like. But he won't ever forget the experience. And that's kind of pleasing.

When I get home there's a message on my answerphone from Alistair, inviting me to spend a weekend with him and his parents in their country mansion.

Alistair, I think to myself, you have to be joking.

9

'Come home and meet the parents.'

The phrase fills me with dread. It signifies an inspection ceremony – parade the girl/boyfriend in front of the parents to see if he/she passes muster. No, no, no, no.

Alistair and I have ... well, I don't know that I even call it a relationship. We meet once a fortnight, usually, have dinner/go to the opera/ballet/races, and then we fuck. It is straightforward, and it works.

I don't know anything about him. I know virtually nothing about his background, practically nothing about his work, or his social life when I'm not around, or what he gets up to at weekends or holidays. I don't know where he went to school, what he studied at university, how he got into banking – nothing. It's not lack of interest. The fact is Alistair and I come from very different backgrounds. It is my privilege to spend time and share his bed with him. And that's it. Whatever conversations we have had have been about trivial, unthreatening things. I don't know how his mind works, I don't know what's important to him and what's not. And that's just fine.

And I know that if this 'arrangement' were to change, in any way, then it would stop working. The more you get to know about a person, the more possessive you risk becoming. And that's where jealousy – the horrible green-eyed slug – starts slithering in under the door and wrecking your life.

So I ring Alistair and says thanks, but no thanks. I try to explain, but he doesn't get it. He thinks, I think he thinks, that I think I'm not good enough for him, that I'm scared his parents won't like me, or approve of me, or something. No matter how hard I try to tell him, I can't persuade him otherwise. Well, so be it.

I have invited Number Six to my place for an evening of seduction and unbridled sex.

I have my 'tools' ready: the candles, the wine, the video, the determination, everything but the vibrator, which I hope I won't be needing. I've cooked a meal for him – I hope he realises how privileged he is.

We get the meal over with first. He talks about architecture, which he seems to know quite a lot about, though happily he keeps off the subject of symmetry and balance.

I fill his glass at every opportunity. By the end of the meal we've got through a bottle of wine between us and the atmosphere is definitely mellow.

We go next door, to the living room, where I light the candles.

I am wearing a loose black dress with buttons down the front. It doesn't look obviously like a seduction outfit, but I happen to know that I can undo those buttons in three seconds flat to reveal, beneath, nothing but skin.

He settles down among the cushions.

'This is extremely nice,' he says.

'Good. I'm glad you're feeling relaxed.' But not too relaxed, hopefully. 'Do you want to watch a video?'

He narrows his eyes slightly as he looks at me. Those iceberg eyes.

'What kind of video?'

'It's a little something I picked up in a shop in Soho one time,' I say.

'You mean pornography.' He laughs. 'Oh yes. That will be amusing.'

Amusing. Huh.

I slot in the video, set it running and settle down on the cushions on the floor right there next to him.

We sit there watching together for several minutes, and he hasn't said a word. Occasionally he makes a sort of grunting noise, which I take to imply disapproval of some kind.

We have just got to the bit where the husband walks in to find his wife being fucked by the handyman when he starts to mutter, 'No, no, no, no, no.'

'What's wrong?'

'That is too much.'

'What is?'

'The husband. His face. Look at him.'

'So?'

'It is ludicrous. Don't you find him ludicrous? That expression on his face?'

I pause the video.

I suppose I'd never really noticed the guy's facial expression before. His mouth is hanging open and his eyes are popping – and yes, now Six mentions it, he does look ludicrous.

'It is laughable,' he says.

'Shut up,' I tell him, and unpause the video.

The next thing that happens, you may remember, is all three men go into the next room and hubby sits down to watch while his wife lies on the sofa and the two men fuck her at either end. And I hate to say it, but Number Six is starting to chuckle.

'Now what?'

'I'm sorry, but this is so bad,' he says, through his chortles. 'This is too quick. There is no foreplay, no anticipation.'

'This is a porn video,' I explain, as if to a five-year-old.

'But it's all so mechanical. Oh, no!'

He's shaking his head and sighing, heavily.

It's the bit where hubby wags his fingers at the two guys and beckons them into the bedroom to watch how it really should be done. I'm getting quite annoyed with Number Six now, because I happen to find this particular scene extremely erotic.

Give him his due, he goes quiet at this.

'That was slightly better,' he pronounces, when it's all over. 'There was perhaps something going on there.'

There is something going on here too, with me at any rate. I'm beginning to feel hot, bothered and decidedly moist. I move my body fractionally closer to his.

What happens next in the video – we didn't get to this bit earlier, when I was On My Own – is a kind of foursome, with hubby leading and the two guys following his every command. It's a bit mechanical, this bit. Even I have difficulty following it, working out which limb belongs to who and so on. Every so often we get a close-up of one of their faces and here – damn him to hell – here is where Number Six really starts to laugh.

OK, that's it. I am seriously angry now. I flick off the video, get to my feet and stand there like a cross housewife, hands on hips, glaring down at him.

'I am very sorry.' He wipes his eyes.

'Are you doing this deliberately?'

'Of course not. I am sorry, but –'

'Tell me what's so damn funny.'

'It's as if it is made by children. Teenagers, perhaps I should say.'

'How do you mean?'

'Pornography,' suddenly he's quite serious. 'Pornography is a marvellous thing, an artistic thing, if you do it right. But this . . .'

'Are you criticising their acting skills?'

'No, no, not really. But they go at it, these film-makers, as if it is a series of gymnastics, you know what I mean?' He mimes leafing through a script. 'Page one, first fuck, man and woman, ordinary position. Page two, second fuck, second man and woman, from behind. Page three, one woman and two men, at either end. And so on. It's too quick. It means nothing.'

'It's pornography, not art.'

'It's meant to turn people on, right?'

'Yes.'

'Well then.' He shrugs.

'It turns me on,' I say.

'Does it?' He's looking up at me. I'm still standing there, right in front of him, feeling a lot less randy now than I did before.

'Are you turned on now?'

'No. Not any more. Thanks to your film criticism.'

'I have seen many videos in my time, most of them laughably bad, like this one. I think perhaps one day I would like to make one myself,' he says.

'Oh? And what would you . . . tell me how you'd go about it.'

This is looking a touch more promising, I think, as I sit back down next to him.

He gets up, goes over to fetch his briefcase from the corner of the room, comes back, sits down and opens it.

Inside, to my surprise, there is no video. He pulls out a bottle of something and a machine, a small round thing of some kind, I don't know what it is. He switches it on. It hums.

'Feel this.' He hands it to me. 'Rub it on your skin.'

I rub it up and down my arm. It's quite nice.

'Let me do it for you.'

He reaches over and undoes a couple of the buttons of my dress. I hold my breath.

He takes the machine from me and starts to rub it very, very gently over my breasts. It's – I can't really describe it, it's – extremely nice.

'What I would do,' he says, 'I would just set the camera running – perhaps two cameras, one in the corner of the room for long and medium shots, and another close to, for close-ups. Lie back on the cushions.'

I do. He undoes more of my buttons and starts to rub his machine over my stomach.

'I would make sure that I had plenty of film, because I want to just keep the cameras running all through the evening, without stopping and without editing. There would be no script, just a man and a woman, and a good atmosphere, that is all.'

The machine has reached my thighs.

'How's that?'

'It's wonderful.'

'Good, isn't it? Now. I'm going to give you a massage.'

I groan slightly as he takes the machine away.

'Sit up.' I do. He undoes the rest of my buttons and removes my dress so I am naked. Naked and horny as hell. He looks at me, my face, then down at my body. Expressionless as ever.

'Lie down on your front,' he tells me.

As I lie on my tummy on the cushions I can hear him squeezing oil from the bottle onto his hands, and then he sits straddling my back.

'Are you comfortable?' he asks in my ear.

'Very.'

'OK.' And he starts, gently, to massage my shoulders.

'I would make sure that the cameramen, both of

them, knew precisely what to do, without being told,' he goes on, as he rubs. 'But if not, then I would instruct the second cameraman, the close-up man, to focus, at this point, on your skin, on your back, very, very close – so close you can see the pores. I would instruct him to stay on your back, quite, quite still, to capture the very slightest movement of your body.'

'I'm not moving.'

'You may not know it, but you are. Very, very slightly. With the movement of your breath, and the touch of my hands.'

'Ah.' His hands are moving slowly down my back, massaging my shoulder blades, pressing on my spine.

'And then I would instruct the cameraman, the same one, to follow the movement of my hands, slowly down your body, to your waist, down to your buttocks.'

I laugh at this. I'm not proud of my buttocks.

His hands are on them now. I can feel his breath on my skin.

'As I touch you here,' he says in a low voice, his hands on the crack in my bum, 'I would ask the cameraman to focus on your face.'

'Well, it's a better bet than my bum.'

'Because I think, now, you are liking this very much.'

True.

His hands move back up my body, in a smooth, circular motion, kneading, stroking, caressing my skin – he knows what to do, this guy.

'How about *you*?' I say. 'What about your face – is the camera on that?''

'Perhaps.'

'What is it showing?'

'Concentration.'

'Just that? No excitement?'

'Not that you would see, no.'

'Of course, you don't do excitement, do you?'

He doesn't rise to this. 'Turn over onto your back now.'

I do. He's still straddling me. Sitting there, resting his weight – his fully clothed weight – very lightly on me.

I reach up and undo a couple of his shirt buttons. Miraculously, he doesn't try to stop me.

'What's the camera doing now? It should be on your face, I think,' I murmur, as I stroke the skin on his chest, what I can get at, that is.

'Perhaps.'

'Very closely. Hunting for signs of something. Anything.'

I try to undo some more of his buttons.

'Lie still. I haven't finished the massage.'

And now his hands are on my breasts, working away at them, quite hard. The pressure on them is … exquisite.

I feel my body start to heave.

'The camera is now where I am, looking down at you,' he says.

'What is it seeing?'

'Your beautiful body, moving, reaching out, wanting …'

'Yes.'

'Wanting something inside it, I think.'

'Yes, you.'

But instead I get his fingers. He's massaging my pussy.

'Now the camera is going to stay on your face, very, very close. Through the expression on your face the viewers will see, will imagine, every little thing that is happening to you.'

'Ah!' A little jerk of my body as his fingers reach deep inside me.

'Yes, just like that.'

'They'll think you're fucking me.'

'Maybe.'

'And you bloody well aren't.'

'Don't you like this?'

'You know I do, I –'

'You like this too . . .' His finger on my clit.

'I hope he's good at focusing, your cameraman.' My body is beginning to move all over the place.

'And the camera, meanwhile, still on your face, watching you, watching your eyes, your mouth, all the time, sensing your approaching climax, watching it, feeling it as it comes ever closer and closer.'

'Yes.'

'And the viewers are there with you, coming with you, sensing what you are sensing –'

'For Christ's sake, fuck me!' I cry out as I come.

'Yes!' he cries, with unmistakable triumph.

Time freezes. Time and sensations freeze in the moment, the glorious, suspended, self-obsessed, oblivious, post-climactic moment.

I am aware of him leaning away from me and muttering something.

'What did you say?'

'Like a cat,' he says. 'I was thinking how like a cat you are, your face, just now. First snarling, as if in agony, as you came. And then, contentment. At least I think it was contentment.'

I sit up and grab him round the neck and push my mouth hard onto his. To my surprise, he responds.

His lips open and slowly, and almost delicately, his tongue enters my throat.

Now I'm sucking his tongue and his mouth so hard it's as if I'm trying to suck his whole body into me. He responds, with restraint. He puts his arms around me gently, all the better to hold my body slightly away from his.

'My turn,' I say, as my hand moves down to his trousers.

'No.' Very gently he takes my hand away from his crotch, which it hadn't quite managed to reach.

'I want to touch you.'

'Not now,' he says, pulling away from me ever so slightly.

'Why not?' I say, trying to keep the desperation from my voice. 'Haven't I shown enough restraint?'

'One thing at a time, I think.'

'Are you trying to drive me crazy?'

'Not at all.'

'Then why won't you let me touch you?'

'It's something to look forward to. For another time perhaps.'

'Another time?' I exclaim. 'What other time? I'll be in an old people's home by the time you let me touch your cock.'

He smiles. 'It will still be there.'

His quiet, almost respectful gentleness is unnerving. I realise there is no point in pursuing this. He is calling the shots here and he, unilaterally, has decided to call it a day, at least as far as sex is concerned.

And the awful thing – the worst thing – is he's right. He knows exactly how to play me along. This game-playing, if that's what it is, and I think it is, works. The more he won't let me touch him, have him, fuck him, the more I want him, have to have him. It makes no sense whatsoever.

I am annoyed. Deeply and disturbingly annoyed. I get up and move away from him.

His face is a picture.

'Did I not satisfy you?' he asks, concerned.

'Of course you did.'

'Then, what is the problem?' That irritating little puzzled smile. 'Usually it is the other way around, isn't it? Usually it is all take and no give. So . . .'

'I want to fuck you. Now.'

'I'm fine. Honestly.'

'I don't care if you're fine or not, I want to fuck you. If you won't let me fuck you then, then . . .'

'Then what?' he asks politely.

'Then that's it,' I finish, lamely, turning my back on him like a spoiled schoolgirl.

I reach for my dress and put it on. My hands are trembling with frustration and desire – strong, unrestrained desire.

By the time I turn back to look at him he has packed up his things. The vibrating machine, the oil, are all neatly packed away inside his briefcase.

'Stay, please,' I say. I can't help myself.

'I have to go. But I very much hope to see you again.'

'Maybe. Maybe not.'

'I hope so. But meanwhile, thank you so much for the lovely evening, for the food and so forth. I can see myself out.'

He stands for a long moment in the doorway, gazing at me.

'You are very beautiful,' he says solemnly. Then he turns and leaves the room.

I hear the front door go.

Damn him to hell.

The following day I ring Alistair and tell him I've changed my mind. If it's still OK by him then yes, I will come and spend the weekend in the country and meet the folks.

I need the distraction.

Barely have I made the decision than I'm regretting it. I don't know what to wear, I won't know what to say or how to behave. I get all my stuff out of my wardrobe in a vain attempt to find whatever it is that a girl wears to a country weekend in Suffolk. Jeans – no. Short skirt – absolutely not. Evening gown – don't have one. Among my 'come hither' clothes and my 'keep away if you don't want to get your fingers burned' clothes there is nothing that's bland enough, that doesn't tell people something about me.

In the end I plump for a smart yet barely worn skirt and jacket ensemble from my old-fashioned, respectable days (yes, they existed, sort of), and an equally forgotten pair of high heels.

Alistair looks vaguely surprised. Surprised, I think, at my outfit, though he doesn't say so, and even more so at my suitcase.

'It's only one night you know,' he says, mildly.

'I didn't know what to bring.'

'You don't have to worry, Hazel. They're not going to bite you.'

Very reassuring, I'm sure.

We drive down together on the Saturday morning. I have a vision of a massive stone mansion, with pillars maybe, a bit like Syon House, set in manicured grounds with lakes and a team of uniformed staff standing on the steps ready to greet us and take from me my cheap, battered, old-fashioned suitcase (I only hope I get to do my own unpacking); Lord and Lady Alistair, silver-haired, descending the grand staircase, she in Chanel, he in Savile Row, gracious, smiling, and trying terribly hard not to show their intense disapproval of Alistair's tart.

I am wrong on all counts.

Alistair has called it a cottage, and that is exactly what it is. It is old, perhaps very old, with genuine beams and wisteria all over the walls, and a large, pretty but slightly overgrown garden. As we crunch up the driveway I hear a dog barking.

'What do I call them?' I whisper to Alistair in panic.

'Who?'

'Your parents, who else?'

'Oh, er, Anthony and Maud. Tony, he likes to be called.'

You have to be joking.

'Ah, there you are!'

A voice emerges from the rose bushes, followed by this tiny, birdlike woman, dog at her side, hair tied up in a scarf, wearing baggy trousers and an old shirt and gardening gloves.

'Alistair, darling, how wonderful, you've caught me completely on the hop. My goodness is that really the time? Oh, do forgive my appearance ... yes, and this must be Hazel.'

'Hazel – my mother.'

'Maud, please. How simply marvellous. Did you have a good journey? Was the traffic dreadful? It usually is at this time of the year, simply everyone away for the weekend I suppose – my goodness you are looking smart, Hazel, you must forgive my appearance – did you come straight from the office?'

'Hello there.'

This is Dad. The spitting image of Alistair plus around thirty years. A full head of grey hair, immensely tall and stooping slightly – not from age, but from having to avoid the low ceilings in his house, so Alistair has told me.

'Dad, this is Hazel,' says Alistair.

'Good to meet you. Good journey?' And so on and so forth, and it's twenty minutes of genial chitchat standing there on the driveway before we've unloaded the car and taken our stuff inside.

'Alistair, show Hazel her room, there's a dear,' says Lady ... Maud. 'Lunch will be in around half an hour. Help yourself to whatever you want, Hazel, make yourself at home.'

'Thanks. Thank you.'

Inside, the house is low-beamed and quite dark. I follow Alistair up the stairs to the landing, he opens the door to a room on the right and, huffing and puffing so as to make a point, he heaves my suitcase up onto the (single) bed.

'This is you,' he says.

I pause in the doorway.

'And where are you?' I ask.

'Just down the passageway.'

'Right. Separate rooms then.'

'Yes. But we get to share a bathroom. I hope that won't be a problem.'

Hell and damnation. What is this?

'The bathroom's next door, through that door there,' he says, pointing.

'Alistair.'

'If you just want to get your stuff unpacked and have a wash and so on, and I'll see you downstairs in around half an hour, how's that?'

'Alistair.'

'Yes?'

'Why do we have separate rooms?'

'I – oh, were you expecting to share?'

'Don't your parents approve or something?'

'I didn't think you'd want to.'

'Want to what?'

'I thought you'd gone off the idea.'

'Of what? Sleeping with you?'

'Yes.'

I stare at him. Has the world gone mad, or is it just me?

'I'll see you in half an hour, OK?'

And he's gone.

I sit myself down on the bed in, frankly, a bit of a sulk. The whole thing feels like a mistake. I'm a fish out of water, I'm dressed all wrong, and I want to go home. I don't want to spend a weekend making small talk with Alistair and his parents and worrying about saying the right thing and sleeping in a single bed knowing he's sleeping in the same house just down the passageway almost close enough that I can touch him, and yet I can't touch him.

I just want to go home. I knew this would be a mistake.

Over lunch I am, in the nicest way possible, interrogated.

Where do I live, what do I do, how did Alistair and I meet? What does my father do, do I have brothers and sisters? Do I have any hobbies, what sort of music do I like? All of this is done by Alistair's mother, while Alistair himself looks on with quiet amusement. I wonder how many other times he's sat there watching while his mother gives his girlfriend the once-over, thinking, How is she coping? Is she passing the test? Does my mother approve? How many points out of ten? Who cares? Do I care?

I actually rather like her, Alistair's mum. Everything

she does is birdlike, the sudden, quick way she moves her head, the way she takes tiny, tiny mouthfuls of her food, the way she speaks, fast, breathy, and not really listening to the answers to her questions. Alistair's father is like Alistair. He's a watcher, too, quietly amused I think, genial, happy to sit back and let his wife do all the work.

After lunch the guys wash up – no dishwasher in this house apparently – while Mum shows me round the garden. It is a riot, a bit like her, unruly and eager and colourful and without much order. 'It's such a mess,' she says, rather unnecessarily. 'But I do hate ordered gardens, don't you? If I see a flower I want I just plant it wherever I can find a space, it's pot luck in a way, either it looks right or it doesn't, you can't really tell until you've planted it. It's very unscientific but I love it. Are you all right in those shoes?'

'Oh, yes, fine.' I'm not of course. I feel like a prime idiot.

'I'm afraid we've become slobs rather, living out here the way we do. I'm hardly ever out of trousers and I can't remember the last time Tony wore a suit, or even a tie come to that.'

'I really love your garden, Mrs . . .'

'Maud. Do you really?' She looks genuinely delighted. 'I'm so glad, it's not to everyone's taste. Let's go in and have a cup of tea.'

'She's a bit exhausting, isn't she? She's always like this, mind you, even when I'm not here. That's why Dad has his summer house.'

I'm sitting in the garden with Alistair. We've had tea, which seemed to follow almost directly on from lunch, and there's barely an hour until the predinner drinks.

'But she really, really loves her garden. I don't know what she'd do if she didn't have it. How are you doing?'

He's looking at me solicitously.

'Fine.'

He reaches out a hand and places it on mine. I clutch on to it, hard.

'You don't feel they're giving you too much of the third degree?'

'Well, yes actually.'

'It's fairly meaningless,' says Alistair. 'Ma doesn't listen to half of what anyone else says anyway. It's not rudeness, her mind is just racing on to the next thing.'

'Right.'

There's a pause. I'm watching the butterflies – there are hordes of them – fluttering among the roses.

'Your shoes don't look too happy.'

'They're old anyway. I hardly wear them.'

He squeezes my hand. I squeeze his back.

'Right. Better be getting ready for dinner then.'

'What do you think I should wear?'

Alistair laughs. 'Wear whatever you feel comfortable in. There's no dress code here, you know.'

That is precisely the trouble with the upper classes. They say there are no 'rules' or 'dress codes', when what they actually mean is there are rules and dress codes galore, and none of them are written down, or discussed, because anyone who is anyone already knows them – they instinctively know what to wear, and how to behave, and which fork to use and all that; and the entire purpose of these unwritten rules is to sort the goats from the sheep and filter out anyone who is not the right sort from their own exclusive social circle.

And the worst thing is, they don't know this. Or, if they do, they don't acknowledge it.

This whole weekend is turning out to be a test of endurance. It's not that I really care – as you might have guessed, I am usually happy ploughing my own furrow and not caring a hoot one way or another what people think of me – but here, here is different. In their cosy, determinedly casual way, Lord and Lady Alistair, Tony and Maud, are tyrants.

And while I'm not so concerned about making a prat of myself, for myself, I am concerned, for some reason, for Alistair. I don't want to let him down I guess. And that's another problem. I never felt that way before, not with Alistair, not with anyone. It's another complication, another distraction from the wonderfully straight-forward lifestyle I thought I had engineered for myself.

As I sort through the piles of ridiculous clothes I've packed for this weekend, it occurs to me that whatever I end up wearing this evening is likely to be wrong – wrong for Alistair's mum, wrong for Alistair, or wrong for me. And since the only person whose taste I'm totally familiar with is me, then I might as well do as Alistair says, and wear exactly what I want to wear.

So that is how I end up wearing my knitted number.

It's jersey silk, silver in colour, and it's sleeveless with a lowish neck and not much of a back, in fact all in all it shows quite a lot of flesh. More, it clings to the body so intimately that anything I wear underneath it is going to show, which is why I cannot wear anything underneath it.

The fact is I love it, I love it to bits. I love it because it suits my mood, which is, right now, as randy as hell. And separate rooms or no separate rooms, I am spending tonight in the same bed as Alistair.

Their reactions are much as expected.

'You look nice,' says Alistair's mum, eyes popping out

of her head. Alistair puts on one of those barely concealed smiles that indicate his delight at being seen with a whore. Alistair's dad doesn't say anything. But I can't help noticing that he spends a good part of the evening, while the rest of the table is prattling on, with his eyes fixed on my boobs.

They talk for a while about people they know, relatives and so on, until someone – Alistair's mum I think it is – mentions that this is of no interest at all to me and they are being really rather rude.

Then Alistair mentions that I am a regular reader of *Hello* magazine and other such populist rags, after which the floor is more or less mine while I regale them with the latest gossip surrounding celebrities from 'A', 'B' and 'C' lists, including which royalty is having affairs with who, and three-in-a-bed romps involving — from — United, and so on, bits of which are actually true – at least according to *Hello*. Alistair's dad perks up at this. '*Really?*' he says, frequently. 'You mean — and —? *Really?* Well I never! I never would have thought – goodness me, what goes on.'

And in the end it turns out to be quite a jolly evening. Alistair's mum's smile wavers from time to time earlier on in the evening. But at the fifth bottle of wine we are all as merry as larks, she included, and the stories are getting so outrageous that even they realise I'm entering fantasy land. But nobody cares.

And soon it's bedtime. We all offer to wash up but Mum – Maud – shoos us all away, saying it can wait till the morning. And so there we are, Alistair and I, mounting the stairs together.

I pause outside my room. He is standing right behind me, so close I can feel his breath on my bare back.

He places his hands lightly on my behind and leans down and kisses me softly on the back of my neck.

Then, pressing me closer to him, his lips move down my bare back, kissing, licking, caressing my skin with his tongue.

'You look gorgeous tonight,' he murmurs.

'Thanks.' I lean back onto him, my eyes closed.

'Do you want the bathroom first or shall I?'

'I'll go first.'

'OK.'

I let myself into my room. I'm out of my dress and into the bathroom and doing the necessaries in as little time as I can. When I'm done I call out, 'All yours,' and his voice, from somewhere in the distance, replies 'Thanks.'

And I climb into bed and wait.

I can hear him in the bathroom. I hear the toilet flushing, the tap running, him cleaning his teeth, the click of the light as it goes off, the gentle clunk of the door.

And I wait.

It's gone totally quiet.

It's beginning to look like I'll have to go hunting him. Perhaps he has a double bed.

Except I realise I don't know precisely which room is his.

Oh, well, not much I can do but go on waiting.

And waiting.

10

The next thing I know is it's morning and there's a light tap on my door and there is Alistair, with a mug of tea.

'Sleep well?' he asks cheerfully as he puts it down on the table by my bed.

I grab hold of his arm before he can escape.

'What happened to you last night?'

'What? I don't know. Did I drink too much? Did I disgrace myself?'

Oh, we're into playtime, are we?

'You know what I mean.'

He sits down on my bed and looks down at me, thoughtfully. God, he can be inscrutable at times.

He's wearing a dressing gown with nothing underneath it. I want to undo his belt and – but, dammit, I'm not going to.

Very slowly he pulls back the sheet, exposing my naked body. He puts a gentle hand on my breasts, then runs it down my body.

'You are so beautiful,' he says.

'Last night.'

'Yes?'

'I wanted you,' I say.

'I wanted you, too.'

'So?'

'So.' He's still running his hand across my body, thoughtfully, like a doctor inspecting a body for blemishes.

'What's going on, Alistair?'

'Well, breakfast is help yourself time I'm afraid. When you're ready I'll show you where things are. You don't take sugar in your tea, do you?'

'Alistair!'

He smiles, stands up, tightens the belt on his dressing gown.

'See you in bit.'

And he's gone.

I don't want to lie there too long because I don't want to do too much thinking. Life up until now used to be pretty straightforward and it isn't me that's complicating things.

I'm quite relieved to find Alistair's dad in the dining room.

'Good morning!' he says cheerily, just like his son. 'What can I get you? No cooked breakfasts I'm afraid, just toast or perhaps some cereal if I can find some.'

'Toast is fine, thanks.'

'Sleep well?'

'Er, yes, thanks.'

'It's very quiet here after London I expect, isn't it?'

You can say that again.

'Can I help with last night's washing up?' I ask.

'Oh no, thanks for asking. Maud was up with the lark. She's done the washing up and picked the vegetables already.'

'She has a lot of energy.'

'Yes, she has.'

I wonder if these two are happy together. I wonder if familiarity, the kind of familiarity they seem to have, is a comforting thing at their age. Or does it secretly drive you mad? I think it would probably drive me mad.

He makes me some toast and pours me coffee and we sit there together, eating our breakfast.

'Sunday paper?' he offers.

'No thanks. But don't let me stop you.'

'I have all day for it. It's not often we have company for breakfast.'

'What do you do normally, when you don't have people staying?' I ask him.

'Well, Maud's in the garden, of course. Sometimes she spends ten hours of the day out there, I barely see her.'

'And you? Meanwhile?'

'I, meanwhile?' He thinks as he eats. 'That's a very good question. I don't know what I do. The time seems to pass quite happily. I have a little summer house – it's down at the bottom of the garden, I'll show it to you later if you like. I spend hours there sometimes, reading, doing not very much at all, except thinking. Or pretending to think.'

'Is it lonely?'

He looks at me in some surprise. 'Well, now you come to mention it, no. Not really. What's lonely? Lonely is . . .' he tails off.

'Are you still working?'

'No, thank God. I'm afraid work for me was always a chore. A duty. I couldn't give it up fast enough. Now, time is precious. I could fill a whole day doing nothing, and feel quite satisfied.'

'That's excellent.'

He smiles at me.

'And how about you? Do you enjoy your work?'

'Oh, not really. It's a job.'

'I'm afraid a lot of jobs are just that. Just jobs. We settle for very little I sometimes think. So, what gives you pleasure?' he goes on. 'If it isn't work?'

Now that's a question and a half. He wouldn't much like the truthful answer I don't think.

'I don't know, really. I like . . .'

'Yes?' He watches me over his toast. Just like Alistair would. His look is disconcerting, but I don't really know why.

'Ah, there you are – how did you get to be here?' Alistair walks in.

'I walked down the stairs.' I didn't mean it to sound catty, but his eyes widen a touch.

'Right. Good. Well, you're being looked after, are you?'

'Yes. Thanks.'

I exchange a look, a rather private look, with Alistair's dad.

Alistair sits down beside his father. 'Morning, Dad.'

'Morning, Al.'

Father and son. So alike. Both eating breakfast. Same mannerisms, same expressions. Even eating the same breakfasts.

'So. What were you two talking about?'

'None of your business,' says Alistair's dad, winking at me.

'Oh. Like that, is it? Fair enough.'

The rest of the morning is taken up with Sunday papers. They seem to have them all – all the posh ones at least – which means there's at least two sections each to go around. Each family member seems to find his or her own little corner, away from the others, and some other unspecified rule says they leave one another alone, for the morning anyway.

Alistair casts me curious looks from time to time. I smile inscrutably back. A bit more of this kind of way of life and I'll be behaving just like them, I'm thinking.

Sunday lunch is roast lamb and spuds (from the garden), beans (ditto) and all the trimmings. Alistair's dad talks to him about work, the state of the market, interest rates and so on. Alistair's mum talks to me about the royal family and whose turn it will be to get married next, and what do I think of the two young princes? (Too young for me, I say, at which she hoots with laughter.) Once again there's wine and, not being used to drinking in the daytime, I am starting to feel decidedly relaxed.

'What time are you off?' asks Alistair's mum.

'Early evening.'

'Oh good. Then we've the afternoon ahead of us. Tony, why don't you show Hazel your summer house? I want to have a chat with Alistair, over the washing up.'

Ah. This will be the reckoning up. The Verdict delivered, no doubt.

'I was planning on doing that anyway, as it happens,' says Dad.

'Here it is, my own private little hideaway. My refuge. Come in.'

They may call it a summer house. You or I could live in it.

There's a sitting room, with wood floors and wood furniture and bright, pretty curtains. Bookshelves, a table, a comfortable chair, and a bed. Off it is a tiny kitchen and a toilet. You could definitely live here.

'Would you like a drink?' he asks me.

'What, now? I don't think so, thanks.'

'Well, I will if you don't mind.'

These aristos, they don't half put it away. He gets out the whisky and pours himself a modest slug.

'It's nice here,' I say. It is, I mean it. There's a real sense of peace. Not usually my thing, as you know.

'I like it. I spend hours in here sometimes, especially on a late summer afternoon like this. I like to sit at the window and watch the shadows on the lawn, see the sun setting. Sit down, do.'

I do. There's a bit of a silence.

'What do you do in here?' I ask him.

'Sometimes I read, sometimes I doze. Sometimes I just sit and think. Or just sit.' He chuckles. 'I'm very good at wasting time.'

He looks at me, rather as Alistair does, with that touch of contained amusement that is just a bit disconcerting.

He's a highly attractive man, I realise. I can see where Alistair gets it from. His looks, and his style. Very contained, very ... deep isn't exactly the word I'm looking for. Confident, perhaps. The kind of quiet confidence that goes with top breeding.

'How long have you known Alistair?' he asks me. It occurs to me we may be about to embark on his version of the parental cross-examination. Afterwards, over their evening sherry, they will compare notes, Lord and Lady Alistair.

'About a year,' I tell him.

'You're not at all like any of the other girlfriends he's brought here.'

'I can imagine.'

'Very refreshing.'

He sees the surprise on my face and laughs.

'They have tended towards the double-barrelled, if you know what I mean. Very upper crust, cut-glass, a bit superior. A bit like us, I suppose.' He chuckles. 'It's nice to meet someone with a bit of spark.'

'Oh. Thank you.'

Dammit, I'm blushing slightly.

'I think you're probably rather good for him. Bring him out of himself a bit. He's a bit tight-arsed, don't you agree? If you'll forgive the language.'

I laugh.

'Well, yes. And then again, no.'

'Oh? Tell me.'

The dirty old man, he wants to know what we get up to in bed. Got up to, should I say.

'Well. Underneath the reserved exterior, he's . . .'

'He's what?'

I can't quite find the right words, the *appropriate* words.

'Is he a good lover?' he asks.

Now I'm really blushing.

'He's fantastic.'

'Oh good. I am relieved. You'll probably think it none of my business, and it isn't, but I do worry. What with his upbringing. We're so out of touch us people nowadays, what with even the royals speaking with estuary accents – isn't that what you call it? – we're a bit of an anachronism, us people now. I rather feared Alistair might be following in our footsteps but, well, apparently not. Not in that way at least.'

'I don't think there's anything old-fashioned about Alistair. Except in the best sense, that is.'

'Which is?'

'He has old-fashioned manners. He treats women – me – like a queen, for the most part. He's always thoughtful, and polite, even to me.'

'What do you mean, even to you?'

'Even to someone like me. Who's a few rungs down the old ladder from him, if you know what I mean.'

'If you mean what I think you mean then you're quite wrong. If by the ladder you mean the class ladder, then I should damn well hope he treats everyone identically – not according to their background, or their position. If I've taught him anything I've taught him that.' He takes a hefty swig of his drink. He's quite fired up.

'Well you have,' I say. 'Alistair is class. Real class.'

'Is that why you like him?'

'I don't know. No. I like him because –' I'm treading in treacle here.

'Because he's a wonderful lover and he treats you like a queen.'

'Well...'

'And quite right too.'

I look across at him – Alistair's dad, who is still looking at me in that steady, rather unnerving way – and suddenly something rather odd starts to happen. I feel something beginning to stir, deep inside me.

'You are lovely, if you don't mind my saying so,' he says.

'Thank you.'

I'm matching his look. There's no question what's going on here.

I get up and walk over to him, kneel down in front of him and kiss him, softly, on the mouth.

He responds by placing his hands on either side of my face and holding me there. He pulls away slightly. He touches my face, runs his fingers lightly over my cheeks, my mouth.

'Do you want to make love to me?' I ask him.

'Oh,' he sighs. 'Oh yes, that would be wonderful. If only...'

I stand up and start to peel off my clothes. His face as he watches me is a picture of wonder and pleasure and delight, though I say it myself.

'Goodness me, I had forgotten,' he says, as he reaches out a hand to touch me, lightly.

'Forgotten what?'

'I had forgotten how lovely a naked woman's body is.'

'Now you.'

'Oh. Do I have to?'

'Yes.'

I pull him to his feet and, like a mum with a small kid, I help him take off his clothes.

He's suddenly shy. He laughs nervously as I pull down his trousers and his Y-fronts, and all the while I'm wondering if this is the right thing to do, if I won't change my mind the moment I see him naked.

He is not in bad shape. For a man of – what? – mid to late sixties? His penis is limp, and he is trying very hard to shield it with his hands, like a small boy.

'I don't know if I can do much,' he says, with a smile.

'We'll have to see.'

I move till I'm close to him and gently rub my pussy against his cock.

'How does that feel?' I whisper.

'That feels very nice. Very nice indeed.'

He closes his eyes and starts to kiss me, on the face, the eyes, the neck and the shoulders. To my surprise I find myself beginning to feel faintly aroused.

'Come,' I say.

I take his hand and lead him like a child to the bed. There's a thin cover on it and it's pretty small – not a coupling couch evidently – and we lie down on it together, close, very close, we have no option. And I kiss him. I kiss him hard, on the mouth and on the cheek and all over the face, and then the neck, and I'm beginning to feel quite turned on now.

I feel down his body, down his chest to his belly, and I'm moving my hands along his hips, his thighs, and I want to take hold of his penis, but somehow ... Somehow it feels a bit *impertinent*. He is the father of my boyfriend. He is the nearly-seventy-year-old father of my lover, whose wife and son are, at this very moment, in the house barely a hundred yards away doing the washing up.

'It's been a long time,' he says.

'So?'

'I don't know if I can ... ah!'

I've done it. I've taken hold of his cock.

'How's that?'

'Oh! Nice.'

I hold it, and squeeze. Then I sit up and I straddle him, still holding his dick, still squeezing. He looks up at me in surprise.

'On top. You're on top,' he says.

'Anything wrong with that?'

'Oh, no. It's just I never ... Is that what women do these days?'

'Some of us, yes.'

'How times have changed.'

I don't know, but I think he may be taking the piss.

He gazes up at me, wide-eyed. He looks somehow innocent, and slightly nervous. Uncertain – apprehensive about what I'm going to do next. Unused to the woman taking the initiative, I think.

'Relax,' I say to him. 'Just relax, I'm not going to do anything you don't want me to do.'

I start to roll his penis against my stomach. Now he's looking startled, startled perhaps at the first signs of movement there. I'm impatient now; I want to suck him, I want to make him hard, quickly. I'm aroused now and I need something inside me.

'May I touch your breasts?' he asks politely.

'Of course.'

Tentatively he reaches up and takes one of my breasts in each hand. He looks at them in wonder, like a child with a new toy.

'Stroke them,' I order him.

'Lovely, lovely.'

'Is this nice, me doing this?' I'm still rubbing his cock against me, resisting the urge to shove it inside me, limp or not.

'Yes, yes.'

His hands flutter down my body to my waist and then up to my breasts again.

'Touch my nipples.'

'Like this?'

'Like that. Squeeze them, hard.'

'Oh.' He's so darn tentative.

His dick is starting to twitch.

'I want to make love to you,' he says.

'You're not hard enough.'

'I'm an old man.'

'That's no excuse.'

'I may have forgotten how.'

'You never forget. You're just not trying.'

'But I am.'

'Then try harder.'

'Yes, oh, yes.'

I'm kneading his cock quite hard now. And yes, it's a cock now, and it's growing, yes, it's growing.

'No one ever . . .'

'Ever what?'

'Did that to me.'

'You mean no one ever massaged your cock before?'

'No, never.'

'Then what did you do, normally?'

'Just – made love. With me on top and –'

'Unbelievable. There's a lot you've missed out on. Like this perhaps.'

I push his cock against the edge of my pussy.

'Oh, my goodness!' His eyes grow ever wider.

'Anyone ever do that to you?'

'Oh! You are very good,' he gasps.

I roll his cock against my cunt, hard, edging it closer.

'I think we may be getting warmer,' say I.

'Oh!'

'Nearly there, but –'

'I'm ready.'

'For what? Say the words. What are you ready for?'

'To make love to you. Is that what you say?'

'To fuck me. Say it.'

'To – fuck you.'

'Spot on. But not yet.'

'Not yet?'

'In a moment.'

'You're teasing me.'

'You bet your life.'

'When? When can I?'

'Now.'

And I push him into me.

I move my body quickly so I am crouched above him, and I begin to ride him. Up and down, slow, sinuous, swaying from side to side. He closes his eyes and lets it all happen, just lies there letting me do whatever I want to do, and there's a smile on his face and, my God, he's in seventh heaven, I know he is.

I guess it never quite leaves you – this desire, this overwhelming desire for the feeling of another body, to be inside another body, it never leaves you no matter what age you are.

I start to move quicker now, lifting my body off his, arching my back. He opens his eyes and reaches up to hold my breasts. His eyes are dancing.

'Oh, you wanton woman,' he says with delight.

'I am that.'

'This is such fun.'

'Fun? Yes.'

'I feel so naughty.'

'You are naughty.'

'You're so soft.'

'Very naughty indeed.'

'Can you feel me? Can you feel me in you?'

'Just about.'

'That's not very nice.'

'Only kidding. I can feel you.'

I shift position a touch.

'Feel this.' I squeeze the muscles in my pussy and his eyes nearly pop out of his head.

'Ah! How did you do that?'

'Good, yes?'

'You are ... quite ... astonishing.'

'How are we doing?'

He starts to jiggle around underneath me.

'I think we're on the home stretch.'

'Yes?'

'Yes. I think I can see ... the finishing post. We're really galloping. Oh, yes! Yes, yes, yes! We're ... oh, oh!'

His eyes start, and everything stops. I'm not sure if he's having a heart attack or a climax.

'Ah. Oh. Ah. Oh, my goodness.'

He lets out a deep sigh. I guess it was a climax.

He lies there for a moment. Then he opens his eyes and smiles at me. Such a sweet smile.

'Did you make it?' I ask.

'Oh, yes, I think so. Oh, thank you. Thank you so much.'

I start to ease myself off him.

'Don't go.'

I lie down next to him. His penis plops out of me.

'Not bad for an old man, eh?' he says.

'Not bad,' says the wanton woman.

We lie there for a while. I can feel his heart beating, steadying, his body relaxing.

'Thank you,' he whispers, and falls asleep.

I move off him and sit there, looking down at him. A man at rest. I have known this man. And, even if it never happens again, and it won't, we will never be quite the same again. We have a secret now.

I climb off him quietly, so as not to disturb him, and I pull the cover up to his chin. He's sleeping like a baby.

I go to sit by the window and look out. It faces west, and I watch as the slowly sinking light turns to an orange glow that filters through the trees, stretching the shadows across the lawn.

How wonderfully, truly English it all is. A late summer evening, the low light of the sun, and my ancient lover asleep in the bed.

I sit there for a long time, still naked on the chair, knees drawn up to my chin, listening to the crows cawing and to my lover's even, deep, untroubled breathing.

That was a nice thing to have done.

I'm woken from my daydream by the sound of voices outside, in the garden.

In a flash I've grabbed my clothes, rushed into the shower room, dressed, and I'm back sitting on the chair like little Miss Innocent with a book in my hand as there's a tap on the door and Alistair pokes his head in.

'So you're still here. We were beginning to get worried,' he says.

He looks at the sleeping body in the bed. His glance goes fleetingly to the pile of clothes on the floor. He looks at me and smiles slightly.

'It's time we were off,' he says quietly, so as not to disturb his father.

'Right.'

We drive for some time in silence. I'm feeling pretty thoughtful, one way and another.

'That wasn't so bad, was it?' Alistair asks me, eventually. 'The weekend?'

'It was fine.'

'Good.'

'Did I pass?' I ask.

'Say again?'

'Did I pass the test? With your mother?'

He gives me a sidelong glance.

'What are you talking about?'

'Your chat, this afternoon. It was about me, wasn't it? Your mum passing sentence on me.'

He laughs. 'Of course not. We were actually talking about work. Among other things.'

'Right.'

'But she did like you, I can tell you that. You said all the right things about her garden, and you made her laugh.'

'Well, that's OK, then.'

'And Dad liked you, as you know.'

There's a silence.

'So, there's only one person I need worry about then.'

He doesn't answer this.

It's dark by the time we get back to London. I wonder if he's going to head to my place, or ...

'Alistair, please tell me what's going on,' I say, before he makes the decision.

He doesn't reply for a while. Then:

'I'm not sure what you mean.'

'Are we over? Is our sex life over?'

'I hope not.'

'Then . . .'

'Then?'

'Take me home, please, to your place.'

'If that's what you want.'

'We've got a lot of catching up to do.'

I've never felt so hungry for him in my life. The moment we're inside the door I'm reaching for him. I've got my hands around his neck before he's even had time to put his bag down, and I'm pushing my mouth onto his and giving him the biggest French kiss he ever had.

'God!' he exclaims, emerging into the air gasping for breath.

I start tearing at his clothes, like an animal, pulling at his jacket, clawing at his shirt. He starts to laugh.

'Hazel.'

'It's your fault, you've driven me to it.'

'*I've* driven you –'

'Playing hard to get like that.'

I yank down his trousers and his underpants. He's standing there naked from the waist down, and he's not even hard.

'What's the matter with you?'

I kneel down and grab his cock in my hands and put it straight in my mouth.

'Hazel, stop that.'

I do. The tone of his voice has surprised me.

'Stand up.'

I do. He pulls up his underpants and his trousers and does himself up.

'Let's start again, shall we?' he says.

'OK.'

'We come in through the door. I put my bag down. I say, would you like a cup of tea? Or a drink?'

'And I say no, no thank you.'

'Anything to eat?'

'No, not hungry. Not for food, that is.'

'No. You are not allowed to touch me.'

'Who says? Oh, OK.'

'So there's nothing I can offer you, then?'

'There's plenty you can offer me.'

'In that case. Well, it is late.'

'Bedtime,' say I.

'In a moment,' he says, very softly, leaning towards me, 'I'm going to go into the bedroom. While I'm getting ready for bed, you can use the bathroom.'

He kisses me on the mouth.

'When you come out of the bathroom,' he goes on, 'I want you to be naked. Naked and smelling sweet and ready for me.'

'Yes.'

He kisses me on the ears.

'And once I'm done in the bathroom I'm going to come back and I want to find you lying in my bed, naked, and wet, and hungry.'

'Yes.'

He kisses me on the neck. He starts to pull my clothes off me, kissing my shoulders, my breasts.

'First I'm going to kiss you, all over. Your face, your mouth, your hair, your breasts.'

He's got half my clothes off now.

'Your stomach, your pussy ... you're opening your legs for me.'

'Oh, yes.'

'And I'm going to lick your pussy. And your clit. I know I'm not very good at it, but you're going to have to lie there while I try to get it right, yes?'

'Yes.'

'You can help me.'

'I will.'

He's kneeling down in front of me now, pulling down my pants.

'I love your cunt.'

'Yes.'

His mouth is on me, buried in my pussy, his tongue pushing its way into me.

'I want to live in your cunt.'

'Oh, Christ, Alistair.'

'Tell me. Tell me what to do.'

His tongue is on my clit, softly circling.

'That. Oh, yes.'

Suddenly he's standing up and his mouth is on mine.

'Taste it. Taste yourself.'

'Not sure I want to.'

'Sweet, sweet juices. Christ, I want you. I want to taste you, to fuck you, to kiss you, to own you . . .'

'Own me?'

'Go. Into the bathroom before I come all over the floor.'

He's waiting for me when I come out. He's lying on the bed, fully erect. I go straight to him and lower myself onto him.

'Is this what you did with my father?' he asks.

I start to move on him, gently.

'Mind your own business,' I say.

'Was he good?'

'Mind your own business.'

'As good as me?'

'No one is as good as you.'

'Tell me about it. I want to hear all about it.'

'No, you don't. You know you don't.'

'Whose idea was it?'

'It was mutual, what do you think?'

'What's he like, in the sack? My dad.'

'Alistair, stop it.' I stop moving on him. There's a curious look in his eye.

'Fuck me,' he says.

'I'm doing my best.' I start moving on him again.

'Fuck me! Hard.'

'God, Alistair, what do you think I'm doing?'

He sits up suddenly and pulls himself out of me. He sits there on the bed, staring at me.

'Have I ever made you come?' he demands.

I hesitate.

'Have I?'

'It's not the beginning and the end you know.'

'So I haven't.'

'Alistair, you drive me wild. You give me the best sex ever. I couldn't want for more.'

'Lie back. Lie back on the bed and tell me what to do. Tell me where I'm going wrong.'

'Don't be daft.'

I lie back. His mouth finds my clit and he starts to chew.

'Calm down! You're hurting me!'

'Sorry.'

And then he starts to lick me, softly, so softly I can hardly feel him.

'Yes. That's wonderful.'

I'm beginning to float. To float away. To a parallel universe.

His tongue on my clit. Every so often he says something. I don't hear him. I'm flying off somewhere quite else.

Then suddenly he moves off me.

'I'm sorry,' he says, as he enters me. 'I have to. I can't wait.'

'Welcome back,' I say.

'Deep in you. I want to go so deep into you, deeper than anyone, deeper than my father.'

'Shut up about your father.'

'Last night, in that dress, I wanted to fuck you right then and there, on the dining-room table, with everyone looking on.'

'Then why didn't you?'

'Because.'

'Where were you, last night?' I ask him.

'I was with you.'

'Like hell you were.'

'Not physically. In every other way.'

'I waited for you.'

'Did you?'

'All bloody night.'

'I made love to you all through the night.'

'In your mind.'

'In my mind, yes.'

'Well, that was no good to me, was it?'

'I thought you didn't want me,' he says.

He's pressing harder into me, pulling my body up, deeper and deeper into me.

'Tell me what we did last night,' I ask him.

'I just fucked you, fucked you and fucked you and fucked you till you screamed.'

'Not nice.'

'You loved it.'

He's beginning to slam into me.

'Jesus, Alistair.'

'Am I hurting you?'

'Just a bit.'

'I'm sorry. I have to do this. Just let me. Let me do this to you.'

His body crashes down on mine so hard he's battering the breath out of me.

'I'm there, I'm so nearly there, I'm sorry to do this, my darling, but I have to, I have to ... Christ!'

He climaxes so hard his whole body shudders. Shudders and shakes. It's quite scary to see.

'Oh, God.'

He rolls off me. His sperm is still spurting from him. I reach down and grab some of it in my mouth. I'm sucking it. Sucking him. Sucking the juice from him.

His body is still shaking, and sweating. I move up to his mouth.

'Taste yourself,' I say to him. He opens his mouth and I dribble his sperm into it. His mouth closes over mine as he sucks it in, sucks me in.

'Oh, Christ. I'm sorry,' he says.

'What for?'

'I didn't mean to do this.' He starts to kiss me all over, little kisses, light, frantic ones, on the face, on the eyes, on the neck, like a nervous little boy who's done something bad and is trying to make amends. 'I wanted to do it for you,' he murmurs. 'I wanted to make you come.'

'Another time.'

'Always another time.'

'There's plenty of it.' I stroke him, calming him. 'I'll give you a tutorial if you like.'

'One day.'

'Yes.'

He lies there, staring at me.

'I will, one day. I'll make you come. If I could only fucking ...' he stops.

'What?'

'If I could only fucking well control myself long enough.'

I put my arms around him, around the whole of him, pinioning him.

His breathing steadies, slows, turns to a snore. He sleeps in my arms.

11

The next morning I wake up and there in the bed next to me, where Alistair should be, is a note. It says, 'I've gone. Early meeting. Help yourself to breakfast, you know where everything is. Cheers, Alistair. PS, when you go please double lock the front door and post the keys back through the letterbox. Thanks.'

'Cheers, Alistair' eh? Well thank *you*.

I've obviously blown it. The coldness of the note tells me as much. But what was it exactly? Was it because of what I did with his dad or was he ashamed of me in front of his parents? Did I wear the wrong things, say the wrong things? Or was it delayed shock when it sunk in that I'd shagged Tony, his father?

And there I was thinking I did quite well, on the whole, all things considered. His mum liked me, so he said. His dad certainly liked me. But you never can tell.

I am upset. Ashamed to admit it, yes, but upset. I have a soft spot for Alistair, quite apart from the sex, and I think I may miss him and that pisses me off. But in the end we all have to find our own level, don't we? What's the expression? Ideas above her station? There I was, wandering into unknown and unfamiliar territory without a passport, what did I expect? Cavorting with one of London's most eligible bachelors – who *do* you think you are, Hazel Cunningham?

I think for a moment, seriously, of spending all day right here, in his bed, in his sheets, basking in the smell of him on his sheets, plunging my head into his pillow, suffocating myself in him, in the absence of him, in the once-presence of him. And at the end of the day he'll come home and find me here and, without a word said, he'll strip off and jump in next to me and I'll seize hold of his hair and thrust my face into it, right into it, and I'll jam his body right up to mine and glue us together, wrap my legs around him, trapping him, entangling him so he can never ever...

Time to get up and go to work. Get a grip, Hazel.

At the end of another nondescript working day I'm sitting there, contemplating, without enthusiasm, the evening ahead – with my father, an invitation from him this time, which makes a change – when I look up and there's someone standing in the doorway.

'Hello, er, Sly,' I say.

'Slyde.'

'With a "y".' We say together, and laugh.

I'm actually rather pleased to see him, I find. He's looking, somehow, younger than I remember him, younger and less cocky, less arrogant – which is ironic when you come to consider. The lopsided grin is still there, but this time it doesn't seem quite so *put on*. In fact, all things considered, he's looking decidedly cute. And I am really pleased to see him, though I can't think what he's doing in my office.

'How've you been?' I ask.

'Excellent, thanks.'

There's a pause.

'What are you doing here?'

'I just wanted to come by. I've come for Janine, but I just wanted to –'

'Janine? How come you know Janine?'

'Er, we ... through Nick. Nick introduced us.'

'Ah. And you and she are ...'

'Yes, we are.'

Well, well, well.

'Well,' I say.

'But I just wanted to drop by to say, you know, thanks,' he says.

'Thanks? What for?'

'For, you know.' He stuffs his hands in his pockets and shifts from one foot to the other.

'Oh, that,' I say.

We smile at one another. I think we're both feeling a tiny bit shy, would you believe.

'It was my pleasure,' I tell him.

'It was great, you know.'

'I just wish it could have been elsewhere.'

'Well, yeah.'

'It shouldn't have happened there, in the ladies toilet for God's sake. We should at least have had a bed, a huge bed, in a bedroom, with silk sheets, and some time. We should have had all the time in the world.'

I see it. The enormous bed, as wide as it's long, covered in layers of brocaded quilts in rich, deep colours. Goose-down pillows, huge and soft, and my good self laid out for all the world to see in my full, naked glory, my pale skin startling against the rich, deep . . .

'We could have gone at it slowly, gently, bit by bit,' I go on. 'Nothing rushed.' He naked and terrified, I soothing, calming, touching. 'We should have made love for hours and hours. And hours. And I could have shown you a thing or two.' My plaything, up for anything — what larks we could have got up to. 'So much I could have shown you. It's a shame.'

He's looking at me, staring at me, very very hard, and, my God, my own words, and that penetrating stare — between them they're beginning to get me highly hot and bothered.

'It shouldn't have happened like that, not your first time. In that sordid toilet.'

'It wasn't sordid,' he says, quite fiercely.

'Don't think badly of me because of it.'

'Think badly of you?' He looks almost outraged. 'You were fantastic.'

'I did my best, in the circumstances.'

'Fantastic. I won't ever forget it.'

I look at him, at his tight, taut, wiry little body and his spiky hair and I start to wonder. Wonder if we can't somehow, you know, find a way of making amends for a slightly dodgy beginning. I'm about to open my big mouth and make a fool of myself when Janine walks in.

'Hi,' she says.

'Hi,' he says.

'I didn't know you were here.'

'I just dropped by to say hi to Hazel.'

And in full view of me, of his mentor, his deflowerer, his teacher and guardian angel, he takes hold of Janine's face and gives her the biggest, hungriest open-mouthed kiss I've seen outside the movies. It goes on for what seems like a fortnight before he eventually pulls back and looks to me as if to say ... To say what? Look at me, look at what I can do. Look what you taught me.

Suddenly I feel very old. Janine turns to me too, and blushes. They stand there together, arms around each other's waists, looking for all the world like a pair of sweet sixteen-year-old kids in love, which I suppose is what they more or less are.

'Have a great evening,' I say, with as much warmth as I can muster.

'Thanks. You too,' they reply, in chorus.

I shouldn't feel depressed. And I don't really. But I don't feel this is turning out to be the best day of my life, and frankly the last person on earth I feel like seeing tonight is my father.

It was he who issued the invitation, for a change. Usually it's my conscience that nudges me, every few months, to get onto the phone to talk to him. He hardly ever calls me, mostly because I suspect he doesn't want to be seen as the interfering old dad. But on this occasion, not only is it not that long since we saw one another, but he sounded positively cheery on the phone as if...? Who knows. All I know is I don't feel in the mood for macrobiotics and I don't feel like spending an evening in the energy-sapping surroundings of his monk's cell, not tonight.

There are surprises afoot, however. First of all, he greets me with a big smile. Then he takes my customary bottles (two) from me without a murmur or his usual 'You enjoy them, sweetheart, you know I don't'. And the moment I step through the door into his living room I know that something is up.

There are flowers. Flowers everywhere, on the tables, the mantelpiece, the windowsills. And brightly coloured rugs where there used to be scrawny little strips of organic hessian. There are other oddities – things I can't quite put my finger on immediately but realise later are, uniquely, bits of *clutter*. There are *things* on shelves where there used to be empty space, cushions and throws on previously bare sofas, *stuff*, furniture and stuff, that is there for no particular purpose other than decoration. The place is, simply, transformed.

Well, I know I gave my dad a hard time last time we met but I never thought he would take my words quite so much to heart. As I stand there gazing at the surroundings with my mouth hanging open he smiles at me and says:

'Different, huh?'

'I'll say.'

'You like it?'

'I love it, Dad, it's – it's actually a nice place to be in, for a change.'

'Thought you'd approve.'

'What's going on?'

'Well, after what you said that time, I looked around and had a little think and thought, well, why not? Flowers don't cost that much. The place could do with a touch of colour.'

'Not very convincing, Dad.'

'So you see I do listen to you, Sox, sometimes.'

He pours two glasses of wine and hands one to me.

'Cheers.'

'Cheers.'

And then another thing hits me, and this time it's a smell. The smell of cooking chicken. It's at that point that the kitchen door opens and this woman enters.

'Sox, this is Elspeth. Elspeth, this is my daughter, Hazel.'

'How do you do, Hazel,' says the woman.

'Hi,' says I.

She's quite a big woman, in her fifties I guess. Handsome rather than pretty. She smiles at me as she holds out her hand to shake mine. It's a broad smile, but at the same time she's wary, watching for my reaction, wondering perhaps why my mouth is still hanging open.

Then I look at my dad and maybe it's the perspective, but I swear he's grown. This is a big woman, as tall if not taller than him and broad in the beam, and yet standing there beside her he looks like a match for her.

Perhaps it's because ... because ... Who the hell is Elspeth, anyway?

'You look shocked, Sox,' he says, amused.

'Sorry. Just taken by surprise, that's all. There's rather a lot to take in.'

'Elspeth and I,' he says, ominously, his arm finding its way around her shoulders, 'are ...' He pauses and looks to her.

Are what, for God's sake?

'What do you call us, darling?' he says to her.

Darling?

'Friends? An item? A couple?' he ventures.

'Yes, we're sort of, yes, a couple, you could say,' she says, with a chuckle.

She's got a deep, warm, chocolatey voice, that suits her rather large, handsome face with its oversized features, its big, liquid eyes, generous mouth and Romanesque nose. She is everything that he is not.

It turns out – to précis a rather long explanation that is related and repeated, almost word for word, by both sides – that they have been working in the same department for years, but only recently 'got together'. Elspeth too has been married, and divorced, and though she implies she had 'admired' David from afar for some time, he had always been friendly but distant and it wasn't until – When was it, darling? A month or so ago? – that they agreed to go out for a drink together.

A *drink*? My *dad*?

Followed some days later by a meal, and then ...

I bet she's not macrobiotic. It would take healthy dollops of animal protein to fill that bulk of hers.

'Are you macrobiotic too?' I ask her.

At which she roars with laughter, and they look at one another as if to say, 'what a question!' and Dad looks at me apologetically and says:

'There are a lot of things that are in the past now, Sox. Food, for instance.'

'He eats meat now, white meat.'

'And fish.'

'And fish. And he drinks.'

'Not much, not drinks as in *drinks*.'

'He enjoys a glass of wine.'

'I do, with a meal, yes.'

'And he's allowed me to make a few changes round here.'

'As you can see.'

'Flowers, for instance.'

'Flowers and a bit of colour.'

'I mean, this place, before, it was . . .'

'Like a monk's cell!' they say together.

'So, as you can see, one or two changes.'

'She has transformed my life.'

At which point they turn their attention from me to each other. And they gaze at one another for, what, not long, but there's a look in their eyes that says quite a lot.

I am speechless.

We have a very jolly supper. The food is delicious, we get through the two bottles in no time and Elspeth immediately produces another one. She matches me glass for glass – which is no mean feat, let me tell you – and she's getting more and more flushed and her laugh is getting louder and louder and her hair, which hitherto has been tucked neatly into some kind of knot on the top of her head, is bit by bit making its escape down both sides of her face like some neglected trailing plant. The more unkempt she becomes, the more I like her.

After the meal is over she banishes David, my dad, to the kitchen to do the washing up. She pours us each yet another glass of wine and sits us down side by side. Clearly she has Something of Importance to impart to me, but her body seems to be suffering odd little jerky spasms of some kind. I realise she has hiccups, which slightly undermine the seriousness of what she is summoning the courage to say to me.

There is a long pause, as she sits there making these funny little jumpy movements in her chair, silently hiccuping; and I sit there trying not to giggle, or to feel too anxious about whatever it is she's about to tell me.

'We are sleeping together, you know,' she says eventually, in a rush between hiccups.

There's a silence.

Well I should damn well hope so, I'm thinking.

She lifts her eyes to look at me. She looks distinctly nervous, embarrassed.

'I'm sorry, I felt you should know. I just –' hiccup '– to be frank, I thought all that was behind me. Ever since I divorced – I was in my forties then – and the kids were growing up, and you know –' hiccup '– you have different priorities. I didn't give it, sex, much –' hiccup '– thought. After all I'm – well, let's say I'm in my fifties.'

There's a pause.

'Good for you,' I say.

'You're not shocked?'

'Why should I be shocked?'

'A woman of my age?' She laughs. Her hiccups have gone, I realise. 'And then there's, well, there's your mother, and I know she was the love of his life and I would never think . . .' She stops.

'Never think what?'

'That I could replace her. Either in his eyes or yours, of course.'

'She wasn't . . .' Whoops, no, I stop myself just in time.

'What? She wasn't what?'

I was about to say she was not the love of his life, that she didn't love him – not in the way he loved her, that is. And that in a way I feel he deserved – deserves – something better and that if anything can be salvaged from the sorry mess that was my parents' marriage, if anything can bring a bit of light to my father's dull existence, then it's high time it happened.

'I'm delighted. I am, truly, delighted.' I reach out and put my hand on hers. This isn't a gesture I normally make. But she needs reassurance, and somehow I feel – and I like this woman – now I'm getting over the shock, I'm absolutely bloody delighted. And sex, too. Well good on them, I say.

'I absolutely adore him,' she says simply. 'I never thought, in a million years, at my age, never thought it would happen. Could happen. I totally adore him.'

'That's wonderful.'

'You don't mind?'

I shake my head. Even the question makes me slightly cross.

'He said you wouldn't mind. He said you'd be pleased, pleased as punch, he said.'

'I am. I think it's fantastic. I can see, already, what you've done for him. To him. He was becoming a total misery to be frank, and I told him so, last time I saw him.'

And I wonder whether and how much that conversation was responsible for this, for Elspeth, and everything she has done to him. I like to think it was, at least partly.

By now we've both got tears in our eyes and we reach out and give each other a big, big hug, and she clings on to me like I'm her long-lost friend, and now she's crying openly and I'm wondering if perhaps she hasn't got a bit of Russian in her too.

I realise when eventually we pull apart that Dad has been standing there for probably some time, watching us. His face is a picture. I don't think I've ever seen that expression before, not on him. I don't think I've ever seen him looking so pleased, so supremely, comfortably, lovingly happy. I guess he looked like that in the early years of his marriage, when I was too young to see, or understand, or remember.

'You should try it, Sox,' says my dad.

'Try what?' As if I didn't know.

'Love. It's the best thing in the world, you know.'

'So you said before.'

Thanks for your advice, Dad. For all of it, all those conflicting bits of advice that are all so much garbage anyway – one man for one woman for God's sake. Remind me one day, not today, to say I told you so. I told you never to give up on things.

Anyway, that's my dad sorted.

And it's good to know that sex still happens even in your fifties. That gives me a good thirty or more years of it, which is a deeply pleasurable thought.

Suddenly the world is full of lovers. Dad and Elspeth, Janine and Slyde. And I'm beginning to feel like – what was her name? – Emma, from the Jane Austen novel, the self-appointed matchmaker who made it her business to find partners for all her friends, sometimes unsuitable ones, while she herself . . .

It is a curious thing, this thing called love. Personally I don't believe in it. I think you can be fond of someone, very fond, and I certainly think you can have great sex with someone. But love? When I looked at my dad's face, and Elspeth's, and the way they looked at one another – well, it's hard to put into words, but I couldn't help wondering, to myself, *where are they*? They are somewhere strange, they are not here, in the here and now, with me, they are somewhere else, in some Unknown Territory. Unknown to me that is, some place I've never gone to. And frankly, don't intend visiting. On account of it inevitably bringing trouble. But we've been into all that before. Time to be moving on.

It occurs to me, as I'm sitting here at my computer, that I haven't seen Nick for ages. Not since the day in the pub, with Slyde. The drink that we were intending to share, the chat we were supposed to have to clear the air between us, so to speak, never really happened, all on account of Slyde, of course. Nick is on my conscience, despite what he told Slyde about me. That's the trouble with Nick, he's always on my conscience, which isn't a good place for anyone to be.

I pick up the phone and dial.

'Information technology,' says the voice at the other end.

'Hello, is that . . .?' No, that's not Nick's voice.

'Who are you looking for?' Never heard that voice in my life.

'Nick. Is he there?'

'Nick's gone,' says the voice.

'He's *what*?'

'He left two weeks ago. Is that Hazel?'

'Er, well, yes. How did you know?'

'Hi, I'm Nick's replacement. My name's Ryan.'

'Oh, right. Hello, Ryan.'

'Did you want Nick in particular, or –'

'How come he left? Just like that?'

There's a bit of a pause.

'Well, I don't really know, but if there's anything I can do for you . . .' He tails off.

He's got a slight mid-Atlantic accent, you know, the sort of pseudo-American twang young things used to adopt – well, people like me used to adopt – when we were teenagers and spent all our waking hours watching *Baywatch* and *Beavis and Butthead*.

'I can drop by if you like. Say hi,' he drawls.

'OK.'

'When?'

'Whenever.'

'At the end of the day, right?'

'Right,' I say, without a lot of conviction.

How curious. So Nick just upped and left, suddenly. No goodbyes, and nobody got round to telling me. I feel – I hate to admit this – I feel bereft. I feel as though Nick and I were unfinished business. No matter what our differences were we had some truly great times together and I thought, if he could only keep things in perspective, we had great times to come. And now I'm beginning to wonder if this, if Nick's sudden departure, isn't my doing, my fault, as well. Am I turning out to be Bad News?

I had totally forgotten about him. I was just packing up to leave – on account of having an Important Date this evening with Number Six – when this guy walks into the room and comes right up to my desk, leans on it and announces, huskily, 'Hi, I'm Ryan.'

'Oh. Yes. Hazel.'

'I've heard a lot about you.'

Oh no, not you too.

He offers this great beefy hand and gives mine a firm, manly shake, while looking me steadily in the eye.

He's standing so close to me I have to pull back slightly to look at him properly. My first impression is – well, let's say he looks nothing like an IT guy, he looks more like a cowboy.

'So, you're Nick's replacement,' I say.

'That's me,' he says with a sly grin.

It's not that he's wearing cowboy boots or anything, but he is what I think they call, on the far side of the pond, what's the word?

'It's good to meet you, Hazel. How're you doing?'

Beefcake. That's what he is.

'And so what – so what – exactly did Nick say about me?'

The stammer isn't put on. He makes me nervous.

'He told me you were a bit of a dummy where computers were concerned.'

'Well, that's true.'

It's his sheer size, I think. The size and the bulk of him.

'He also said . . .' He pauses. For effect presumably.

'Yes?'

That sly grin again. This man fancies himself.

'He also said you were . . . that you, uh, liked to –'

'To what?' He's getting on my nerves now.

'I tell you what. Seeing as it's packing up time, how's about we head down to the pub and get acquainted over a beer?'

'I . . .'

OK, I'm tempted. Despite my best efforts I find my eyes, disconnected from my better judgment, sliding down his body, from his grinning face down past his open-neck shirt to his jeans (Nick would never wear jeans to the office, in fact I've never seen anyone in this office wear jeans, ever), to the undoubted great bulge in his crotch where, again entirely of their own accord, they hover momentarily.

He misses none of this. His grin exposes perfect white teeth. He has to be American.

There are few things in life that annoy me more than a man who fancies himself. In this case, however, despite his arrogance, his cheeky grin, his assumption, the double entendres and the well-honed flirtatious manner, I have to admit he is, unfortunately, gorgeous.

'I can't, I'm sorry, I have to be somewhere else,' I say eventually.

'Shame. Another time perhaps.'

I nod, vaguely, I hope.

He turns away to go and then stops in the doorway.

'Oh, hey. When you called up to talk to Nick, did you have a problem?'

'A problem?'

'Yeah, a computer problem. Is that why you called up wanting to talk to him?'

'I . . . no. No problem.'

'So you were just calling up to . . .'

'I was just calling up to say . . .'

'Hi.'

'You could say, yes.'

'Right.'

And, dammit, he winks at me as he opens the door and saunters, cowboy-style, out of the room.

I don't know why I decided to see Number Six again. After the last time, with the video and the oils and the massage and so on, when he had so deftly 'serviced' me but refused to allow me to so much as touch him in return, I had decided that was it. Whatever game it was he was playing I had neither the time nor the energy for it. Moreover, I like to fool myself that I am, usually, in control when it comes to sex.

However, Six is, still, a challenge unmet. And I am still, though I hate to admit it even to myself, intrigued, fascinated even. Worse, since we're into admissions, is acknowledging that his game is working. He has me on the end of some tenuous, invisible thread and he has pulled it and – well, here I am, sitting next to him in this little Greek place just round the corner from my flat, where something rather remarkable is happening.

I have my hand inside Six's trousers and it is cradling his cock. His cock is not hard. But the important thing is, he is not complaining, he is not stopping me, and I have every reason to believe that before the evening is out . . .

To go back a bit:

We've been playing this game. We'd eaten our meal and drunk our wine – a bottle between us – and we were into the coffee. The conversation had been polite, even a touch banal, and I realised if the evening wasn't going to be a total washout that I was going to have to do something to liven things up. So I watched him quietly stirring the sugar into his coffee and then I asked him who, of all the people in the restaurant, he would most like to fuck.

He stopped stirring and looked slowly round the room, gazing carefully at each person – male and female – in turn, before his eyes came to rest upon this voluptuous, raven-haired, Latin-looking woman wearing a bright orange peasant-style blouse showing a massive cleavage. She was sitting across the restaurant at an all-woman table.

'Why her?' I asked.

'She has magnificent breasts,' he said, staring.

'I didn't know you went for big boobs.'

'It is not the size, it is the way she uses them.' He lifted his coffee cup and took a tiny sip.

'*Uses* them?'

'She wears them with much pride,' he said, in all seriousness. 'She is wearing, I expect, one of those bras – what do you call them – that lift and enhance and push the breasts upwards and upwards until they are exposed, or semi-exposed, like two great globes, for the world to gaze upon.'

The fact that of all the women in the room she was the one least like me was not lost on me. It's at this moment that I laid my hand casually on his thigh and asked:

'What would you like to do to her?'

'I would like to bury my head in her breasts,' he said, carefully replacing the cup in its saucer.

'And then?'

'And then, I would like her to drag her long, black, coarse hair over the length of my body.' He leaned his elbows on the table and clasped both hands together, thoughtfully.

'Drag her hair over your body. Your naked body.'

'Yes.'

Slowly, and I hope deftly, I undid his flies.

'Where are you?' I asked.

'Where? Oh, I see. We are in a palace, in Spain somewhere, perhaps Granada. The palace of the King, in the nineteenth century, I think. I am the King's chancellor, his right-hand man. And she is his favourite courtesan.' He took another sip of his coffee.

'Sounds dangerous,' I said.

'Perhaps.'

My hand was inside his trousers now, feeling its way through the opening in his underpants.

'What if you are found out?' I asked him.

'Execution, without a doubt. By garrotte, probably.'

'For who?'

'For both of us.'

'You like to play dangerous games, then?'

'Not really. It is a calculated risk. The King is not at home, the odds are against us being caught. That is, if we do not make too much noise,' he added, with a smile.

That is the point where I took his cock in my hand. His limp cock. And that is where it is now.

'Excuse me, but would you like anything else?' comes a strange voice.

This is the waiter. Unsuspecting, naturally. What we're doing is under the table, literally, and butter isn't melting in either of our mouths.

'Brandy?' suggests Six.

'No thanks.'

'Then just the bill, thank you.'

I start to stroke him, gently. There is no reaction, either above or below the table.

'What does she look like?' I ask as soon as the waiter's back is turned. 'Her naked body, describe it.'

He turns to look at the woman across the room. She throws back her head to laugh and her cleavage – her bosom – heaves alarmingly and threatens to escape from its covering.

'She's quite large,' he says. 'Her bosoms are like small mountains, you could lose yourself in them.'

'Are you going to fuck her?'

'Fuck her?'

'Yes. Because you're going to have to do a bit better than this.'

I give him a sharp squeeze, for emphasis. He lets out a tiny gasp, which is the first sign he's given that he's aware of anything – anything unusual that is – going on inside his trousers.

'She won't want this inside her,' I say.

'We have some way to go before that.'

'You can say that again.'

'There are other things to do first,' he says. He's taking this particular game very seriously.

'Such as.'

'To begin with she is not aroused. She is lying there, naked, her arms above her head, looking – how shall I say – slightly bored.'

'She's done this too often before, perhaps.'

'I'm afraid so, yes.'

'You're going to have to be very inventive.'

'All suggestions are welcome.' He turns to me and smiles slightly.

'Perhaps ... Perhaps she likes to be tied up.' I'm still squeezing him. But there's not much going on.

'Good idea,' he says.

'Is there anything to hand?'

He frowns.

'As a matter of fact, there is', he says after a moment. 'There is the silk cord belonging to her robe. In fact –' he smiles now '– there are four of them as it happens, I cannot imagine why.'

'How lucky.'

'Yes. So now I am attaching her hands, one by one, and now her feet, to the four corners of the bed, so her naked body is spreadeagled.' He demonstrates, with precise movements of his hands, over the table. I rub my thumb over the tip of his cock.

'Does she like that?'

'She is not complaining.'

'And now?'

'I am going to pass my tongue very lightly across her body, breathe upon her.'

'Very minimalist,' I say, squeezing the tip of his cock hard between my fingers. He opens his legs wide.

'Her nipples are growing hard,' he says.

'Good sign.'

'So I give them a little nibble, on each one.'

'Ouch!' I say. I give his cock a sudden nip with my fingernails.

'She likes it. Now I am sucking them.'

'And she?'

I start kneading him.

'Her body is beginning to move a little. Her eyes are closed. I take one of her great bosoms in my mouth. It is soft, and her skin, it's very sweet, it tastes of cinnamon.'

'Yummy,' I say. I feel movement, as I knead.

'Now she is starting to push her body, with her body she is trying to push herself into me and, as I move my hand down her stomach, she is murmuring something.'

'What?'

He says something incomprehensible, in Spanish.

His cock begins to dance. I squeeze harder and step up the pace.

'Which means?' I ask.

'"Fuck me".'

'Your bill, sir.'

'Oh. Thank you.'

The waiter stands there, by the table, as Number Six peers at the bill. I stop kneading momentarily and grip him hard, as hard as I can, as he signs.

'Here you are,' he says to the waiter. 'The signature looks a bit strange I'm afraid but –'

'Thank you, sir.' The waiter goes.

'Go on.'

I lean one elbow on the table, turn all my attention to his face, and resume the pumping movement. I'm pumping him quite hard now and his cock is growing and growing.

'OK, so she wants you to fuck her,' I say.

'I believe she does, yes.'

'So what's stopping you? You're hard enough.' It's true.

'I want to ... prolong ... for slightly longer.'

His breath is shortening.

'You're teasing her.'

'A little.'

'You want to wait until she's crying out for you.'

'Perhaps.'

'It's the only way you can get a hard-on, when you know the woman is desperate for you.'

'You know me well.'

'Except in this case, if she does cry out, it might attract attention.'

'Yes.'

'So now?'

'She is wet,' he says. 'I can feel she is wet.'

So can I. I'm pumping and squeezing with all the strength I have.

'But she's not desperate,' I say, 'not yet.'

'Oh yes, she's quite desperate.' He pushes his knees together, crushing my hand and everything within it.

'She's about to cry out?'

'I think so.'

'Any moment?'

'Any moment.'

'So you'd better not wait.'

'My cock ...'

'Your cock is ...?'

'Inside her!'

'Yes!'

He comes into my hand.

We sit there, side by side, for a moment. He is breathing heavily. He closes his eyes.

His cock, his soaking, coated cock, subsides very, very slowly.

It is soft, when it is limp. A nice cock. I don't really want to let it go.

'Thank you,' he says.

I want to give a little whoop of satisfaction. Well, a half-whoop anyway.

We did it. I did it. That makes it, what, 2–1 to him. Now there's nowhere else to go but total consummation.

I turn to look out of the window at the pigs flying across the sky.

12

I'm sitting in the pub listening – or part-listening – to Ryan's life history.

He has an American father apparently, and an English mother. He was born and brought up in Wisconsin and was Best At Everything at junior school and then high school and was heading for a career as a professional baseball player when his parents split and his mother brought him over here, to dull old non-baseball-playing England, thereby ruining his career. He contemplated becoming a male model, but decided that really was beneath him and opted for computer science instead, which seems an odd substitute but there you go. He works out regularly in the gym and still plays sports. He plans one day to run his own computer company and make an obscene amount of money.

Some of it, I realise, even with only half my mind occupied, does not quite add up. Why he did not return to his beloved US, for instance, when he was of an age to do so. Why, if he's that ambitious, he has come to work for a tin-pot little company like ours. But I don't really care, because I know this is simply the hors d'oeuvre, and my mind is on the main dish that's to come.

So when, out of the blue, I hear him say, 'OK, your place or mine?' I really have no right to think, now hang on just a minute, aren't you making a few assumptions here? This doesn't stop me acting the Miss Prim, however.

'I beg your pardon?' I say, in my archest manner.

'I said, where are we heading now? Your place or mine?' He looks at me innocently over his nearly empty beer mug.

'I'm sorry, I don't remember agreeing to go anywhere.'

'Oh, come on, Hazel!'

'What?' It snaps out like a shot from a gun.

'You know what.'

'I don't know what people have been saying about me –' my eyes are flashing now '– but I'm not impressed by your assumption.'

'What assumption?'

'The assumption that I'm an easy lay.'

'No, look, I never assumed, look, hey.'

'Well?'

'I just thought you were ... there was something about you, about your body language. I thought you were up for it. OK, so I misread –'

'What did Nick tell you about me?'

'Nothing.' He holds up his hands in protest.

'Are you sure?'

'He said – he just said you were not the kind of girl to get entangled with, that's to say with your heart. He said you just liked, you liked to get it on, and I thought, that sounds like my kind of girl.'

'Nick has a big mouth.'

'You could say.'

There's a pause.

'I'm sorry,' he says.

At last. It's easier to get blood out of a stone than an apology out of a man. My point is made.

'OK. Let's go to your place,' I say.

He looks up at me, in surprise.

'You mean it?'

I give him a big, broad, false smile.

'Great,' he says. 'Let's go.'

Games, games, games, we all play them. Playing hard to get isn't one of my regulars, because being mistaken – taken – for a whore, for a good-time girl as they used to say, doesn't offend me in the slightest as a rule, as by now you will have realised.

This guy just needed a bit of deflating, that's all, in the ego department at least.

You know when you're walking down the street and you see someone coming towards you and you think, hey, I know him, or her, and you stop to say something and they look back at you blankly and you realise, hey, I don't know him/her at all, this is just someone I've seen on TV, a *celebrity*, a famous person?

Imagine what it's like to be that celebrity, knowing that every second person you pass in the street knows you, or thinks they know you. They know who you are, they've seen you on TV, they *own* you, or they think they do. They know all about you, or they *think* they do.

Well this, in a watered-down sort of a way, is how I'm beginning to feel now, thanks to Nick and his ever-open mouth. As we arrive at his apartment building, Ryan and me, and we're standing there in the lift together, our bodies almost touching, saying nothing, I'm wondering how much he knows, or thinks he knows, about me already. What kind of an unfair advantage has he got on me?

Everything Ryan does, every movement he makes with his body, is suggestive. In the lift he stands a little closer to me than necessary. As he opens the lift door for me he positions himself so that our bodies brush against one another as I exit. As we pause outside his apartment door his eyes – in a manner which he probably thinks is seductive but to me looks simply drugged – slowly travel the length of my body, mentally undressing me.

'OK?' he says to me softly, as he clicks the key in the lock.

No complaints so far.

It's a bachelor apartment, all right. Clutter and chaos. Empty beer bottles, dirty plates and glasses on the floor, tables piled high with men's magazines, the lingering smell of last night's curry.

'What can I get you?' he asks.

'Nothing,' I say.

He comes straight at me, grabs my face in his hands and kisses me on the mouth. It's a huge, open-mouthed, tongue-down-the-throat, Wisconsin-style kiss, like they do in the movies. I feel as if he's eating me.

He pulls back. He's breathing heavily.

'What are we waiting for?' he breathes into my ear. Then he takes my hand and leads me to the bedroom.

'Make yourself truly at home,' he says. 'I'll be right back.'

And off he goes, who knows where.

So I go and lie there, on the enormous bed, gazing around me at the posters on the walls. There's Stallone, and Bruce Willis, a Pamela Anderson lookalike and a couple of guys I don't recognise. It's a teenager's bedroom. A kid's bedroom in every way but for the size of the bed.

I start to take my clothes off, and as I'm doing so I'm asking myself why, what am I doing here? I don't feel particularly horny, it all seems a bit … Is it just habit? Or curiosity?

I lay myself down on the bed, trying not to look too resigned. I think I know how that Spanish lady was feeling.

'Oh, wow.'

He's back in the room again, a drink in his hand, looking down at me.

'Your turn,' I say.

'You want music with this?' he asks.

'Music? OK, why not?'

He goes over to the hi-fi in the corner of the room, flits briefly through an untidy pile of CDs and slots one into the player. It's a quiet jazzy number.

'OK, here we go.'

He takes a swig of his drink, puts it down, and gets to it.

First he takes off his shoes. Then he pulls his shirt out from his trousers and undoes the buttons. He takes his time. He shrugs the open shirt from his shoulders and runs his hands down his – OK, I have to admit it – beautiful, naked torso. He works out, he told me. It shows.

This is not a man taking his clothes off. This is a striptease. I wonder if he does this professionally.

His hands go to his belt.

'You sure you don't want to do this for me?' he asks.

I shake my head. 'Keep going,' I say.

As he undoes the buckle he starts swaying slightly, moving his hips from side to side in time to the music.

The belt takes a very long time. He pulls it slowly and quite unnecessarily through the belt holders on his jeans and, gently rotating his hips all the while, rolls it up neatly and puts it aside. Then he unzips his fly, and stops.

He's looking at me. I look back with what I hope is nonchalance at this half-naked man standing there, legs apart, hips swaying, flies undone but nothing revealed. His hand goes to his crotch and he holds himself. His eyes are locked on to mine as if to say, I bet you wish this was your hand, you lucky, lucky lady.

He eases his jeans down his legs and off, and there he is, in his boxer shorts, tight boxer shorts that emphasise his enormous bulge. He puts both hands inside his shorts and moves them down himself very slowly. Every movement he makes is slow, and deliberate, and separate. His unmoving hands are now right down inside his boxer shorts and I can only guess that they're holding his cock. He's watching me, as if awaiting instructions.

'Are you touching yourself?' I ask him.

'I am. I'm big.'

'So I can just about see.'

Still inside his boxer shorts, with both hands he starts to stroke himself.

His body – his hips – are moving more now as he arouses himself. He is rubbing himself quite hard now and I can see him almost bursting out of his shorts.

'You like this?' he asks me. 'You like to watch me do this?'

'It's OK,' I say, with a shrug. My apparent indifference is lost on him.

'I'm growing – boy, am I growing,' he says, his breath coming faster.

'Let me see it,' I say. 'I want to see what you're doing.'

'You do?'

'Yes.'

'OK, here we go.'

He stops what he's doing and pulls down his shorts. I let out an involuntary little gasp.

His body – well, it's what you'd expect from someone who works out, who puts all his time and energy into the love and devotion of his physical appearance. It's about as perfect, I have to admit, as they come.

As for his manhood...

This is not a word I generally use, but in this case it is the only way to describe the throbbing, alert, expectant and beautifully proportioned instrument that is now revealed before me in full – and I mean full.

Its owner stands there, hands on his hips, allowing me to ogle.

'You want to touch him?' he asks.

'No, it's OK. Why don't you do it instead?'

'Tell you what, we'll do it together. Talk dirty to me, tell me what you'd like to do to me. Let's see if we can make Johnny grow erect without touching him.'

And I had thought – to be honest I thought Johnny was pretty much erect already.

'OK,' I say.

'What do you think of him?' He asks me as he stands there, he and Johnny, a few feet away from me.

'He's pretty good.'

'He likes you, too.' His cock moves. He looks down at it in surprise.

'I can see he does,' I say.

'He'd like to pay a visit to you. He'd like to explore you, wouldn't you, Johnny? Yes?' he asks his friend. 'Yes,' he nods to me in confirmation.

'I thought he might,' I say.

'Johnny says – what's that Johnny?' He looks down at his cock and appears to be listening. 'Johnny says he'd like you to open up your legs to him and show him your pussy. Yeah?'

Involuntarily – other forces are obviously in charge here – I part my legs, just the tiniest bit.

'That's good,' says Ryan. 'Isn't that good, Johnny? Oh yes, he likes that, he likes that. See him grow?'

I do.

'OK. Now he's walking up your garden path to your front entrance. Here he comes now, he's real close now, he's knocking at your front door right now. Do you feel that?'

'Er, yes, I feel that.'

I'm going along with his fantasy. He's still some feet away from me, he and his friend.

'Hey, you're wet!' he says. 'You're horny. You must be ready for him.'

Slowly slowly, up he comes. We're both watching him – it, rather – as if it's something disconnected from either of us.

Ryan takes his by now rampant cock in his hand and holds it, as if it's a prize trophy.

'OK,' he says, 'here he comes, he's coming to you now.'

He walks a couple of paces towards me. I am, needless to say, transfixed.

'He's pausing at your entrance.' He stops. 'He's pushing his head in to take a look around. Yep, there we are, Johnny.'

And, dammit, with his cock in his hand he twists it this way and that – for all the world like it's a puppet or some live thing on a day's outing to Disneyworld, taking a look around. Bizarre is far too mild a word for what I'm witnessing here.

'Nice. Yes, he likes it here. He's going to come in a little bit more now, inch by inch' He edges slowly towards me. 'And you're lubricating for him, lubricating nicely – oh, wow, yes, this is good, this is a good fit, a good, tight fit.' Now he holds his cock so it protrudes at right angles from him and pretends to give it a little shove.

'Ooh! Now he's fully in. Feel how tight that is. He is filling you, Johnny is, filling every square inch of you. It's good, it's warm in here. How does that feel? How does that feel?'

Gripping his cock tightly, he starts to move his body

slowly backwards and forwards, as if he's fucking the air.

'OK, boy, easy now, easy, steady. In and out, feel it? Feel that. He wants to hold on, but he don't know if he can.'

He's starting to pant and his body is starting to quiver.

'Johnny wants to come in. It's cold out here, he wants to be inside, somewhere warm.'

Together they advance towards me. Ryan and Johnny. And despite myself, despite my intentions, I open my legs wide and prepare myself, just in time.

He thrusts into me with such force he sends my entire body hurtling back against the headboard.

And he starts to fuck me. He fucks me hard, in and out, rhythmically, powerfully, me on my back on the bed, the headboard banging against the wall.

Then he pulls out of me, whips me over onto my front like a pancake and crashes into me from behind, his hands gripping my waist, pushing me, pulling me, now flat on the bed, now pulling me so I'm on all fours, now lifting me so I'm upright, we're both upright, and still he keeps on pumping.

Suddenly, without warning, he turns me around, puts his hands on my waist and lifts me, lifts me right off the bed so I'm sitting on the rim of the headboard; he hooks my legs over his shoulders and pounds into me while my back hammers against the wall. Now his arms are around my back and he's lifting me again, lifting me into the air and taking the whole of the weight of my body as he keeps pounding, pounding, and I'm clutching on to him for dear life as he drops me down onto the bed again. Then, still inside me, he drags my body to the edge of the bed, plants his feet on the floor, spreads my legs wide, as wide as they'll go, and then off he goes again – thrusting, pumping, like an unstoppable, inexhaustible piston – the sweat pouring down his face and his chest and dripping onto me, my body bouncing up and down on the bed beneath him like a rag doll until, suddenly, he pauses.

'Are you ready for me?' he gasps.

'Ready for you?'

'Are you ready for me to come?'

'Yes.'

'OK, baby, here we go.'

And with one – two – three – no, four great, almighty final thrusts he comes, crashing into me, smashing me almost to pieces. As he comes his body goes into spasm and he opens his mouth and howls like a wolf as he releases everything into me.

Well.

Two, three minutes pass and he continues to stand there on the floor, by the bed, still inside me, his body heaving as he struggles for breath. Then he takes a step back and I feel his great cock slowly sliding out of me, and my cunt, so recently and so fully accommodated, sighs as it empties.

He stands there looking down at me, still breathing heavily. His cock hangs there, quivering slightly, glistening with the combination of our juices.

I lower my legs, stiffly, and lie back on the bed. I'm not at all sure I'll ever walk again.

'How was it for you?' he asks, huskily.

The truth is there was a time when he would have been the answer to my prayers. To have been banged – and 'banged' is the word – for hours on end by a man with the strength of a horse, the stamina of a long-distance runner, the athleticism of an acrobat and the sexual appetite of a rampant bull – all this would have simply blown my mind.

But now ... Maybe I'm getting old, but being penetrated and hammered to within an inch of my life till I'm limp and wrung out like an old rag doesn't seem to do it for me any more. I want a bit more gentleness, please, a bit more of the teasing, the anticipation, the toying with each other's bodies, the build-up, the touching in exquisite places, the slowly growing desire.

Yes, I'm definitely getting old.

Of course, I say none of this to Ryan. When I feel I can move again I ease my poor old body off the bed and give him a smile that he takes to be a sign of satisfaction for services rendered. He nods and turns away from me, and so I make my way to his bathroom, wash and dress and make my exit as swiftly as I conveniently can, in case – as I'm afraid he might – he's planning a repeat performance the moment he's got his breath back.

The bar is crowded, fortunately. I say fortunately because the more crowded a place is, the more anonymous you can be. I buy myself a drink and find a spare seat in a corner.

I spot Alistair on the far side of the room, but I don't want to go over to him, not yet, because as long as he hasn't seen me I can watch him. It's a rare treat to be able to watch someone without them knowing.

He is talking, unfortunately, to Number Six. I say unfortunately because, for some reason I can't quite explain, while I know they are acquainted, work colleagues, in my mind I like to keep them completely apart. Ever since Alistair made it clear he is not interested in hearing what I get up to with Number Six I have made a point of keeping the two of them in separate compartments of my slightly complicated life. To see them together is, illogically, a bit of a shock.

Still, I can watch them both together, double treat.

They are alike in many ways. Two businessmen, in suits, in a bar full of not dissimilar businessmen, in suits. Tall, elegant, urbane, at ease with their surroundings. Talking quietly, casually and easily to one another and smiling occasionally.

Yet there are differences, almost imperceptible at first glance. Number Six's attention is only partly on his drinking companion. Every so often his eyes, those arctic eyes, turn their attention away from Alistair and scan the room, like a beam from a searchlight. As Alistair talks to him he smiles, and nods in his direction, yet without moving his head those eyes, alert and remote at the same time, are constantly on the move, now looking in this direction, now in that, not wanting to miss anything. He makes an appearance of listening, of laughing, of enjoying the jokes, the pleasantries. But there is something not completely convincing about him, I realise. He is not totally where he appears to be.

There is a lull in the conversation. Alistair leans back with both elbows on the bar behind him, crosses one elegantly trousered leg over the other and smiles genially at the world in general. He is gorgeous. If he only knew how gorgeous he was.

Over in the corner, unbeknown to him, a huddled collective of bright young females is ogling him. These are the clever smart young women with money, hard-earned – or more likely borrowed – money they are prepared to burn in pursuit of The Ultimate Night Out. As I watch, one of them, a sleek, toned blonde wearing a figure-hugging black number, schmoozes her way across the floor right up to the two men. Her companions follow at a tiny distance.

This will be interesting. I wonder how my lovers will deal with this one.

They form a friendly little crowd right there by the bar. There are introductions, nods, smiles, handshakes. Alistair smiles warmly at something the blonde girl says and, dammit it to hell, I feel a pang of something unfamiliar. Jealousy, for goodness' sake.

These are the sharp young working women – successful, self-assured, at ease with the world around them and ready for anything. Their clothes have never seen the inside of a chain store and more money has gone into the maintenance of their hair, their teeth and the honing of their bodies in a week than most ordinary people spend in a month in the supermarket.

The blonde is a touchy-feely person, the kind of girl who finds any excuse to lay a hand on a male shoulder, or sleeve, or anything at all within reach. Alistair says something and she throws back her head as she laughs (trying just a bit too hard, I can't help thinking) and reaches out to touch him as if to say, Get along with you! But the hand remains there, on his jacket, on the buttons of his jacket right there on his chest, touching him, touching my ... Touching my what?

I'm suddenly filled with uncharacteristic self-doubt. I really have no right to be there. I feel shabby and out of place. What chance do I have against these glittering, golden things with their slinky bodies and their careless manner and their wandering hands? These are million-dollar babes, with penthouses in Docklands and a five-figure continental soft top sitting on a double-yellow line right outside. These are Alistair's kind of women, these glitter-babes. These are the sort of women he mixes with all the time. Theirs is the sort of lifestyle he is used to. Me? Who do I think I am?

I have to get out of there. I'm reaching down to my

feet to grab my stuff and getting to my feet when I look up to see Alistair standing right there, smiling at me.

Standing next to him, also smiling, is Number Six.

'Are you off?' asks Alistair.

'Oh, hi. I didn't notice you there.'

'You looked as if you were in a rush to go somewhere.'

'I – well no, not really,' I say, sitting down again for no reason other than that I don't know what else to do.

Of the four women there is no sign, no sign at all. It's as if they've dematerialised. Or maybe I dreamed them.

The two men are still smiling at me.

'May we join you?' Alistair asks.

'Of course.'

'You do know each other, don't you?' says Alistair. 'Hazel, this is –'

'Yes, we've met.'

'Indeed we have,' says Six, with a funny little bow.

They pull up a couple of chairs, seat themselves, place their drinks down on my little table and turn to look at me.

My two lovers.

'Were you looking for someone?' asks Alistair.

I was looking over his shoulder, as I thought, surreptitiously, to see if I could spot the glitter-girls.

'No,' I say. 'I just thought . . . I thought I saw you with someone.'

The two men glance at one another and laugh lightly.

'So what brings you here?' asks Alistair.

'I, er, I just came in for a drink.'

He nods at me, smiling, not taken in for a second.

'It is an amusing place, I like it here,' says Number Six. 'It is a place where interesting things happen.'

'Such as?' I ask, wide-eyed.

'Last time I was in here – well, one of the last times – I bumped into an old colleague of mine. Or perhaps colleague is not the correct word. You remember Geoffrey?' He asks Alistair.

'Geoffrey?'

'He used to work for the National Bank.'

'Geoffrey Malcolm-Smith. Good God.'

'Indeed.'

'I wonder he has the nerve to talk to you,' says Alistair.

'It is not a problem for Geoffrey. Nothing is a problem for him, he is without shame. He has no conscience and the skin of a hippopotamus.'

'A rhinoceros,' I offer.

Alistair looks at me.

'Fortunately I was able to – how do you say it – get my own back on him,' says Six.

'Good for you. What did you do?'

I feel a foot, under the table, pressing into mine. Such is the layout, the position in which the guys are both sitting, I've no idea who the foot belongs to.

'I gave him something,' says Six. 'Something he thought he wanted very much, but in reality the moment he had it he decided he did not want it at all.'

There is a pause.

Alistair looks at Number Six. Then he looks at me.

'And what was this thing?' he asks.

'He's very greedy, is Geoffrey,' I say, without really meaning to.

'You've met him?' Alistair's eyes widen.

'I think I have.' I turn to Number Six for assistance.

'Hazel was here that time, she was witness to Geoffrey's humiliation,' says Number Six. 'In fact, you could say she was partly responsible.'

'Oh?'

'You want to tell him?' Number Six asks me. 'Or shall I?'

'Well, I don't know that –'

'Let's just say he bited off more than he could chew.'

'Bit,' I say.

'Bit? Yes, of course. I thought it sounded odd – "bited".'

Alistair watches us, his head swivelling between us like a spectator at a tennis match.

Number Six takes a sip of his drink. 'It is a tricky language, your language,' he says. 'The moment you think you have it licked, up it jumps and bites you in the face, so to speak.'

He laughs. 'Of course it is "bit". As in "hit". Only "hit" is both the present and the past participle of the verb "to hit", is it not? He "hit" a good shot. I am going to "hit" you if you don't stop that. I'm only joking, of course. It is all quite confusing.'

I realise what Number Six is up to, and I join in.

'Then what about "lit"?' I say.

'"Lit"?'

'"Lit" is the past of light. He "lit" the candle.'

'Indeed, yes. Except that in America I believe they say "lighted".'

'But no one says "fit".'

'"Fit"?'

'As in "fighted". He "fighted" a good match. And did you know –' I can't stop myself now '– there are four different ways of pronouncing "o-u-g-h" at the end of a word? As in "cough", "plough", "though" and "enough" – all spelt, the same way and all pronounced quite differently.'

'And then there is "ought",' says Six.

'That's another one, yes.'

'It is no wonder we make mistakes. I believe you do it deliberately, you Brits, you make up silly rules with your language just to confuse the foreigner.'

And on we go. And all the while Alistair watches us, the two of us, wondering why it is we've suddenly taken to talking total gibberish.

We never do get back onto the subject of Geoffrey, thank God. And it is interesting, and characteristic of Alistair, that he doesn't pursue the subject. But he does give us some highly curious looks and, when eventually Number Six makes his apologies and gets up and goes (and with him, unsurprisingly, goes the foot under the table), and we're sitting there together just the two of us, he says nothing for rather a long time.

Silences between Alistair and me are rare things. It's not so much that we've got endless things to talk about, but Alistair is far too genial a person, far too good a conversationalist, to allow something as significant as a silence to come between us. Silences are such loaded things, and in this one my imagination is running all over the place. First it tells me that he is no longer turned on by my whorish behaviour, that on the contrary he finds it despicable, particularly where it concerns a colleague of his; that he is so bored with me he can no longer be bothered to make conversation; that he is quietly hunting for the kindest yet most decisive way to tell me, sorry, but he's found a replacement for me – a blonder, more glittery replacement with a body to die for and a six-figure coupé outside the door.

When he eventually opens his mouth to speak I am such a nervous wreck that what he does say doesn't register for a considerable while.

'Have you had your holidays yet this year?' he asks, for all the world like a chatty hairdresser.

'Sorry?'

'I said, have you taken your holidays yet?'

'Er, holidays?' I'm staring at him like an idiot.

'Yes, you know, those things where you pack up work for a couple of weeks and swan off into the sunshine.' He smiles.

'Yes, yes, of course. Sorry. No. Er, no, I hadn't given it much thought.'

'A friend of mine has a place on a Greek island. I wondered if you'd fancy a couple of weeks in the Aegean.'

Yes, the smallest feather could send me flying.

'Well. I'll check, at work. Well yes, that sounds great. I'd love to.'

'Good.'

I look at him and he smiles inscrutably back.

I'm not usually lost for words. Usually I'd have no difficulty telling him what was on my mind, which in this case is something along the lines of 'Where the hell have you been? Why haven't I heard from you?' Or, worse, 'I've missed you. What was it, was it something I did?'

But thank God I say none of that. Instead, I smile warmly back and bask in the prospect of spending two weeks in the Mediterranean sunshine fucking Alistair all day and all night until we are both completely off our heads.

Eat your hearts out, glitter-babes.

13

This morning I slept through the alarm, so I'm late for work. Believe it or not I am not usually late, not even for work – I have a bit of a thing about it. I decide to take the bus to the tube station to make up a bit of time.

Being that time of day it's full of elderly people with Freedom passes and mums with small babies in pushchairs. It's crowded, and one of these (pushchairs) is being annoyingly shoved into my ankles. I look down to complain to its occupant, and this little thing looks up at me and gives me the biggest smile I have ever been on the receiving end of.

Thinking it must be a fluke, or a case of mistaken identity, I look away and look back, and it happens all over again. There is this dazzling smile, and it's just for me, and this time it's accompanied by a dirty little gurgle. Hooked now, I smile back, and play the game again, and each time the smile gets bigger, and the gurgle dirtier. You couldn't have melted my heart more effectively if you'd had it surgically removed and placed in the oven at Mark 4 for 35 minutes.

I'm so absorbed in our little game that I miss my stop and have to jump off and walk back several hundred yards to the tube station, which makes me later than ever. But what the hell.

When I see Barbara at work I want to tell her about the baby, but something about her expression discourages conversation. Instead she growls:

'Ryan was asking for you.'

'Ryan? What for?'

She gives me one of those looks that says, 'If you don't know then I'm sure I can't tell you,' which drives me absolutely spitting mad. So I sit down at my desk and switch on my computer with dread and foreboding, because I know there will be at least one sexy email from Ryan and, frankly, I'm not up to it.

It's now at least a week since we got it together and I've managed, so far, to just about avoid him. He, however, is not getting the message.

This is odd, I admit. Odd that I should want to avoid him. Him of the men's magazine body and the super-human sexual prowess. What more could a woman want? Moreover, he offers sex without ties, a man after my own heart you'd think. As for his selfish sexual behaviour, that could be fixed in no time, it would be a pleasure, a challenge. It *would have been* a challenge, if I could be bothered. And that's just it, I can't. I can't be bothered.

Something is going seriously awry in my life, I realise.

'I think we ought to have a talk,' says Barbara to me later that day, as if she's been reading my thoughts.

Oh doom and despondency. I don't suppose she intends talking about the weather or inviting me to dinner. She's either going to give me a dressing-down about my behaviour or the sack, probably both.

'Do you ever give much thought to your future?' she asks, ominously.

We're sitting together over café lattes at the local Costa's.

'Not really.'

'You intend staying in this job, do you? How old are you? Twenty-five, twenty-six?'

'Are you sacking me?'

'Where do you see yourself in a year's time? In five years' time?'

I shrug. 'I'm a day-by-day sort of person, Barbara.'

'And you think that's good enough?'

My hackles are starting to rise. I'm not sure what makes her think that what I do or where I go in my life has anything to do with her.

'Look, Barbara, if you're giving me the sack then just do it, and get on with it.'

She doesn't immediately respond to this.

'Do you see yourself getting married one day?'

I laugh so suddenly I spray latte all over the table.

'It's not a laughing matter, Hazel.'

'Sorry. Sorry, sorry, I didn't mean ...'

She takes a very deep breath.

'I don't know where you get your ideas about life from, Hazel, but in my view they are something short of what a young person like yourself might be expected to have.'

'I'm sorry, Barbara, but I can't see –'

'This job, when you do it, when you put your mind to it, you can do perfectly well. When you put your mind to it.'

'Yes, I know I've had my off days –'

'But I'm very much aware of the fact that for half the time, for most of the time, your mind simply is not on the job, which is why you so often fall short.'

'OK, I don't deny it.'

'The reason your mind is not on the job is because the job, this job, is beneath you. Once perhaps, in the early days, it presented a challenge. Now the challenge is no longer there, all you are left with is the same routine more or less day after day. Which understandably is getting you down. That is why – no, please don't interrupt – that is why you seek your pleasures ... elsewhere, shall we say. Or rather – as often as not – not elsewhere, but *in other ways*, and very often, all too often, right there in the office under my nose, so to speak. Don't think I'm a complete fool, Hazel.'

'I don't, I ...' I'm stuck for words again.

'It's not my business to question the way you lead your life, but I simply feel, since you have no mother, and your father by all accounts is ... Well, let's say I feel you lack a guiding hand.'

She doesn't look at me as she says this, and to my surprise I realise she isn't finding this, any of this, easy to say. I'm suddenly touched.

'You are an intelligent woman, Hazel, underneath it all, you could – you should – be making something of your life. You are also a much nicer woman than you pretend to be. Or you could be, if you allowed yourself.'

'What do you mean?'

'If you were not so ... if you allowed yourself to be slightly less brazen. To show your vulnerability.'

'I don't have any.'

'None at all? Don't be ridiculous. Are you trying to tell me you never feel unsure, insecure, unhappy?'

'Pissed off, maybe.'

'Yes. Perhaps that's the modern way of putting it.'

'Sorry for myself, you mean? No.'

But I'm remembering the moment in the bar, with Alistair, and the silence. And then for no particular reason, because there's a slight break in the flow of the conversation, I find myself telling her about the baby on the bus, and the way it smiled at me – at me, a total stranger – with complete trust, complete openness.

'You would make a marvellous mother, Hazel.'

Trust Barbara to completely miss the point.

She goes all misty-eyed.

'You know there is nothing, absolutely nothing, like the love of a small child. It is the most unselfish, honest love there is. It is impossible to describe. Nothing, nothing in the world is more life-affirming than knowing you are capable of love. You may never have loved a man, not completely, not unselfishly. You may not have really loved your parents, not in the way that you should – well, perhaps from time to time, but it can be complicated. But the love of a child is the purest, most wonderful love of all and the best experience in the entire world.'

Well, what do you say to that?

She brings out a hanky and dabs at her eyes.

I'm kind of dumbfounded, as you might imagine. I would quite like to take her hand, like I did Elspeth's, and comfort her – if comfort is what she's looking for. But she's not the sort of person you do that kind of thing to. She is, in her own peculiar way, untouchable. I sense that beneath her slightly stern exterior lurk deep wells of profound and complex Russian-style emotions that are beyond the reach, and the understanding, of any other human being – certainly of this human being. But she is a good sort, on the whole.

'So, Barbara, what is it exactly that you wanted to say to me?' I ask her eventually.

'I've said it. Haven't I? I thought I'd made myself plain.'

'Are you sacking me?'

She sighs, deeply, like you do with a small child who is resolutely refusing to get the point.

'I'm simply asking you, Hazel – suggesting to you – that you give a little thought to your life, and where it might be leading. That's all. No, of course I'm not giving you the sack. It's not my position to sack you, you know that.'

Dear Barbara. I don't really know what to say to her. I've no doubt she expects something from me but I don't really know what. So I smile at her as warmly as I know how, and we sit there in silence for a bit, and then we talk about the weather, and about her garden, which is clearly the love of her life, and then eventually we get the bill and we go to our separate homes.

And I think about what she said. Or about what I think she said. And then I think, thank God I'm going on holiday soon and I won't have to think about anything.

There is no better feeling in the world (bar one) than the feeling of the sun on the skin.

It's been a long haul getting here. A very early morning start, a flight to Athens, a taxi trip to the port, and now here we are, sitting on a ferry for four hours crossing a sea – the Aegean perhaps? – on our way to some island whose name I can never remember let alone pronounce.

And I am sitting here on the deck, basking in the warmth, lifting up my face to the sun and letting it do whatever horrors it wants to do to my skin. The sky is a deep, ludicrously deep blue, and it seems to grow more and more vivid with every mile we travel.

A few feet away from me, leaning against the railing, is the most gorgeous man in the world. He is dressed in a loose-fitting linen suit, his tall, lean outline silhouetted against the sun, and he gazes out over the sea beyond the horizon. He's like something out of a novel by Scott Fitzgerald. And this beautiful specimen is going to be mine, mine, mine for the next two weeks.

Paradise, now I know what you are.

The island appears and grows bigger as we approach. We dock at a tiny port and everywhere you look it's like a painting done by a child: every colour is a bit too bright, every house a bit too crooked. Small groups of old men gather in the shade of the trees. A dog barks. Otherwise, everything, including the insects, sleeps.

A taxi takes us, bouncing so our heads bang against the roof, down this dusty, pitted road to our holiday home. We arrive as the sun is just beginning to sink. Those same children have brushed their ridiculous paints all over this unlikely, deepening blue sky, washing the canvas orange towards the west.

It's a house from a picture book: single-storey, white walls partly covered by some vivid, violet-coloured creeping plant, a red roof, and a terrace overlooking the sea.

I climb out of the taxi and do a circuit of the house. At the back of it I find a flight of steps leading directly from the house right down onto the beach. Onto this small and completely inaccessible (from anywhere else) beach go I and, before anyone has time to stop me, I'm down those steps and flipping off my shoes to feel the glorious, wonderful, warm slither of the sand between my toes.

I wander to the sea's edge and allow the water to caress my feet. It laps, almost silently. As the sun sets – so quickly – so the colours, those bright, primary-school colours gradually darken around me and, before I completely lose my sense of where I am, I clamber back up those stairs again to the little house at the top.

There is a car parked outside the house that wasn't there before, and for just about the first time I start to think about Alistair's friends, whoever they may be, and I wonder what and who they are and how we're going to get on. It occurs to me I've never been exposed to his friends before. This will be a new experience; will I have to be on my best behaviour? Whatever that is.

As I walk round the side of the house I see Alistair standing by the front door talking to another man, and as I approach I realise, with just a bit of a shock, it's Number Six.

I shouldn't have been surprised, I should have expected it, of course. Number Six. Who else could it have been? I'm not sure how pleased I am to see him.

They turn as I approach.

'Hazel!' says Alistair. 'We were wondering where you were. You've met –?'

'Yes.'

How many times do I get to be introduced to this guy?

I go to stand by Alistair and he puts his arm around me.

'I've been on the beach,' I say, a bit breathlessly after all those stairs.

'It's nice, isn't it?' says Number Six.

'Beautiful, just beautiful.'

'And it's all ours. No one else can get to it,' he says.

'It's all perfect.'

Well. It was. It was perfect, until Number Six . . .

As we go into the house and he shows us around, all I can think of is – now what? What happens now? What is my role here? Have I been brought here as the whore? The domestic whore, to be shared between them – alternate nights, first with Alistair, then with Six? Or perhaps – and here the mind begins to boggle – we'll be a threesome? Will I like that? Was I consulted?

That's, of course, presuming there isn't a fourth member of the party, that Number Six hasn't brought a girlfriend. Foursomes – now that is a place I'm not sure I want to go.

'And here, this is your room,' announces Six, to Alistair and me. Well, that clears one thing up anyway.

The bedroom is bare, plain, a wooden floor, a low bed with a thin covering, a crucifix on the wall. And the best view in the entire world, looking right out over the sea.

The sea is a hypnotist. It hypnotises me every time I see it, which isn't often, and every time, every time I see it I wonder to myself how I can bear not to live right beside it and wake up to it outside my bedroom window every day.

'Supper will be ready in about half an hour,' says Number Six, and leaves us to it.

I'm standing there mesmerised, gazing out through the window, lost to the world. I can feel Alistair standing close, just behind me, his breath faintly on the back of my neck, not quite touching me.

'You didn't tell me,' I say.

'Tell you what?'

I want to know why he didn't tell me about Number Six. At the same time I don't want anything to break this spell.

'You didn't tell me how beautiful it was.'

He puts his arms around me and I sink back into his linen jacket. He kisses me softly on the neck.

'Do you want a shower?' he murmurs into my ear.

'No. I want you.'

And before he has time to protest I turn and gently remove his jacket and his shirt and allow my hands, my hungry hands, to run swiftly over his chest, to grip the waistband of his trousers and rip them open, to pull down the zip, my mouth reaching for his. And there's a pause, a long, still moment, as our mouths connect, and open, and I feel his gentle tongue down my throat and my body starting to float away. Then we are naked on the bed – on the low, hard bed – pawing one another, exploring, feeling, stroking, and he's inside me, so gently, it all feels so natural, so wonderfully familiar, so *comfortable*; and I squirm my pleasure and we writhe together for a bit and then he fucks me, poetically, balletically – or so it seems, perhaps it's the atmosphere that's got to me – and he comes majestically, quietly, and quickly. We lie there for a bit, just a bit, looking at each other's faces, and then we get up, silently, and we shower – first me, then him – and we dress and moments later we're sitting on the terrace, at this little table, with our glasses of red wine and a Greek salad, and we're watching the moon – a child's moon, bright yellow and half full – slowly lifting up out of the sea into the sky.

Number Six is wearing a suit. Perhaps it is the only kind of clothing he possesses. It's a lightweight suit, but it's still a suit, and though he isn't actually wearing a tie he's done his best to look as if he's only just taken it off.

He's been here a week already apparently, and the tan suits him. It sets off his pale blue eyes and his fair, light brown hair. But he still is, even here in this unearthly paradise, a businessman.

And there's no sign of anybody else. No reference to a fourth person, no place laid, no mention of anyone.

A threesome. I gaze out over the sea and ponder on it.

It seems unseemly. Yes, a strange word for me to use perhaps, especially since I've been there before as you may remember, many months ago, in my dreams, in the boardroom, Alistair and him, and others. But that was then, way back when I didn't know him – Six, I mean. So much easier to fantasise about people you don't know.

It would have to be in a darkened room. Alistair and Number Six. Shadows, indistinguishable, one at each end of me as I lie on the low, hard bed. One touching my breasts, another my legs, one mouth on my mouth, another on my cunt, a tongue down my throat, the other on my clit, two pairs of hands, two mouths, all over me, touching my body, inside me, exploring me. And then I would open my legs and I would open my mouth and a cock would slide into each end of me and I wouldn't know which was which or who was where. Or would I? Would I? They'd fuck me, together, in rhythm, in slow motion. I would suck them deep into me, into each end of me. And then one of them would draw out of me, out of my mouth. And there's just the two of us, fucking, harder now, and he – he is standing there watching us, I can see his eyes, his eyes catch the light, his pale blue eyes watching us, Alistair and me, fucking, and coming, and holding each other. I watch him to see the expression on his face and there isn't one, none at all.

I look out over the sea. The moon's up high now, its reflection bouncing in little pieces on the gently moving water. A dark shape flies across the sky. A bat, perhaps.

My two lovers are talking to one another, quietly, so quietly I can barely hear them above the cicadas. They seem so very far away, there on the other side of the table. I reach out for my glass and my hand feels suddenly so heavy I can barely lift it. I realise I'm only just on the conscious side of falling fast asleep.

Alistair looks over to me.

'Tired?' he asks.

'Exhausted.'

'Go to bed,' he says. 'I'll follow you.'

And I do. And he doesn't. Or rather, I'm asleep before he does, and he doesn't wake me. And I sleep the deep sleep of the innocent, all through the night, without moving or dreaming.

I also sleep through Alistair getting up. I can only assume he did come to bed last night – there's certainly the imprint of a body on the sheets.

I go in search of him and find Six, on the terrace, clearing up after breakfast.

He's wearing shorts and a T-shirt. He looks almost indecent. I've never seen any bit of him naked before, you understand, not so much as a bare arm, let alone a leg. Seeing him now, like this, I almost find myself apologising for catching him without his clothes on.

'Sleep well?' he asks.

'Fabulous, thanks. You?'

'I always sleep well.'

Of course.

'Have you seen Alistair?'

'He's gone. He said to say to you, sorry he didn't speak to you this morning, he left quite early.'

'Gone?' I feel my blood stop. Am I stupid, or . . .?

'He's taken the car and gone for a tour of the island,' Six goes on. 'He said he may be gone all morning. He didn't want to wake you.'

'Oh. Right.' Odd though, I'm thinking.

'Breakfast?' Six offers.

'Yes, thanks. Just – anything will do.'

'There are some fresh oranges. And bread, and coffee of course.'

'You're very kind.'

He smiles at me as he turns to go, hesitating a tiny second to run his eyes swiftly over my body.

It is not a desirable body, not at this time of the morning, not when it's only just staggered out of bed, unwashed, hair everywhere, eyes still gluey with sleep, breath stale, appearance unchecked.

I eat my breakfast alone, gazing out over paradise. He joins me for a cup of coffee and we sit there, either side of the table, not talking. Not out loud at least.

'Have you been here before?' I ask. A daft question really.

'Yes, I try to come every year,' he says.

'Only once a year?'

'The house does not belong to me. It belongs to the company.'

'Ah. Oh. I didn't know.'

He's looking at me. I realise the cotton kimono I have on has slipped slightly to reveal perhaps a half-nipple. Instinctively I reach up to pull it around me – not that there isn't any small part of my body he hasn't already seen, touched, licked – and then for some reason decide against.

Instead, I lean over the table towards him, and the kimono parts slightly and I know now he can see, if he looks, he can see my breasts. My hand goes to the tie of the kimono and toys with it. I could be naked in two seconds.

But he isn't looking at my breasts, he's watching my face, and smiling.

'So,' he says. 'What are you going to do this morning?'

'I hadn't thought.'

'The beach is yours.'

'Well, in that case . . .'

'No one ever comes here. It is almost impossible to

get to except by the steps here. You could sunbathe naked if you wanted, nobody would see you.'

'Except you,' I say.

'Except me, perhaps.'

He looks away from me.

'But I could avert my eyes, if you wish it,' he says.

'Is that what you've been doing for the past week? Sunbathing naked?'

'Perhaps.'

'So you're tanned all over?'

'You could say so.'

His arm is resting on the table by me. I look down at it, at the brown, healthy skin, the golden hairs moving very slightly in the breeze. It's a strong arm. I move a hand over it lightly, brushing the hairs.

'I don't want to get in your way,' I say.

'You could also avert your eyes.'

'Why should I want to do that?'

He looks at me properly now. His eyes move from my face, slowly, down my body to my breasts.

What is Alistair doing? Going off like that and leaving the two of us alone? What's going on?

'I'm going to have a shower,' I say, before I find myself saying – or doing – anything else.

The sun is halfway up now. Once again the children have been having fun with the colour of the sky. It must absorb a lot of blue that sky, it is deep, as deep as infinity.

I stand there on the sand, in my bikini, exhilarating in the sun on my skin. I can feel it penetrating right through me, tanning my bones, melting my muscles. I stretch out my arms so it can reach every part of me.

'Do you have protection?' comes a voice from behind me.

'Protection?'

'You should have protection. Your pale London skin. This sun is very harsh, you know.'

'Yes, of course.'

He comes up to me. He wears swimming trunks and carries a towel, a tube of sun cream and a book, just like any old tourist. Well, not like any old tourist. He's got a surprisingly good body. For a businessman, I mean. A city-based businessman. In fact, for the first time, I realise, he no longer looks in the least like a business-man. He looks like a beach bum.

I'm quite enjoying looking at him, actually. He's beef-ier than I would have expected, he has a strong, muscu-lar chest and powerful shoulders and there's not a trace of the businessman's belly.

'Lie down,' he tells me. 'On your front.'

So I do. I spread my towel and lie down on it, on my stomach.

He puts his things down on the sand, kneels down so he straddles my back, and begins to apply sun cream to my body. My memory drifts back to my flat, and the cushions, and the video, and his hands – soft hands, hands that never did any harsh manual work, anything harsher than what he's doing right now – his soft hands on my back.

He begins with the back of my neck, smoothing the cream with both hands up to my hairline, then down again to the curve of my neck, and along my shoulders, pushing aside the shoulder straps of my bikini as he goes.

He moves down my back, rubbing, caressing, both hands working on me, like the masseur he is. I feel his fingers on my bikini strap, undoing it. 'You don't need this,' he murmurs as he snaps it open.

There's a pause as he replenishes his fingers – I can

hear the faint 'squeak' of the tube as he squeezes it – and then his hands are on me again, running down my back, reaching around under my arms to the curve of my breasts. I can feel the warmth of his skin, the skin of his thighs against mine, his breath on my back as he leans over me.

His hands move down to my waist, to my hips, reaching inside my bikini to the curve of my bum. Helpfully, I lift my bottom half off the sand so he can pull my bikini bottom down my legs and off.

His hands are on my buttocks now, rubbing, stroking, his fingers moving fleetingly into the crevice of my bum, tickling slightly, before travelling on down my thighs to my calves.

'Turn over,' he says, and I do.

The bikini top falls off me and I am naked, lying there on my back, on the sand, with him straddling me.

He looks down at my face for a moment as he squeezes more cream onto his hands. The tube makes a funny little farting noise as he squashes it. Still he watches me, his face neutral, unsmiling.

'Close your eyes,' he says, and I do.

He starts to smooth the cream onto my face, his fingers moving lightly over my eyes, my cheeks, my chin, brushing my hair back from my forehead, softly caressing my lips, under my chin, down my neck to my breastbone, across the front of my chest to my shoulders, and then there's a pause.

I open my eyes a crack, he's squeezing more cream onto his hands, his face as always expressionless, concentrated – he's doing a very thorough job here. As he rubs cream into my breasts I can feel my heart pumping, hard. Bang, bang it goes as his fingers move lightly over my nipples, around the curve of my breasts and on, down my body to my stomach, rubbing, smoothing, all the way down to my pussy. Then he stops.

He squeezes some more, then takes one of my arms in his hands, applies the cream from top to bottom, then the other arm.

I close my eyes again and concentrate on keeping my body still. I am wet now. Boy am I wet.

Now he's onto my legs, and I part them to help him. He's doing this like a professional, carefully, conscientiously, making sure he covers every square inch. Every square inch but one, that is. The one place his hand does not cover is the place that most wants it, that is quivering, weeping, crying out for it.

'All done,' he says, finally, screwing the cap back onto the tube of sun cream.

'Thank you,' I say, reaching out for the tube. 'And now it's my turn.'

The fact that his body is already tanned a burnished brown from head to foot is by the way.

'Stand up, I'll start with your back,' I tell him.

Now it's my hands on the back of his neck, moving down it to his shoulders, his strong shoulders, kneading the muscles of his back and down to his waist.

My fingers linger on the waistband of his trunks. Gently I pull them down half an inch.

As expected, the tan continues.

I pull them down a little more.

'You won't be needing these,' I murmur into his ear as I pull his trunks down over his buttocks. He parts his legs a touch so I can ease them down over his thighs and off.

He has beautiful buttocks. They are round and perfectly brown, all over, and it is my utmost pleasure to be able to take them in my hands and spend rather a long time smoothing the (quite unnecessary) cream all over them, reaching with my thumbs into his crevice and moving them down around the curve to between his legs, brushing my fingers lightly against his balls before moving on down his thighs, down the muscles on the back of his legs to his ankles.

'Turn round,' I say, and he does.

I try not to look down. I concentrate on his face, as he closes his eyes and allows me to spread the cream over his skin, my fingers lingering on his mouth, hoping perhaps he might part his lips and give them a gentle nibble. But he doesn't.

Round his chin to his neck and down his chest go my fingers, wiping, stroking, rubbing, feeling the muscles under them, feeling those muscles tighten as they touch. I kneel down in the sand as I move my hands down his torso to his waist, rubbing the heel of my thumbs gently into his navel in passing. My face is so close to him I can see the movement of my breath on the wiry fuzz of his pubic hair.

His naked body, tanned golden from head to foot. My naked body kneeling before him, my mouth inches from his cock, his flaccid cock, my breath on his cock.

I only have to open my mouth. Only have to open my mouth and move towards him a touch. Put out my tongue, touch him, lightly. Lick him around the tip, in the crack at the tip of his cock ... along the shaft of his cock, along the length of it. He's standing there, still, right in front of me, and I could do anything I want, I could take him in my mouth and suck him, hard, suck his entire body into my mouth and swallow him whole.

But I don't. Instead I stand up and eyeball him.

I am as horny as I have ever been. I am naked, standing there before him. He has stripped me, run his hands over my entire body, caressed my breasts, moved his fingers lightly between my legs. And in turn I have rubbed him, stroked him, touched him all over, placed my mouth so close to him he could feel my breath on his cock. I have all but offered myself to him, prostrated myself before him.

And still he isn't hard.

I sigh, very profoundly.

'I don't do it for you, do I?' I say to him.

'What makes you say that?'

'I've done everything I can think of for you, to you – every trick I've got. And look at you. You're like a damp sock.'

I nod in the direction of his nether regions. He looks down. He laughs.

'There is one thing you haven't tried,' he says.

'Which is?'

'Nothing.'

I stare at him. 'What do you mean, nothing?'

'You think about sex all the time, don't you, Hazel? You're a very, very sexy woman, I know you are. But you try too hard. Do you understand?'

'No, I don't.'

'If you could forget about it, about sex, just for a moment. It would present perhaps a challenge. I personally would find that totally sexy.'

'Huh.'

It's not much of a proposition. Not when you're standing there, wet, desperate, naked. And he's standing there naked, brown all over, six inches away.

'Otherwise . . .' he shrugs, as if in regret.

I look at him for a moment. And then I turn away from him and plunge into the sea.

14

I've made myself a little pile of mother-of-pearl shells. It's taken me quite a while. I am a little kid again.

I am reminded of holidays by the sea when I was little. I collected the shells and my mother, my dear, painstaking, clever mother, made little holes in them somehow – I don't know how – threaded them with nylon thread and created these exquisite little necklaces for me. They were the most beautiful things you ever saw and I wore them all day and all night until they disintegrated.

And now, on this tiny rocky beach, around the headland and away and out of sight of the other rocky beach and of Number Six, I have discovered little rock pools, puddles of warm, crystal-clear water, the kind of puddles I used to love to play in when I was a child. There are no crabs in them, not here, but there is an abundance of shells; and this time I'm going to make my very own necklace, all by myself, and tonight I will go to bed wearing nothing else and see what that does for Alistair.

I have swum here to get away from Six, from his ever-watchful face, away from the humiliation of Six. Here, on this little beach, which is even more inaccessible than our little beach, I am truly alone. There is no one and nothing in sight but the sand, the sea, the rocks, and acres of the ridiculously coloured sky. I feel totally liberated.

I lean back so I am draped over the rocks, my naked

body stretched out in the sun. The water laps against my legs, and I position myself so that every so often, say one wave in every four or five, it washes up over my legs and tickles my pussy. I part my legs to allow the sea to sluice me, to enter me. The anticipation, waiting for the next wave to touch me, to fuck me, is thrilling. I idly wonder if it is possible to be fucked by the sea, to be brought to orgasm by the movement of the water. I feel lazily aroused. I feel the urge to touch myself, to . . .

'So this is where you got to.'

The sun has gone in, suddenly. I lift my head and squint up at this dark shadow that is blocking out the sun, and there is Number Six. He is standing over me, his feet either side of my naked body, his eyes – his ever-amused eyes – smiling into mine.

'I came all this way to get away from you,' I say.

'You did. Get away from me. You were totally absorbed, with your shells.'

'Have you been spying on me?'

'I was concerned about you, when you disappeared around the rocks, out of sight.'

He kneels down on the rocks – boy, that must be uncomfortable – so he straddles me. I can feel the warmth of the skin on his legs against my thighs.

'I'm quite a strong swimmer, actually,' I tell him.

'I was not worried about that,' he says. 'I didn't think you might drown. But I thought perhaps you had disappeared forever, like a mermaid.'

'Like a what?'

'Like a mermaid.'

What an odd thing to say.

'I was . . . I was being a child again,' I say.

'So I could see,' he says. 'Is that what you used to do, when you were a child? Collect shells?'

'Yes. My mother used to make necklaces for me out of them.'

His cock dangles very close to my pussy. He takes it in his hand and gently, and almost absent-mindedly, plays with himself.

'Did you enjoy those holidays?' he asks politely.

'They were all right. I always loved the sea, being by the sea.'

He lightly touches the tip of his cock against my cunt. I gasp, involuntarily.

'I used to enjoy holidays by the sea, also,' he says, as his cock makes little circling movements against my clit.

'Did you?'

'Although the weather was not much good. Not like here, of course.'

'Where – whereabouts did you go?'

He begins to tease me, his cock playing tag with my clit, touching it, rubbing it lightly and then running away.

'We used to go to this little place on the north coast. We would go there every year, year after year, to stay with my aunt.'

I lean back against the rock again. Close my eyes, shut down every part of me; my mind, my brain, my body, my entire consciousness concentrated on the feeling of his cock against my clit.

'Who was "we"?' I whisper.

'My brother and I. My parents meanwhile went elsewhere, to the south of France, to stay with their friends on yachts. They did not want us horrible little kids with them.'

His cock is no longer on my clit. I open my eyes and there it is, hovering above my face. I reach out with my tongue and lick it.

'My brother and I, we would quarrel, nonstop, from the moment we arrived.'

He's holding it there, just out of reach.

'So in the end, I used to take myself off on my own, to the beach. I found a favourite spot on a deserted beach, like this one – well, not like this, but deserted, just like this.'

Slowly, and deliberately, he lowers his cock towards my mouth. I suck the end of it. It is dry.

'I would sit on a rock and play with myself,' he continues. 'I thought, I will spill my sperm into the sea and it will turn into Aphrodite, and I will jump into the water and make love to a goddess.'

His cock slowly edges further towards my mouth. I reach up with my hands and grab hold of his body so he can't move away.

'One day I met a mermaid, there, by the rocks,' his soft voice goes on. 'I fell in love with her immediately. She was beautiful. She had the softest, loveliest, most symmetrical breasts I have ever seen.'

Slowly, slowly, his cock enters my mouth. I gently scrape my teeth against it, resisting the urge to bite.

'But unfortunately, being a mermaid, her bottom half was like that of a fish, which made certain things difficult.'

I start to suck him, hard, as hard as I can, stretching and pulling at his cock with my mouth. Slowly, inexorably, I feel him hardening, growing, moving inside my mouth.

'She would take my cock in her mouth, she was happy to do that, and she would suck me, slowly, sensuously, inventively, thrilling me with her tongue – just as you are doing.'

There is not a break in his voice.

'And I would say to her, you are so good to me, you bring me off whenever I want it, whenever I need it, you are there. But what about you, what about your needs? I would like to satisfy you in the way you satisfy me.'

He pulls his cock out of my mouth and with one strong, swift movement, he lifts my body and carries me over and away from the rocks and lays me down on the sand.

He sits there, by me, perfectly still, looking down at me.

'So?' I ask. 'What did she say, your mermaid?'

'She said, "There is a way to satisfy me, but very few, very few know how".'

'That was some challenge.'

'It certainly was.'

'Did she smell like a fish, this mermaid?' I ask him.

'Not at all. She smelled like the sea. Her scales, her scaly tail, was rough, hard, exciting.'

'You obviously got quite close to it, this tail.'

'I did,' he says. He moves his body so it is over mine.

'And?' I say, spreading my legs, ready to receive him. 'Did you do it? Did you manage to satisfy her?'

'I believe I did.'

He takes his cock in his hand again and holds it, in readiness.

'How?'

'I never really knew.'

He touches his cock against the edge of my cunt.

'Then how did you know she was satisfied?' I ask, fighting to control my breathing.

'Some things remain a mystery,' he says. He leans his body over me so his mouth is an inch away from mine.

'But I know I satisfied her because . . .' His mouth

touches mine lightly. 'Because, after a particularly exciting coupling, I never saw her again.'

And slowly, very slowly, he slides into me.

I sigh, very deeply, I cannot help myself, as I feel the length of him inside me.

At last.

'What kept you?' I breathe. 'Why now?'

'Because now is the right time,' he says.

Then, still inside me, he sits back and, with his thumb, he gently starts to rub my clit.

I look up at him, at his ice-blue eyes. His eyes, hard with concentration, burn into mine as he strokes, a little harder now, with the ball of his thumb, watching me all the time, watching as I edge towards that place where nothing else exists, not him, not the world, nothing but the sensation of my own body, my own ecstasy. I come quickly: eyes closed, my mouth open in a silent scream.

Then he starts to fuck me.

He fucks me slowly, rhythmically, building, all the while building, penetrating deeper, his hips circling, pushing, as he reaches to touch every bit of the inside of me. He fucks with his whole body and his whole being, with nothing of him left out. He fucks without restraint, with a kind of animal need, every muscle of him taut. He pumps into me, faster, harder, his eyes always locked on to mine, and the noise he makes as he comes, spilling into me, his body arching over me, his pale eyes darkening in surprise, is like a great sigh of relief.

He sits back. He sits there for a moment, staring at me, breathing hard, his hand resting lightly on my stomach.

'So,' he says at last.

'So.'

Very slowly, with a little 'plop', his cock slides out of me.

He smiles at me, politely almost. And then he gets up and reaches out a hand to help me to my feet and we stand there, a touch awkwardly, two naked bodies quite close to one another and yet not close; and for one awful moment I think he's going to shake my hand.

'Thank you,' he says, finally.

'Thank *you*,' I reply, resisting the urge to curtsey.

And then, for something to do as much as anything, I turn away from him and plunge my body – my exhausted, fucked and satisfied body – into the water. As I twist over onto my back and let the sea float me away, out and away from him, I have the sensation, an odd sensation, not so much of the beginning of something but of something coming to an end. What the Americans call closure.

When I turn to look back at the beach I can see him walking back over the rocks. He turns to wave at me. I wave back. And he's gone.

Some time later – perhaps an hour, perhaps more – I make my own way back to the house, my shells held loosely in my towel, slightly apprehensive about what or who I might find there.

The house is empty and the car is not there. I shower and put on a dress – a long-sleeved, Indian cotton number that feels soothing to my slightly battered skin. And then, eager still to be on my own, to get out of the house before anyone can get back in time to stop me, I take myself for a walk.

I take a path that leads away from the house in the opposite direction from the one we arrived at yesterday. The path follows the top of the cliff for a while and then sort of peters out. I suppose it would be an exaggeration to call it a cliff path, not many people would have had reason to tread it before me. I keep walking anyway, for a while, my legs brushing through the spiky grass, till I find a clump of trees that offers some delightful and much needed shade, where I sit down for a bit of a rest and a think.

I realise I now find myself in a Difficult Situation. Now that we have consummated, Six and I, I find, to my slight dismay, that – not to put too fine a point on it – I have lost interest in him. It was a game, a wonderful game that we both enjoyed playing. But it was a game with an objective, a powerful objective, and now that objective has been reached the game, as I see it, is over.

Yet Six is our host, Alistair's and mine, in a sense anyway, and there are another two weeks to get through. I don't know what will be expected of me, but whatever it is, I'm not sure I'm going to find myself up to it.

So what's going on? Am I losing interest in sex? Can it be possible? Can a bird lose interest in flying? Can a fish no longer be bothered to swim? Sex is what's kept me going after all, it's my reason for being, it's what gets me up in the morning. What else is there, when all's said and done?

I lean back against a tree and I start thinking of the men in my life. Of Ryan. Of his gorgeous, perfect body and his insatiable energy, his rapacious – not a good word, perhaps, in the circumstances – his voracious sexual appetite. His amazing strength, his uncomplicated arrogance, his great, unstoppable cock. Ryan, the answer to many girls' dreams.

And Nick. Awkward, uncontrollable, perhaps the most clumsy lover I've ever known, but a great lover all the same, in his own special, unique way. Nick, who loved to fuck in the office, on the desk, among the cables

and the terminals and the computer accessories, prefer-
ably when there was someone else in the room, a third
party, looking on perhaps. Nick and Janine. Their young,
slim frames, mouths glued together, limbs entwined,
bodies joined. Nick and Janine, lost to the world.

And – why can I never remember his name? – Slyde.
With a 'y'. Shy Slyde, who thought he so fancied himself,
with his small, taut body and his spiky hair and his
wicked grin and his *Sex and the City* fantasies. Slyde the
shy, uncertain virgin. Ex-virgin.

Slyde and Janine. They were not like Nick and Janine.
Slyde and Janine were more like . . . more like my father
and – whatshername.

And I think of Six, who in some ways understood me
best of all. Who presented the greatest challenge of
them all. Who taunted, teased and tantalised and finally
gave in. And having given in . . .

I love them all. I really do, I've loved them all, we've
had some fantastic times, I have the fondest, best memories of all of them.

It's just that . . .

I can vaguely hear the sea, somewhere quite close
but just out of sight, over the brow of the cliff. The trunk
of the tree feels warm and hard behind my back. The
ground is dry and prickly beneath me.

I'm suddenly feeling unbelievably sleepy. That's what
thinking does, it exhausts you, I must remember not to
. . . not to . . .

I dream about Alistair. He's disembodied, it's just his
face, somehow everywhere, in the midst of everything –
not a part of anything, yet always there. I look into the
pushchair to smile at the baby and Alistair's face smiles
back at me. I lean down to pat the dog and Alistair wags
his tail. His face looks down at me, up at me, sideways

at me, from the lampposts, from my dinner plate, from inside the teapot when I take off the lid to stir the tea, from behind my mother's shoulder. I'm trying to ignore him because he isn't there, he has no right to be there, but it's like white rabbits on the first of the month – the more you try not to think of them, the more you do. Alistair's face emerging from the shadows under the trees, coming closer.

This is not a dream. This is Alistair in the flesh.

'Good God,' he says.

A funny thing to say. I squint up at him. I'm disoriented and uncomfortably aware of the spiky grass sticking into my bum.

'Hi,' I say. 'What are you doing here?'

'I was going to ask the same thing. I've been looking everywhere for you.'

'Oh.'

He comes to sit by me on the ground.

'God,' he says again. 'I was beginning to be worried.'

'Sorry,' I say.

I have absolutely no idea of the time or how long I've been here. From the prickly feeling on my skin, and the position of the sun in the sky, I would surmise quite a long time.

'I must have dropped off. I didn't intend to be out here this long,' I say.

'Are you OK?'

'Fine. Fine.'

'Then I think we ought to be getting back. It'll be dark pretty soon.'

'Right.'

He gets up. I don't.

I don't know if it's the dream that's disoriented me, or the rather random and meaningless thoughts that were swimming around in my head before I dropped off, but one way or another, despite the intense prickliness of the grass beneath my bum, I feel unable to move.

'What's up?' he asks.

'I don't know.'

He sits down again, close to me, facing me, opposite me, and looks into my face.

'Tell me.'

'There's nothing to tell.'

He puts his hand to my face and, with a gesture of surprising tenderness, he strokes my cheek.

'Sorry,' I say, unable to look him in the eye. 'I'll be all right in a minute. Just a bit stiff, I think.'

'I love you,' he says.

He said it. And I heard it. But that doesn't mean it makes sense.

'What?'

'I said I love you.'

There's a pause.

'No,' is all I can think of.

'Yes.'

'But – I'm your whore.'

'So you keep saying.'

'Your fortnightly whore.'

'Well, I suppose ... I have to admit it was a bit like that to begin with.'

He takes his hand from my face and he sits there, knees drawn up to his chin, arms now clasped around them, not looking at me.

'When I first met you I thought you were the sexiest, most sensuous, exciting lover I'd ever had. That was it really I suppose, that was all it was, but that was quite something. Nobody has ever thrilled me and satisfied me and aroused me so completely in bed, I've never enjoyed making love with anyone as much as I do with you.'

He looks at me, briefly, shyly almost. He picks up one of my hands and starts toying with my fingers.

'I used to look forward to our next fuck, in a mildly anticipatory, pleasurable way. Knowing I would see you, make love to you, spend a night with you once every other week, it was thrilling. It suited me. I'm sorry if that sounds selfish, but it was true.'

'It suited me, too.'

'As I thought.'

'So when did –'

'At the opera. That night.'

'Dido and . . . Thingy.'

'Aeneas.'

'I cried, I remember.' I had all but forgotten.

'Yes, you did. And I realised . . . I saw a different side to you. I guess I saw you.'

'I'm your humble kitchen maid, sir, ready to be of service at any time.'

'Yes, exactly, that's exactly it. That's how you saw yourself. That was what was so disturbing. You saw yourself as my whore, as you put it.'

Click. Things begin to slot into place. I remember him not making love to me that morning and me not understanding why.

'Why do you think I took you down to meet my parents?' he asks, after a pause.

'I thought perhaps you wanted a second opinion.'

'Why should I care what my parents think about my whore?'

'We didn't make love that night.'

'I know. I was . . . disturbed. I can't explain it.'

'And your father? Did that upset you?'

'Yes. Very much.'

'I'm sorry. It was a bit like making love to you, actually – you are quite alike, in some ways.'

'It upset me because I realised how much you were not and never would be a one-man woman.'

'Oh. Don't tell me you were jealous.'

'Of course I was.'

'Oh.'

'I found myself wanting you more, and wanting you for myself. I wanted you to clear the decks, and I knew that would be impossible.'

He grips my hand, tightly, in both of his.

'I don't know what I'm trying to say. I want you to come and live with me, but I want you for myself. I know you're a woman who needs a lot of sex, and I'll give you a lot of sex, as much as I am capable of giving, which is a lot. But it may not be enough. There are too many people in the cast.'

I'm not about to tell him, but there aren't, not any more. Not now.

'When I saw you with Danny, and I realised –'

'Who's Danny?' I ask.

'Who's Danny? Danny Kraaten.'

'Oh, you mean Number Six.'

'Is that what you called him?'

'Yes, because he was, er . . . I never actually knew his name.'

He laughs.

'That's over, anyway,' I say.

'What is?'

'Him and me. It was a game. And now it's over. A nice game, mind you. But . . .'

'But what?'

'Well, to be honest, I'm kind of embarrassed, being in the same place as him. With the two of you.' I give his hand a bit of a squeeze.

'He's gone,' Alistair says.

'He's what?'

'He went this afternoon. He said to say goodbye, he couldn't find you, he didn't know where you were.'

'Why? Why did he go?'

'He was going anyway. The house isn't his, it belongs to the bank. He came here for a week and we overlapped by a day, as it happened. He's gone back. It's ours now.'

'Just you and me?'

'Just you and me.'

And then he reaches towards me and kisses me on the mouth, softly, sweetly.

'When we made love yesterday evening,' he says, 'I looked at your face and there was the most intense feeling of tenderness.'

He stops.

I realise that, without my noticing it, the sun has almost gone down. Alistair's face, which is so close to mine, is in shadow and I can't make out his expression.

'Come on,' he says, getting suddenly to his feet. 'Let's go back and get something to eat.'

Over a scratch supper of exotic-tasting sausages and cheeses and other unidentifiable foodstuffs ('I just raided the fridge and this is what I found,' he explained), Alistair tells me about his trip around the island that morning, of the little herd of three-legged goats he came upon and their twelve-year-old goatherd who, as he saw it, should have been at school, and so on, and it's as if our conversation under the trees that afternoon had never happened. It's an absolute marvel, I'm thinking, the English ability to dissemble, to carry on in the most *extreme* circumstances acting as if everything is absolutely normal.

'You're not eating much,' he says, in a pause.

Well, are you surprised? I'm thinking.

My mind is in turmoil.

While I've been showering, and dressing, I've been having intense conversations with my mother, and quite separately with my father, and even in passing with Barbara, and all the other people I know who have visited this strange, unknown territory that I have so far managed so successfully to avoid.

They have been trying to tell me, these people, what a glorious place it is; what a wonderful, all-consuming, fulfilling thing it is to love someone, and love them completely, with no holds barred; to give yourself totally to someone else and never mind the consequences.

I've been arguing with them, of course. I tell them all I can see of that wonderful place they talk about is the ugly bit, the bit where the monsters live, monsters like jealousy and mistrust and deceit and loss and uncertainty. And I tell them I don't want to go there, no thanks very much. But they keep arguing back. 'How can you tell until you try it?' they say. And then they start accusing me of cowardice and, well, that's not fair.

So here we are, Alistair and I. He has made this monstrous suggestion – the outrageous suggestion that he and I might make a couple. A couple, ha! He and I – what do we have in common, other than sex? The most glorious, mind-blowing sex, maybe, in fact I'd safely say the best sex I have ever had and perhaps, just perhaps, the best I will ever have, Number Six or no Number Six. But a relationship? One to one? Supermarket shopping together? Arguing over the bills? Meeting his posh friends? I mean, come on . . .

And he's sitting there rabbiting on as if everything's normal, nothing has changed, as if those words, and in particular the 'l' word, never passed his lips. In fact, he's rabbiting on rather more than usual, and it occurs to me that perhaps, just perhaps, he's talking this much because he's embarrassed, he's trying to pretend he never said those things because he thinks I'm ... No, it's ridiculous to even think of it. He thinks I'm laughing at him.

I tell you, life never used to be this complicated. Barely twenty-four hours ago, the most complicated thing I had to deal with was the prospect of spending two weeks living in a house with two lovers. But this ...

When we've finished eating I say I fancy a walk on the beach, so we go down there together.

It is a steaming, sticky, hot night. There is a wind blowing, quite a strong wind, but it's a hot wind and it feels – weird, tropical, unworldly, exotic. We stand together, he and I, by the water's edge, barefoot, the sea swirling between our toes. The moon is up, the half-moon, the children's moon, and I glance at Alistair's face, which glows white in the moonlight, and I would give the world to know what he is thinking.

He turns to look at me.

I undo the buttons on the front of my dress and slip out of it. Then I pull my knickers down, and off, and I am naked. He watches me as I walk into the sea.

The sea is warm – warmer even than earlier that day. The feeling of the water on my naked skin sends me into paroxysms of sensual pleasure, and I lie back on top of it, floating, gazing up at the moon, my legs and arms stretched out like a starfish. I feel the waves caressing my body, rippling against my breasts, lapping against my cunt. I open my legs to the sea and abandon myself to it, happy to let it take me wherever it likes.

I feel Alistair's arms under my arms, and then his body under my body, his naked body, somehow supporting me; and I'm lying there on the water, on top of him, and he is holding me, holding me round the waist, and I am as relaxed as a person can be, he is my life-saver and I am not drowning.

A wave lifts us both and twists my body towards him. He is upright now, standing, and I am straddling him with my legs, and my mouth is on his and very, very gently, I feel him enter me. I grip him tightly with my legs, and we stand there together, swaying slightly with the movement of the waves. Then I let go of him with the upper part of my body and lean back so I am lying on the water again, and his rhythm as he moves in and out of me matches the rhythm of the waves.

A wave crashes over us and I clench the muscles in my cunt to keep him from being torn from me. He reaches out and grabs me and holds me once more very tightly to him. He is thrusting now, and the waves are beginning to pummel us and I'm swallowing every other one and spluttering and gasping for breath – but still he keeps a tight hold of me.

Now our feet have left the safety of the ground and we are completely at the mercy of the surf. His arms are clamped around my body and I know he will never, never let me go and that if the waves take me, they'll take him too, and I don't care. I don't know where we are, we are moving away from the shore, we could be halfway to Africa for all I know, or care. I can feel the water stinging my eyes, and my body tingles from the combination of the battering waves and the force of Alistair's arms around me.

He is still in me, not thrusting any more but hard, still hard, and we are clamped together as if our lives depended on it, on each other. Then a mighty wave picks us up, holds us for a moment, and sends us crashing down, our bodies swirling and twisting together in the water, gasping, choking, still clutched on to one another, somersaulting together away from the water onto the sand.

And there we lie. Like beached whales. Gasping for breath.

He lifts his body so he can look at me. And without a word, and never taking his eyes from mine, he gently moves in and out of me. As I lie there feeling him, and watching him, I'm aware of the frenzy falling away from me, and a kind of tenderness starts to suffuse my body. I move in response to him, in concert with him, my arms linked loosely around his neck, my body moving with him and for him. And as we do this together, I begin to feel something strange, something that ... I can't quite put a finger on.

He pauses in his lovemaking for a moment, leans down and kisses me. It is a soft kiss, just lips meeting, and parting a little. Then he moves his mouth to my cheek, to my eyes, and he's kissing them and kissing my neck and my shoulders; and all the while he is still inside me and I can still feel him, still feel the throbbing, as if his heart is inside me, in his cock, inside my cunt. I'm aware of a feeling of the most intense calm, a feeling I would like to preserve, to stay with, to not move on from. He gently lowers his body onto mine and I hold him. And I think something I've never thought in my life before: I think I don't ever, ever want this moment to end.

'I love you,' he whispers.

Before I can reply he kneels up. He caresses my breasts, and moves his hands down to my clit. He starts to stroke me, slowly.

'Oh yes,' I breathe, and close my eyes.

'Tell me,' he says, 'tell me what to do.'

But I don't. I don't need to. I only have to breathe, and let it happen.

I am lying there, on a beach like this one, less than twelve hours ago. On my back, with a man inside me. Another man, a very different man. And a totally different feeling. I don't know why. I can't understand why it should all feel so – new.

As he strokes me I tighten my cunt, in rhythm. I wonder if I can make him come simply by squeezing his cock. I open my eyes and look up at him. His face is beginning to show signs of agitation, and I realise he is fighting to hold on. He closes his eyes and starts to move in me again, almost imperceptibly at first, and now it's me trying to hold on, to delay the moment, to freeze the moment, but soon he's fucking me hard, and harder, and stroking me still, and I can feel a pressure building inside my head and I want his skin to melt into mine and his body to become mine, and now his fingers abandon me so he can concentrate on thrusting – so hard that between each thrust he leaves me completely – and it's as if I'm being hammered, and each hammer makes me want to scream out loud and I never ever want him to stop, my pelvis is lifting right off the ground, I'm pushing him into me, locking my legs around his neck now so he can go deeper, slamming together, two bodies hurtling themselves at each other and I think – let it never, ever end, let this go on forever – and then suddenly he's like a train thundering down the track, rhythmic, relentless, unstoppable.

And we come. Together.

His body collapses onto mine and I wrap my arms around him and hold him, firmly, possessively, protectively. There's total silence as we lie there together. Panting, together. Bodies, together.

Oh, Christ. That was a first. A first in every way.

* * *

I am the man in the moon. Painted, of course, by children. I am looking down at the beach below me, the beach I have washed with my light, with my pale, white light. I zoom in on an object lying there on the sand, and as I get closer I can see it is not one object but two. Two objects, bound together, so close I cannot see where one ends and the other begins.

I zoom in with my imaginary camera on their faces. They are lying side by side, on the white sand. Their faces are very close together and they are looking at one another. Their lower limbs are entwined and somehow fused, like conjoined twins. They lie perfectly still, doing nothing.

One of them opens a mouth to speak. A single word, only:

'Yes.'

Spoken so quietly I can barely hear it.

'Yes?' whispers the other.

'I love you.'

'Do you?'

'I think so,' says the girl. 'I guess that's what it is, this peculiar feeling. I've never felt it before so I don't know, but I guess –'

He leans towards her and stops the words with his mouth. And his mouth stays on her mouth so she cannot say anything more.

They stay like that for some time, totally still. As I zoom back to my rightful place in the sky, the sky the children have painted the deepest black, I look down and their bodies have merged once more into one unmoving shape. And I wonder to myself if they will remain there, together, forever more.

Visit the Black Lace website at
www.blacklace-books.co.uk

LOOK OUT FOR THE ALL-NEW BLACK LACE BOOKS – AVAILABLE NOW!

All books priced £6.99 in the UK. Please note publication dates apply to the UK only. For other territories, please contact your retailer.

A GENTLEMAN'S WAGER
Madelynne Ellis
ISBN 0 352 33800 8

When Bella Rushdale finds herself fiercely attracted to landowner Lucerne Marlinscar, she doesn't expect that the rival for his affections will be another man. Handsome and decadent, Marquis Pennerley has desired Lucerne for years and now, at the remote Lauwine Hall, he intends to claim him. This leads to a passionate struggle for dominance – at the risk of scandal – between a high-spirited lady and a debauched aristocrat. Who will Lucerne choose? **A wonderfully decadent piece of historical erotica with a twist.**

VIRTUOSO
Katrina Vincenzi-Thyne
ISBN 0 352 32907 6

Mika and Serena, young ambitious members of classical music's jet-set, inhabit a world of secluded passion and privilege. However, since Mika's tragic injury, which halted his meteoric rise to fame as a solo violinist, he has retired embittered. Serena is determined to change things. A dedicated voluptuary, her sensuality cannot be ignored as she rekindles Mika's zest for life. Together they share a dark secret. **A beautifully written story of opulence and exotic, passionate indulgence.**

Coming in June

DRIVEN BY DESIRE
Savannah Smythe
ISBN 0 352 33799 0

When Rachel's husband abandons both her and his taxi-cab business
and flees the country, she is left to pick up the pieces. However, this is a
blessing in disguise as Rachel, along with her friend Sharma, transforms
his business into an exclusive chauffeur service for discerning gentlemen
– with all the perks that offers. What Rachel doesn't know is that two of
her regular clients are jewel thieves with exotic tastes in sexual
experimentation. As Rachel is lured into an underworld lifestyle of
champagne, diamonds and lustful indulgence, she finds a familiar face is
involved in some very shady activity! **Another cracking story of strong
women and sexy double dealing from Savannah Smythe.**

FIGHTING OVER YOU
Laura Hamilton
ISBN 0 352 33795 8

Yasmin and U seem like the perfect couple. She's a scriptwriter and he's
a magazine editor who has a knack for tapping into the latest trends.
One evening, however, U confesses to Yasmin that he's 'having a thing'
with a nineteen-year-old violinist – the precocious niece of Yasmin and
U's old boss, the formidable Pandora Fairchild. Amelia, the violinist, turns
out to be a catalyst for a whole series of erotic experiments that even
Yasmin finds intriguing. In a haze of absinthe, lust and wild abandon, all
parties find answers to questions about their sexuality they were once
too afraid to ask. **Contemporary erotica at its best from the author of the
bestselling *Fire and Ice*.**

THE LION LOVER
Mercedes Kelly
ISBN 0 352 33162 3

Settling into life in 1930s Kenya, Mathilde Valentine finds herself sent to a harem where the Sultan, his sadistic brother and adolescent son all make sexual demands on her. Meanwhile, Olensky – the rugged game hunter and 'lion lover' – plot her escape, but will she want to be rescued? **A wonderful exploration of 'White Mischief' goings on in 1930s Africa.**

Coming in July

COUNTRY PLEASURES
Primula Bond
ISBN 0 352 33810 5

Janie and Sally escape to the countryside hoping to get some sun and relaxation. When the weather turns nasty, the two women find themselves confined to their remote cottage with little to do except eat, drink and talk about men. They soon become the focus of attention for the lusty farmers in the area who are well-built, down-to-earth and very different from the boys they have been dating in town. **Lust-filled pursuits in the English countryside.**

THE RELUCTANT PRINCESS
Patty Glenn
ISBN 0 532 33809 1

Martha's a rich valley girl who's living on the wrong side of the tracks and hanging out with Hollywood hustlers. Things were OK when her bodyguard Gus was looking after her, but now he's in hospital Martha's gone back to her bad old ways. When she meets mean, moody and magnificent private investigator Joaquin Lee, the sexual attraction between them is instant and intense. If Martha can keep herself on the straight and narrow for a year, her family will let her have access to her inheritance. Lee reckons he can help out while pocketing a cut for himself. **A dynamic battle of wills between two very stubborn, very sexy characters.**

ARIA APPASSIONATA
Juliet Hastings
ISBN 0 352 33056 2

Tess Challoner has made it. She is going to play Carmen in a new production of the opera that promises to be as raunchy and explicit as it is intelligent. But Tess needs to learn a lot about passion and desire before the opening night. Tony Varguez, the handsome but jealous Spanish tenor, takes on the task of her education. When Tess finds herself drawn to a desirable new member of the cast, she knows she's playing with fire. **Life imitating art – with dramatically sexual consequences.**

Black Lace Booklist

Information is correct at time of printing. To avoid disappointment
check availability before ordering. Go to www.blacklace-books.co.uk.
All books are priced £6.99 unless another price is given.

BLACK LACE BOOKS WITH A CONTEMPORARY SETTING

☐ IN THE FLESH Emma Holly   ISBN 0 352 33498 3   £5.99
☐ A PRIVATE VIEW Crystalle Valentino   ISBN 0 352 33308 1   £5.99
☐ SHAMELESS Stella Black   ISBN 0 352 33485 1   £5.99
☐ INTENSE BLUE Lyn Wood   ISBN 0 352 33496 7   £5.99
☐ THE NAKED TRUTH Natasha Rostova   ISBN 0 352 33497 5   £5.99
☐ A SPORTING CHANCE Susie Raymond   ISBN 0 352 33501 7   £5.99
☐ TAKING LIBERTIES Susie Raymond   ISBN 0 352 33357 X   £5.99
☐ A SCANDALOUS AFFAIR Holly Graham   ISBN 0 352 33523 8   £5.99
☐ THE NAKED FLAME Crystalle Valentino   ISBN 0 352 33528 9   £5.99
☐ ON THE EDGE Laura Hamilton   ISBN 0 352 33534 3   £5.99
☐ LURED BY LUST Tania Picarda   ISBN 0 352 33533 5   £5.99
☐ THE HOTTEST PLACE Tabitha Flyte   ISBN 0 352 33536 X   £5.99
☐ THE NINETY DAYS OF GENEVIEVE Lucinda   ISBN 0 352 33070 8   £5.99
   Carrington
☐ DREAMING SPIRES Juliet Hastings   ISBN 0 352 33584 X
☐ THE TRANSFORMATION Natasha Rostova   ISBN 0 352 33311 1
☐ SIN.NET Helena Ravenscroft   ISBN 0 352 33598 X
☐ TWO WEEKS IN TANGIER Annabel Lee   ISBN 0 352 33599 8
☐ HIGHLAND FLING Jane Justine   ISBN 0 352 33616 1
☐ PLAYING HARD Tina Troy   ISBN 0 352 33617 X
☐ SYMPHONY X Jasmine Stone   ISBN 0 352 33629 3
☐ STRICTLY CONFIDENTIAL Alison Tyler   ISBN 0 352 33624 2
☐ SUMMER FEVER Anna Ricci   ISBN 0 352 33625 0
☐ CONTINUUM Portia Da Costa   ISBN 0 352 33120 8
☐ OPENING ACTS Suki Cunningham   ISBN 0 352 33630 7
☐ FULL STEAM AHEAD Tabitha Flyte   ISBN 0 352 33637 4
☐ A SECRET PLACE Ella Broussard   ISBN 0 352 33307 3
☐ GAME FOR ANYTHING Lyn Wood   ISBN 0 352 33639 0

To find out the latest information about Black Lace titles, check out the website: www.blacklace-books.co.uk or send for a booklist with complete synopses by writing to:

Black Lace Booklist, Virgin Books Ltd
Thames Wharf Studios
Rainville Road
London W6 9HA

Please include an SAE of decent size. Please note only British stamps are valid.

Our privacy policy
We will not disclose information you supply us to any other parties. We will not disclose any information which identifies you personally to any person without your express consent.

From time to time we may send out information about Black Lace books and special offers. Please tick here if you do <u>not</u> wish to receive Black Lace information. ❑

Please send me the books I have ticked above.

Name ....

Address ....

....

....

....

Post Code ....

Send to: Cash Sales, Black Lace Books, Thames Wharf Studios, Rainville Road, London W6 9HA.

US customers: for prices and details of how to order books for delivery by mail, call 1-800-343-4499.

Please enclose a cheque or postal order, made payable to Virgin Books Ltd, to the value of the books you have ordered plus postage and packing costs as follows:

UK and BFPO – £1.00 for the first book, 50p for each subsequent book.

Overseas (including Republic of Ireland) – £2.00 for the first book, £1.00 for each subsequent book.

If you would prefer to pay by VISA, ACCESS/MASTERCARD, DINERS CLUB, AMEX or SWITCH, please write your card number and expiry date here:

....

Signature ....

Please allow up to 28 days for delivery.